NECROPOLIS

NECROPOLIS

TIM WAGGONER

Five Star • Waterville, Maine

Published in 2004 in conjunction with
Tekno Books and Ed Gorman.

Set in 11 pt. Plantin

Printed in the United States on permanent paper.

ISBN 1-59414-140-1 (hc : alk. paper)
ISBN 1-4104-0215-0 (sc : alk. paper)

*To my father, who taught me
how to draw the Wolfman.*

–ONE–

I was sitting in Skully's, nursing a beer that I couldn't taste, and which I'd have to throw up later, and trying real hard to look like I was minding my own business when the lyke walked in.

He (I knew it was male only because I'd been told) stood well over seven feet tall. But he didn't have to stoop to enter the bar. Since Skully's is located close to the Wyldwood, a lot of his customers are lykes, who usually wear their wildforms, and he'd designed the nine-foot-high entranceway to accommodate the specialized—and mutable—physiognomy of his clientele.

The lyke, Honani by name, stone-cold killer by rep, was one of the newer Breeds, a mixblood—lyke biology tweaked by the hand of genetic engineering. But as far as I was concerned, he was an ugly mess. I could pick out badger, puma, crow and what I thought was a bit of snake around the eyes. He looked almost as ugly as one of Lady Varvara's demon kin. Almost.

Honani stomped across the hardwood floor, the boards creaking beneath his considerable weight. Even for a lyke, he was massive, and the other bar patrons, who'd all looked up when the nightmarish hodge-podge had entered, suddenly found much more interesting corners of the room to direct their attention to.

I noticed that the lykes Honani passed wrinkled their noses in disgust, and I was glad my own olfactory senses were as dead as the rest of me.

Honani walked up to the bar, slapped a paw on the

7

shoulder of an insectine demon with tangleglow-delivery tubes implanted in his temples, and threw him/her/it backwards. The demon squealed in fright as it sailed across the room and smashed into a table, disrupting a game of bloodshards between several vampires with holo implants. The table collapsed, the bloodshards winked out of existence and the vampires hissed in cold anger, displayed their incisors, and turned to glare at Honani. But as much as they might've liked to, they didn't make a move toward the lyke. He was just too damn big.

"Jim Beam," he growled, the words barely recognizable coming out of his inhuman mouth.

Skully, who so far had eyed, or perhaps a better word in his case might be socketed, the situation dispassionately (which is the only way he could react, given his complete lack of facial muscle and skin), looked at Honani for a long moment before finally nodding his ossified pate and setting a bottle of the requested liquor on the counter in front of Honani. Skully unscrewed the cap with his fully fleshed fingers, set it down, and then reached for a glass.

"Leave it," Honani said, then grabbed the bottle and drank the entire contents down in three gulps. He tossed the empty over his shoulder, and it shattered against the floorboards, the brown remnants of the whiskey mixing with the other less identifiable substances which had soaked into the wood over the years.

Skully normally doesn't put up with much shit. He keeps a silver broadaxe behind the counter, but he hardly ever has to use it. Rumor is that he has ties to the Dominari, Necropolis' version of the Mafia, and while he's never admitted it to me, he hasn't denied it, either. If the Descension celebration hadn't been in full swing—and Honani already likely drunk before he even came in here—

he would've had more sense than to act like such a dick. Probably. But Skully didn't reach for his axe. Instead he looked over at me (at least I think he looked at me; it's kind of hard to tell when the person you're talking about doesn't have any eyes) and I nodded. Show time. If I still had a pulse, it would have been racing.

I stood up.

"My friend," I said just a bit too loudly, "you are the butt-ugliest sonofabitch in the city." And considering the citizenry of Necropolis, that was saying something.

The thick muscles in Honani's shoulders rippled and tensed beneath his fur. The other people (and I use the term extremely loosely) in the bar drew in surprised gasps of air. Those that breathed, anyway.

Honani turned around. His lips curled back from his sizable teeth in a snarl, and his eyes burned feral yellow.

"I ain't your friend."

"If you were, I'd suggest you have a surgeon remove your ass and graft it onto your face. It'd be a vast improvement."

The big lyke just stood there a moment, blinking in confusion while his alcohol-sodden brain struggled to process what I'd said. Either he figured it out or decided to give up and just assume I'd insulted him. Either way, he let out an ear-splitting shriek and came at me.

You know the old cliché about how time seems to slow down when you're in danger? It's true. Unfortunately, being dead, my reflexes aren't what they once were, so the shift in time perception didn't do me any good. But twenty years' experience as a cop can make up for a whole hell of a lot, and thus I was able to sidestep just as Honani's claws—which had lengthened to twice their previous size and were still growing—raked the air where my chest had been a moment earlier.

I was a bit slow, however, and the lyke's razor-sharp talons sliced through my Marvin the Martian tie, decapitating the cartoon spaceman. I watched Marvin's headless body flutter to the floor.

"Goddamnit! Do you know how hard it is to come by ties like that around here?"

Honani didn't sympathize with my sartorial loss. Instead, he lunged forward, mouth wide open, jaw distended farther than should have been anatomically possible, and fastened his twisted yellow teeth on my shoulder. I didn't feel a thing—except regret that along with my tie, I'd also lost a perfectly good suit jacket and shirt.

But before he could take a hunk out of me, he pulled back, his face scrunched up in disgust, and spit great gobs of foam and saliva to the floor. "You're a deader!" he accused.

"Guilty as charged. You'd have known that if you'd bothered to smell me." Mixbloods' patchwork physiology doesn't always function properly. It was quite possible his sense of smell was no better than an ordinary human's.

Though the idiot should've been able to tell just by looking. It'd been a while since my last application of preservative spells, and I wasn't too fresh—skin gray, dry, and beginning to flake. I probably didn't taste too good either.

As if emphasizing this last point, Honani spit once more then looked at me with disdain. "Go back to the Boneyard, zombie. Your kind isn't wanted around here." And then he turned and walked toward the bar.

Honani's reaction was understandable. Most zombies are little more than undead automatons under the control of whoever raised them, and hardly a threat to a lyke as strong as Honani. But I'm not most zombies.

I removed a glass vial full of gray dust from the inner pocket of my suit jacket and pried off the cork. And

10

then I made a leap for Honani.

My reflexes may be slower, and I'm no stronger than I was when alive, but I can get the job done when I have to. I threw my left arm around Honani's chest and with my right jammed the vial into the lyke's massive maw and emptied the contents. There wasn't much in the vial, but a little was all that I needed.

Honani choked and sputtered and then I felt a distant tearing sensation. I stepped back from the lyke, still clutching the mostly empty vial. Something was . . . and then I realized what had happened: my left arm was gone. The preservative spells were breaking down fast.

Honani whirled around and brandished my detached limb like a club. Behind him, I saw Skully lifting his silver axe, ready to strike, but I shook my head and he lowered his weapon.

"You—fucking—corpse!" Honani advanced on me, no doubt intending to pound me into grave mold with my own arm. But he only managed a few steps before he doubled over in pain. He dropped my arm and it hit the floor with a meaty plap! His breathing became harsh, labored, and he started whining like a wounded animal, which, I suppose, he was.

"You shouldn't have killed her, Honani," I said. "Lyra was a simple working girl; it wasn't her fault you couldn't get it up." Like I said, mixblood physiology doesn't always work right.

He fell to his knees, breathing rapidly now. His entire body shook, as if a great struggle were occurring within him.

"That dust I dumped into your mouth was part of Lyra's ashes. Not much, but enough. You took her life; now you're going to give it back."

11

He rolled onto his side, quivering uncontrollably in the throes of a violent seizure. His eyes had lost all of their anger and wildness and were now rolled up in their sockets.

This was it.

With my remaining hand, I reached into one of my jacket's outer pockets and removed a small clay jar. I shook off the lid, which was attached by a short length of twine, then knelt down next to Honani's head and held the open jar in front of his mouth.

His exertions lessened bit by bit and finally his body grew still. And then, as I watched, thin whitish wisps curled forth from between his teeth, lazily at first, but then the jar's magic began to draw them in, and they flowed out of his mouth faster and faster, until at last they were done. I sat the jar on the floor, put the lid back on tight, and then slipped Honani's soul into my pocket.

Honani—or rather his body—began to stir. I put my right hand beneath one of the lyke's sweaty armpits and lifted. I don't know how much help I was, but a few moments later, the body was on its feet again.

Lyra swayed dizzily and for a moment I thought she might fall, but then she steadied herself and gave me a toothy smile.

"It worked!" The voice was Honani's, but yet it wasn't.

I nodded. "Of course. Didn't Papa Chatha say it would?" I decided not to tell her that sometime Papa's spells failed, often in quite spectacular—and deadly—fashion. Why spoil the moment?

She ran her hands across her new body. Luckily, Honani's claws had retracted during the struggle for possession of his form, or else she would have sliced herself to ribbons.

"It feels so strange . . . and I'm male now, aren't I?"

"Yes. But it's better than being dead, isn't it?"

"Oh, yes, much!" And then she looked at me. "I'm sorry, I didn't mean—"

I held up my remaining hand. "That's okay. I know what you meant." Would I have traded in my undead carcass for Honani's body? Maybe. Probably. I don't know.

She pointed at my empty, ragged left sleeve. "Your arm!"

"Don't worry about it. Occupational hazard. Papa'll fix it up for me." I hoped.

She regarded me for a moment, and I could see the confusion in her eyes.

"Something wrong?" I asked.

"I . . . I don't know what to do now." She shrugged her massive shoulders.

"You're alive; do whatever you want."

She grinned, and even though I knew it was Lyra inside the body, the sight of all those teeth being bared still unnerved me. "You're right." She came forward and gave me a hug that, if I hadn't been dead, most likely would have killed me on the spot.

"Thank you, Matthew."

I wanted to respond, but I couldn't pull any air into my dead lungs to do it. She released me, then with a wave, left the bar for whatever her new life held in store for her. I couldn't help but envy her.

Everyone watched her go, and then Skully said, "All right, show's over," and his customers returned to drinking, talking, laughing, the incident well on its way to being forgotten. Just another day in Necropolis.

I walked up to the bar and sat on one of the stools.

"Looked pretty hairy there for a minute," Skully said. "Pun intended." He grinned at that, but then he always looks like he's grinning.

"You know, I can never figure out how you talk

13

without lips or a tongue."

"Just talented, I guess."

"Right." I got off the stool. "Thanks for letting me conduct my business here."

"No sweat. What're friends for?"

"Gotta go. Papa's waiting." I started to leave.

"Matt? Don't forget your arm."

"Oh, yeah. Right." I bent down to retrieve it, more than a little embarrassed, and then continued toward the door. I was half aware of some of the bar-goers watching me as I left, especially a reed-thin, attractive blonde woman dressed in tight black leather sitting in the corner. If I'd still been alive—but I wasn't, so I continued on my way.

However, it wasn't until later that I discovered that as soon as I'd walked out the door, the blonde got up and followed.

– TWO –

Papa Chatha's shop was on the other side of the Sprawl from Skully's, and while navigating the maze of cramped streets was never easy, this time of year it was a nightmare, both figuratively and literally. For it was the anniversary of the Descension, and the Sprawl, always party central for Necropolis, had become a mix of Las Vegas and Disneyland (assuming the Haunted Mansion had exploded and taken over the entire park) during both Mardi Gras and New Year's Eve. Beings of every description—and quite a few who defied description—choked the streets, drinking, shouting, singing, groping, slapping, hitting, dancing, screwing . . . You name the verb, they were doing it. It was Halloween as scripted by Franz Kafka, with costumes and set design by Salvador Dali.

Umbriel, the shadowsun, hung motionless in the starless sky, fixed in the same position it holds day in, day out, its strange diffuse light maintaining the city's perpetual dusk. And directly below Umbriel, rising forth from the ground like a gigantic obsidian talon, visible from anywhere in Necropolis, rested the Nightspire, home to Father Dis, founder of Necropolis and its absolute ruler. And in many ways, its God.

Over three hundred years ago, the Darkfolk, rather than deal with an increasingly populous, aggressive, and technologically advanced mankind, decided to leave Earth. Led by Father Dis and the five lesser Lords, they traveled to a distant dark dimension where Necropolis was born. This

15

leavetaking, which the Darkfolk call the Descension, is Necropolis' most sacred holiday. But as far as I'm concerned, it's a gigantic pain in the ass.

"Hey, check it out!" a bald man with spider legs growing out of his head shouted, pointing at me. "He's been disarmed!"

His friends—a being who looked like a lobster in a leisure suit and a well-built woman with pythons instead of arms— laughed. I stopped.

"I only need one arm to yank those legs off your head and shove them where Umbriel doesn't shine."

The laughter died in their throats and I continued on my way to Papa Chatha's, doing my best to negotiate the twisting, winding crowd-choked streets of the aptly named Sprawl.

The architecture there is a mad conglomeration of styles—Art Deco, Tudor, Baroque, Victorian, Post-Modern, Frank Lloyd Wright, and buildings which look like structures made from regurgitated insect resin. The whole place is like an M. C. Escher fever dream. But the Sprawl is Lady Varvara's domain, and zoning isn't exactly high on the demon queen's list of priorities.

After struggling through the drunken, drugged-up throngs for what could only have been an hour or so but which felt more like a handful of eternities, I saw the greenish tint against the sky which told me I was nearing the flaming river Phlegethon and the Bridge of Nine Sorrows. Papa Chatha's was close by—finally.

And then I felt a hand on my shoulder; or rather, I felt the pressure of a hand on my shoulder, that being all the sensation my dead nerves were capable of conveying.

"Excuse me."

The voice was soft, feminine, and nervous. But while I'd

been in Necropolis only a couple years, I'd been here long enough to know that in this place, appearances mean jack. So I stepped forward, and whirled about, body tensed, ready to fight, holding my detached arm out before me like a weapon.

The woman—the leather-clad blonde I'd seen at Skully's—took a step back, startled by my action. But then she regained her composure, or at least a good portion of it, and said, "I watched you handle that lyke in the bar. A most impressive performance, Mr. Adrion."

She was barely five feet tall, slim to the point of being model-thin, with pale, washed-out skin. Her short hair was bright blonde, almost white. Her eyes were large and red, as if from crying. Or perhaps too much celebrating. "Yeah, well the next show isn't till midnight. Now if you'll pardon me, I have to go see my houngan." I turned to go.

"Wait, please!"

The urgency in her voice, almost panic, made me hesitate. "Look, whatever it is, can't it wait? I'm no expert, but as I understand these things, if I don't get my arm reattached soon, I'll lose it for good."

"I . . . it's just . . ." She looked around, as if afraid someone might be listening, though how anyone could overhear us talking in the din of celebration, I didn't know. Hell, I could barely hear us. She leaned forward and mumbled something.

"I'm sorry, you'll have to speak up."

She looked around once more and then said, with exaggerated lip movements so I'd be sure not to miss it this time, "I need you."

"Sorry, I don't go in for that kind of thing anymore. I'm dead. And I don't get off on fulfilling other people's necrophiliac fantasies. Enjoy the festival." This time I did go, forging a path through the partiers in the general direction of Papa Chatha's.

"You don't understand." Her words sounded in my ear, and although I couldn't feel her breath, I was sure it was cold, like a draft from an open grave.

"Vampire, right?" I said without turning around. "That's why I didn't hear you come up behind me just now."

"Please, we prefer the term Bloodborn."

"And I'd rather be referred to as Previously Living, but at the end of the day I'm still just a damn walking corpse." I would've loved to shake her off my trail, but even if the street hadn't been so crowded, I probably couldn't. I'm not as fast as I used to be, and at my fastest, I'm still standing still compared to a vampire . . . excuse me, one of the *Bloodborn.*

So I just kept on slogging through the crowd toward Papa Chatha's, and hoped she'd get bored soon and go find another dead man to put the moves on.

"They say you're a detective."

"They say wrong," I countered. "When I was alive, I was a cop, yes. But I'm not alive anymore." I wiggled my detached arm to emphasize my point.

"But you helped that woman, the one the lycanthrope killed."

"Sometimes I do favors for people—for a fee. Preservative spells don't come cheap, you know."

"I am in desperate need of a favor. And I can pay. Please!"

She sounded as if she might burst into tears at any moment. But that wasn't what made me stop. I knew Papa Chatha would only give me so much for Honani's soul. And now thanks to that miserable lyke ripping off my arm, I needed more work done than when I'd decided to help

Lyra. More work than Honani's rotten spirit would pay for.

It wasn't the threat of her tears. It was the money. Really.

I turned around. "All right, Miss . . . ?"

"Devona," she supplied. "Devona Kanti."

"You can come along, Devona. We can talk after I see Papa. But I'm not promising anything," I cautioned.

"Of course." But she smiled in relief just the same.

I rotated my left arm and then flexed it a couple times.

"How's it feel?" Papa Chatha asked.

"A bit loose," I admitted.

Papa ran long, slender black fingers through his short gray hair, and then sighed. "That's what I was afraid of."

"I don't like the sound of that."

Papa Chatha was a dignified, handsome black man in his sixties, with a tattoo of a blue butterfly spread across his smooth-shaven face. The edges of the butterfly's wings seemed to ripple, but it was probably just my imagination.

Papa sat on the only chair in his workroom, a simple wooden stool, and smoothed his loose white pants which matched his pullover shirt. He then tapped his bare toes on the wooden floor.

I had the impression he was stalling.

"You're a self-willed zombie, Matt. Do you have any idea how rare that is?" He had a deep, resonant voice that was usually full of good humor. But he was somber today.

"From what you've told me, pretty damn rare."

He nodded. "Most zombies are merely reanimated corpses, bereft of souls, linked to the lifeforce of the sorcerer who raised them from the dead. It's this link, this sharing of a living being's lifeforce, which prevents their dead flesh from withering away. But you have no master." He frowned. "How did you become a zombie, anyway, Matt? You've never told me."

"Just too stubborn to die, I suppose."

Papa looked at me a long moment before going on. "Since you have no master—"

"I know," I interrupted. "I need you and your magic to keep my body in tip-top condition."

Papa gestured at the collection of odds and ends that cluttered the shelves and benches of his workroom—rodent skulls and chicken feet, candles of all sizes and colors, varying lengths of rope tied in complicated patterns of knots, and small dolls of corn shucks and horsehair.

"My meager arts can only do so much, Matt. And I fear they've done all they can for you."

I don't feel emotions the same way I did when I was alive, but I felt an echo of fear at Papa Chatha's words. "What do you mean?"

"That this last application of preservative spells almost didn't take. And they may not last more than two, three days."

"You mean—"

"We've staved off the inevitable as long as we could, my friend. I'm sorry."

I felt like a man who'd just been told by his doctor that he only had a short time to live. And I suppose in a way, I was.

"Nothing personal, Papa, but is there anyone else who might be able to help me? After all, Necropolis is lousy with all sorts of witches and magicians. Maybe one of them—"

Papa shook his head. "I'm afraid not. While it's true there are others more powerful than I, there is only so much power can do."

I thought for a moment. "Could my spirit be caught, like

Honani's, and implanted into a second body?"

"Perhaps," Papa allowed. "If you are willing to steal another's form."

So much for that. After what he'd done to Lyra, Honani deserved to be evicted from his body. But I couldn't do that to someone else just to save my own life. If I did, I'd be in effect a killer, no better than Honani.

I stood there, trying to come to terms with what Papa had told me. I wasn't going to die. I couldn't; I was already dead. But my body was going to . . . what? Collapse into a puddle of putrefaction? Or just flake away to dust? And when it was gone, what would happen to me? Would I end up wandering Necropolis, a disembodied spirit like Lyra? Or would my soul depart for some manner of afterlife? Assuming, of course, that there was any beyond Necropolis. Or would I just cease to be, my spirit rotting away to nothing along with my body?

As much as I hated my mockery of a life, it was the only mockery I had, and I didn't particularly want to lose it. There had to be a way for me to continue existing, a way that wouldn't result in my having to steal another's body. I'd just have to find it within the next couple days.

I shook Papa's hand. "I appreciate everything you've done for me." I reached into my pocket, intending to hand over the soul jar containing Honani's spirit to pay for Papa's services.

"Keep it, Matt." He smiled sadly. "This one's on the house, okay?"

I didn't know what I'd do with Honani's soul, but Papa refused to take it, so in the end I walked out with the jar still in my pocket. I had two souls now, when what I needed was another body. Life—and death—is full of little ironies, isn't it?

* * * * *

Devona was waiting for me outside, leaning up against the wooden wall of Papa's shack, arms crossed, surveying the crowd with a wary, nervous gaze.

Her leather outfit clung to her like a second skin, and even though I no longer had any libido to speak of, I had to admit she looked pretty good.

I had my own problem now, and no time for hers. But I thought I could at least hear her out. Maybe her problem would turn out to be something simple. And I could use the darkgems; I would need them if I was going to find someone else—someone more powerful than Papa—to extend my unlife.

"All done. I'm ready to talk." I didn't feel a need to mention the bad news I'd received. After all, Devona and I had just met.

"Not here. We need someplace private."

Like I'd told her, I wasn't a detective, no matter what she'd heard from them, whoever the hell they were, and I didn't have an office. But I did live not too far from Papa Chatha's.

"How about my place?"

She nodded.

A few more blocks of negotiating our way through the chaotic riot of celebrants—which for Devona meant slapping more than a few males of various species and states of life and death who decided to grab her shapely leather-clad posterior—and we were there.

My neighborhood is actually one of the more mundane sections of the Sprawl, a street of urban townhouses, which, except for the fact that the bricks appear to be made of gristle, looks perfectly ordinary.

We went up the front steps, inside, and up more steps to

my apartment. I had unlocked the door and was just about to grip the knob when a voice behind us said, "Hey, Matt!"

"Hell," I muttered, and turned around to greet my neighbor. "Hi, Carl," I said without enthusiasm. "What's up?"

Carl was a grizzled old fart in a rumpled seersucker suit which had probably once been white but was now mostly yellow.

He grabbed a sheet of mimeographed paper from the stack under his arm and thrust it into my hand.

"Just finished the latest edition of the *Night Stalker News*. I'm breaking a major story this week."

I glanced at the blue-ink headline: WATCHERS FROM OUTSIDE PLOT CITY'S DESTRUCTION.

"Sounds ominous, Carl. I'll be sure to read it."

I quickly opened the door and gestured for Devona to go in; she did and I hurried after her.

Carl scowled. "Don't you humor me now, Matt. It's true! And if we don't do something about it soon, we'll all be—"

I closed the door in Carl's rapidly reddening face, cutting him off.

"Just you wait!" came his muffled voice from the other side of the door. "You'll be singing a different tune when the Watchers come!"

He shouted a bit more before finally moving off, grumbling to himself about idiot zombie cops.

"Who was that?" Devona asked.

"Just some nut who lives upstairs. Used to be some sort of tabloid reporter back on Earth. He won't bother us anymore. He'll no doubt head out into the street to harangue the festival-goers with his latest paranoid exposé." I crumpled Carl's so-called "paper" into a wad and tossed it into an

23

empty corner while Devona surveyed the room.

"It's better than a tomb, even if it does have about as much personality." A threadbare couch, a single wooden chair (with one leg shorter than the others), and a small black and white TV that sat on the floor comprised the sole contents of the living room. No pictures, no rugs, not even curtains. No toilet facilities, either, but then I don't need them. One of the perks of being dead.

"Do you have a bed?" she asked.

"I told you: I don't do those kind of favors."

She gave me a look which said I was being less than amusing. "I'm just curious. Do zombies sleep? I've never thought about it before. But then, I've never been to a zombie's apartment, either."

"I have a bed." Though it was just a lumpy mattress sitting on the floor, no sheets, no covers. "I don't sleep, exactly, but sometimes I feel a need to . . . rest. To relax."

"And so you just lie there and stare at the ceiling?"

"Sometimes. Sometimes I close my eyes. So tell me, what's it like to sleep in a coffin? Ever feel like a sardine?"

"Bloodborn don't sleep in coffins," she said disdainfully.

"Even when they're half human?"

Her eyes widened in surprise. "How did you know?"

I shrugged, the gesture a bit lopsided thanks to the bite Honani had taken out of my shoulder, which Papa couldn't completely repair. "Little things. You don't move as gracefully as other vampires. Your pallor isn't as white. And whatever your problem is, it's got you tied up in knots inside. I've never seen a full-blooded vampire afraid. It doesn't seem to be an emotion they're capable of."

I went into the bedroom, and she followed. I removed the soul jar from my pocket, and placed it on my mattress. I then took off my torn jacket, tie, and shirt, and opened the closet door. I dropped my ruined garments on the floor of the closet next to my footlocker and scanned my pitifully small collection of clothes for replacements. If Devona felt any disgust upon seeing so much of my bare zombie skin with its slight grayish cast revealed, she showed no sign.

"Vampires feel fear," she said. "They just don't like to show it. But you're right; I'm only half Bloodborn. My mother was human."

From my closet's meager offerings, I chose a brown shirt, yellow paisley tie, and a brown jacket. I could wear whatever I want, I suppose. I'm not a cop anymore, and besides, I'm dead. Who cares how I dress? But old habits— and old cops like me—die hard, I guess. And besides, wearing the sort of clothes I wore in life makes me feel more . . . well, human.

I dressed and stood before the cracked mirror hanging on the wall and adjusted my tie. Thanks to Papa Chatha's latest round of spells, I didn't look too much different than I had in life, grayish skin aside. Black hair, brown eyes, features on the ordinary side of handsome (or so I'd been told by my ex-wife; I'm no judge of such things). Face a bit thinner than when I'd been alive. Death is a great diet plan.

I put the soul jar in the pocket of my new jacket. I'm not really sure why; it just didn't seem like the sort of thing a person should leave lying around, then turned to face my guest. "And who's your father?"

She hesitated a moment before answering. "Lord Galm."

-THREE-

"I think you'd better leave now," I said.

Confusion spread across her face. "Why?"

"It's nothing personal; I just make it a policy never to get involved with Darklords if I can avoid it. And that includes getting involved with their relatives."

Lord Galm is an ancient, powerful vampire, ruler of the Bloodborn, and of Gothtown, the section of the city where the vampires live, or rather, exist. And like any Darklord, he's dangerous as hell. I'd rather run up to a Mafia don in his favorite restaurant, dump his spaghetti marinara in his lap, and accuse him of diddling his grandchildren than I would mess with a Darklord.

"Please, at least let me—"

I held up a hand to cut her off. "I'm sorry. Really, I am. But getting involved with a Darklord is what got me killed and resurrected as a zombie. I hate to think what might happen to me the next time. Being dead isn't all that much fun, but I've lived in Necropolis long enough to know it could be worse. A lot worse."

She cocked her head to one side and looked at me as if seeing me for the first time. "I hadn't heard about that. Which Darklord was it?"

"I'd rather not talk about it, if you don't mind. And I don't want to talk about your problem either, not if it involves Lord Galm."

She crossed her arms and gave me a calculating look. It didn't appear as if she were in a hurry to leave.

26

"I don't know a lot about zombies, but I know they need to have preservative spells regularly applied to keep them from rotting. And spells cost money."

"I can get darkgems elsewhere," I said, trying to sound more confident about my ability to do so than I felt. And besides, I wasn't worried about mere preservative spells now. I needed to find a way to keep my body from rotting away to nothing. I imagined I could already feel the slight itch of decay—one of the few sensations I can feel.

"One hundred? Two? Three hundred?" she countered. "Three hundred darkgems would pay for quite a lot of spells."

"They would at that," I was forced to admit. But would even three hundred be enough to buy the kind of magic I would need to keep my body intact?

And then it hit me. I needed the kind of power few beings in Necropolis possessed: the power of a Darklord. If I helped Devona, perhaps she would intercede with her father on my behalf—and Lord Galm could use his magic to "cure" me.

I cautioned myself not to get excited, that it was a long shot, that even if Devona asked, Lord Galm might not help me. But right then it looked like the best—and only—shot I had. Besides, if I did have only a few days left in my existence, I'd rather spend them working than sitting around my place staring at the walls.

"All right, Devona, tell me about your problem."

"I'm seventy-three years old. Surprised?"

"Not really," I said. "Seventy-three is young for a vampire."

We were sitting in the living room, Devona on the couch, I in the chair. The sounds of the Descension celebration out

27

in the street a muted background to our conversation.

"Although I have to admit, you're the best looking seventy-three-year-old I've ever seen."

She blushed slightly. Another sign that she was half human. A full-blooded vampire can't blush.

"Lord Galm didn't exactly love my mother. But he came as close to it as a being like him can, and when I was born, he brought me from Earth to Necropolis."

"And your mother?"

"Died delivering me," she said softly. "Human women usually do when giving birth to a half-Bloodborn child." She looked down at her lap, where the thin, fine fingers of her delicate hands played nervously with each other. "We have our teeth early, you see, and we're born hungry . . ."

"I understand. Go on."

"I was raised in the Cathedral. I didn't see my father very often—he was usually busy ruling Gothtown or engaging in power struggles with the other Lords. I was cared for and taught by Father's staff, and I grew and learned."

"I thought vampires didn't age."

"Those that were originally human and transformed into Bloodborn do not. But those like me, who are half human, do age, only very, very slowly."

"So you'll die one day?"

She nodded. "And afterward, I may rise as one completely Bloodborn. Or I may not. No one can say."

"Could your father transform you, make you a full vampire?"

"He could try. But there's no guarantee I would survive the process and be reborn. At this point, I'd rather wait and take my chances."

"I don't blame you."

"When I reached my forty-fifth birthday, Father called

me in to his study and told me that he wished me to join the staff of the Cathedral and serve him. It was a great honor, and I accepted thankfully."

"What did he want you to do?"

"I was given charge of his Collection, and I have taken care of it for the last twenty-eight years."

I noticed a black spot on the far wall—a spot which hadn't been there when we'd started talking. It was a roach-like insect. Gregor, or rather one of his little informants. I nearly waved hello, but I didn't want to appear as if I wasn't listening to Devona. Besides, Gregor probably didn't care if I acknowledged his presence or not. All he wanted to do was observe.

"His . . . Collection?" I said, returning to the conversation.

"Father is incredibly ancient, how old, even he isn't certain. Thousands and thousands of years, at least. And in all that time, he has acquired quite a number of items. Some are merely mementos of lives lived, countries and cities long dead; others are trophies: of triumphs, conquests, battles won, enemies defeated. Still others are tokens of magic, mystical objects of great power—any of which the other Darklords would dearly love to get their hands on in order to increase their own strength.

"As I said, I have watched over, cared for, and guarded the Collection for nearly three decades. And I have never had any problems," she said proudly. But then she lowered her head. "Until yesterday."

"Let me guess. You went to check on the Collection and found something missing."

"How did—of course, you're a detective."

I almost protested that I wasn't, that I was just an ex-cop (and ex-human) who did favors for people, but I decided to let it lie.

"Yes, something was missing. And I want you to help me get it back."

I thought for a moment. "Why come to me? Why not go to Lord Galm? He's a Darklord, with the powers at his command, I should think he'd be able to locate the object easily."

"Perhaps. But I cannot go to my father. Lord Galm is not especially . . . understanding of failure. Or forgiving. My only hope is to recover the object on my own, or at least discover what has happened to it. If I am unable to do either . . ." she trailed off, shuddering.

"But you're his daughter."

"Yes, but the Bloodborn have a different set of values when it comes to determining family relationships. Those who are chosen for transformation are considered true children, and are closest to their sires' hearts. Half-human get like me . . . well, I suppose the closest human equivalent would be children born out of wedlock. Our sires still care for us, just not as deeply.

"Most of Lord Galm's staff are children of his, whether fully Bloodborn or partially. And there is a great deal of competition among us for our father's favor."

"And so you can't turn to any of them, either."

She nodded. "That's why I need your help. You have a reputation for not only getting the job done, but for keeping quiet about it as well."

"I didn't know I had a reputation. I don't suppose you heard anything about my sparkling personality or my dazzling wit?"

She smiled. "Unfortunately not."

She had a beautiful smile, the effect spoiled only slightly by her revealed canine teeth.

"Tell me about the object."

"It's a crystal a little larger than my fist called the Dawnstone. What it does precisely, I'm not certain. While I tend his Collection, Lord Galm doesn't entrust me with complete knowledge of it, and the Dawnstone is one of those items whose secrets he wishes to keep to himself."

I thought it ironic a vampire would own an artifact called a "Dawnstone."

"But you know it's powerful," I said.

"Of course. Why else would Father be so secretive about it? And the wardspells which protect it are among the most potent in the Cathedral."

"Yet someone got past those spells."

"Yes."

"How do you know Lord Galm didn't just take the Dawnstone himself and forgot to tell you?"

"Father is a stickler for procedure. In twenty-eight years he has never failed to inform me when he removed an item from the Collection."

"Still, there's always a first time," I pointed out.

"I suppose. But I can hardly go up and ask him, can I? If he hasn't removed the Dawnstone, my asking after it would alert him to its disappearance."

"And buy you a world of trouble."

"Yes."

She definitely needed help—and I needed the aid of a Darklord if I was to survive. I stood. "I have more questions, but I can ask them on the way."

"The way to where?"

"The Cathedral, of course. One of the first steps in any investigation is to examine the scene of the crime."

I looked over at the spot on the wall where the bug had been, but it was gone now. Gregor had probably gotten bored.

She stood and, smiling, took my hand and gave it a squeeze. "Thank you, Mr. Adrion."

I could only feel the pressure of her hand, but I could imagine how smooth and soft her skin was. "Call me Matthew."

Detective or not, I was on the job once more—and this time, I was working not only to help my "client," but to save my own life.

Talk about incentive.

–FOUR–

Before leaving, I made a few selections from the foot locker on the floor of my closet, and secreted them in various places about my person (mostly in extra pockets sewn into my suit jacket). And then I was ready, or at least as ready as I was going to get.

As we walked down the front steps of my building, Devona eyed the streetful of drunken, noisy revelers. "It's going to take some time to get through this mess."

"You could go on ahead, and I could meet you."

"Go on? Oh, you mean shapeshift. I don't possess the capability of assuming a travel form. Not many half-human Bloodborn do. Although I do have other . . . talents."

Before I could think of a witty reply, a shriek went up from the festivalgoers at the far end of the street, and the crowd began to part like water before a large yellow object careening toward us.

"Oh, no," I moaned. "It's Lazlo."

Sure enough, with a rattling and knocking of the engine and a roar of purplish exhaust, Lazlo's cab carved a path through the suddenly terrified partiers, only running down one or two in the process. Lazlo pulled up to the curb in front of my building with a pitiful squeal of brakes begging to be replaced and sent on to car-part heaven.

"Heya, Matt! How's it hanging?"

"I'm dead, Lazlo, remember? Hanging is all it does anymore."

Lazlo guffawed violently, his laughter a combination of

genuine amusement and someone in desperate need of the Heimlich maneuver. Lazlo's a demon whose face looks something like a cross between a mandrill and a ferret, with a little carp thrown in for good measure. And although I can't testify to this personally, I've heard he smells like a toxic waste dump.

Evidently the rumors were true, for Devona recoiled as if she'd just took a sledge hammer blow to the side of the head.

"Need a ride, pal?" Lazlo asked.

"You know I do. When else do you show up?"

He guffawed again, sounding this time like he was about to cough up a kidney. "You slay me, Matt." He put the engine in park, hopped out, opened the rear door, and gestured for us to climb in, bowing as he did so.

"Your chariot awaits."

Lazlo, despite my attempts to convince him that it would be in the best interest of the entire citizenry of Necropolis, does not wear clothing. His body resembles a spider that's been turned inside out and then stomped on. I've gotten somewhat accustomed to his rather, er, unique anatomy over the years. But Devona's eyes goggled.

"No offense," she said, "but I'd prefer to walk."

"Every moment we waste is another moment for your father to find out what's happened," I said softly.

She hesitated, but finally agreed. "I may have to hold my nose the whole trip, though."

"Go right ahead." I didn't tell her it wouldn't help. She'd find out soon enough.

We got into the cab; Lazlo closed the door, hopped behind the driver's seat, and put the car in gear.

"Surprise me, Lazlo," I said, "and try not to drive like a maniac for a ch—" That's as far as I got before Lazlo slammed on the gas and I was thrown back against the seat.

He hung half out of his open window, shouting, "Outta the way, morons!"

Most of the celebrants scattered, but a massive bull-headed man wearing an I'M HORNY T-shirt wasn't—pardon the expression—cowed so easily. He planted his feet firmly on the ground and braced himself for impact.

"Look at the size of him!" Devona cried. "Swerve, damn you!"

But there was no point shouting at Lazlo. He never listened to passenger protests.

"Hold on," I warned Devona, and then there was a loud crash and the cab shuddered and jerked; but it kept moving. Behind us, falling quickly away in the distance, came the wounded bellow of one very unhappy—but lucky to be alive—minotaur.

"Hah!" Lazlo barked in triumph. "That'll teach that dumbass to play chicken with me!" He turned around to look at us, and grinned. "So where we headed, folks?"

"Put your eyes back on the road, and I'll tell you," I said nervously. The last time Lazlo turned around to talk to me, we almost ended up taking a flame bath in Phlegethon.

Lazlo laughed, but did as I asked, so I said, "The Cathedral. And we'd like to get there in as close to one piece as possible."

"Gotcha. You two just sit back and enjoy the ride." He pointed his cab in the general direction of the Bridge of Nine Sorrows—the crossing point between the Sprawl and Gothtown—and pressed down on the accelerator.

"Enjoy the ride?" Devona said, her nails digging into the greasy fabric of the seat. "Not until it's over!"

I had to agree.

A few blocks from my townhouse, Lazlo was forced to stop when a fight erupted between a group of lykes and several vampires. Even Lazlo wouldn't try to drive through that mess. Things got pretty bloody for a bit, until a Sentinel came charging through the crowd, knocking aside those who didn't get out of its way fast enough, and broke the conflict up, basically by breaking the combatants up. The Sentinels are Father Dis' police force: eight feet tall, massive, gray-fleshed, featureless golems that are strong as hell and, as far as I know, completely invulnerable. The lykes and vamps tried to fight back, but they never had a chance. When it was over, the Sentinel tossed their bloody, broken bodies into an alley and stomped off. The fighters would heal, eventually, but in the meantime, they wouldn't be bothering anyone.

As Lazlo pulled away from the scene, I said, "Every time I see a Sentinel in action, I can't help thinking we could've used a few during my days on the force in Cleveland. Sure would've made life a lot easier."

"For the cops, maybe," Lazlo said. "But the morticians would've been a hell of a lot busier!" He laughed and laughed, as if it were the funniest thing he'd ever heard.

"I've never seen a Sentinel before," Devona said quietly.

I looked at her, surprised. "You're kidding."

She gave a small shrug. "I don't get out of Gothtown, much."

From her tone, I knew she wanted that to be the end of it, so I leaned forward and said to Lazlo, "Hear anything interesting on the street lately?"

"I hear lots of things, Matt." He yanked the steering wheel to the right just in time to miss a skeletal being in a sombrero who looked like a picture on a Mexican Day of the Dead postcard.

"Hear anything about any big thefts recently?"

Devona frowned, but she didn't object to my asking.

"Big thefts? How big?"

"Big. We're talking about an object of power, Lazlo. A lot of power."

He shook his head and gunned the engine to avoid a group of what looked like shadowy box kites with glowing red eyes. The things were darting up and down, in and out, in a complex formation. The cab bumped up and over the curb and suddenly we were driving along the sidewalk.

"Can't say as I have, Matt. But I'll keep my ear to the ground."

"Just so long as you keep your wheels on the ground, Lazlo."

The demon guffawed and continued barrel-assing down the sidewalk, honking his horn like a maniac.

Once we entered Gothtown, the crowds thinned out considerably. The Sprawl is to Necropolis what the French Quarter is to New Orleans—which is exactly the way Lady Varvara likes it—and thus the majority of the Descension celebration was taking place there. But that didn't mean Gothtown was deserted. Lazlo passed a number of horse-drawn carriages likely bearing their occupants to various private parties. The older vampires tend to keep to themselves and their section of the city; it's the younger ones who seek out the more decadent lifestyle offered by the Sprawl.

Gothtown itself lives up to its name: every street looks like a set-piece for an old Universal horror flick, buildings of gray stone sporting arches, spikes, towers, turrets, and gargoyles. Quaint enough in its own way, but I really could've done without the cobblestone streets, especially at the speed at which Lazlo drove over them. By the time the Cathedral hove into view, even my dead kidneys were starting to ache from the abuse.

"Let us off a couple blocks away, Lazlo," I said.

"Will do, Matt."

Lazlo slowed and actually came to a stop without slamming on the brakes and fishtailing for a half dozen yards as he usually does. Maybe his driving skills were beginning to improve. Or maybe he figured we'd suffered enough for one ride and decided to take pity on us. Whichever, he stopped and we got out. Being dead, I guess my sense of balance was less affected by the tumultuous ride than Devona's. As soon as her feet touched the cobblestones, her knees buckled under her. She would've fallen if I hadn't managed to catch her in time.

I helped her stand, and she nodded to indicate she was okay. I wasn't so certain, but I took my hands away. She stood a trifle unsteadily, but she stood.

She faced to Lazlo. "How much do we owe you?"

His fur turned crimson. "Owe me?" he said, as if grievously insulted. "Lady, Matthew Adrion and his friends never have to pay to ride in my cab—not after what he did for me!" And with a wave, and a wink of a bulbous bloodshot eye to me, he roared off to endanger lives elsewhere in the city.

"What did he mean by that?" Devona asked.

"I've done favors for other people besides you. But I don't think Lazlo would appreciate me discussing the particulars."

She scowled. "You didn't seem too reluctant to discuss my problem when you were asking him questions. 'Hear anything about any big thefts recently?' I told you I don't want anyone to find out what's happened—especially Lord Galm."

"One of the things I hated the most when I was alive was people trying to tell me how to do my job. And that hasn't changed now that I'm dead. You want me to find the

Dawnstone? Then I'm going to have to ask questions. And you'll just have to trust me to do so as discreetly as possible. You don't have to worry about Lazlo. He won't say anything; he's good people, even if he is a demon."

She looked like she was going to say something, but then thought better about it. "All right. I'm sorry I questioned you. Now let's go."

We started walking toward the Cathedral.

"By the way," Devona asked, "how did he know to come get us?"

"I have no idea. Sometimes he just shows up when I need him."

"That's odd," she said.

I laughed. "You're a half-human vampire who's asked a zombie ex-cop to help you track down a stolen magic crystal—and you think Lazlo's odd?"

She smiled. "You've got a point."

We walked to the end of the street, turned the corner, and before us lay the Cathedral. I've never been to Europe, but I've seen pictures of the great Gothic cathedrals. But this place made them all look like tarpaper shacks. It rose four, maybe five hundred feet into the sky (Umbriel's strange shadowlight sometimes makes it hard to judge distances correctly). I'd never been this close before, and if I still breathed, the sheer insane scope of the structure would have taken my breath away. If I hadn't known this was Lord Galm's home, I wouldn't have been surprised to discover the name "Jehovah" stenciled on the mailbox.

A number of carriages were lined up outside the Cathedral and various good-looking men and women, mostly in period dress, were disembarking and entering through the vast entranceway between twin black oak doors at least fifty feet tall.

"Lord Galm always hosts a reception for the elite of the Bloodborn before the Renewal Ceremony," Devona said. "A number of dignitaries even return from Earth to attend."

"There are still vampires on Earth? I thought all the Darkfolk, vampires included, had migrated to Necropolis."

"Most did. But some remained behind, hidden, to look after the Lords' interests on Earth—and to keep clandestine trade routes open."

That explained how so much modern technology had found its way to Necropolis. Even across dimensions, the law of supply and demand still held sway.

I felt a pang at the thought of the dimensional portal housed within the Cathedral. Each Darklord had one; I had entered Necropolis through Lady Varvara's. But any one of them would return me to Earth, if not to my hometown of Cleveland. But they wouldn't do me any good now. Now that I was dead.

I had heard mention of the Renewal Ceremony before, but didn't know much about it. But I had more immediate concerns right then. "Maybe this isn't the best time to examine the Collection. Things look awfully busy right now."

"No, it's the perfect time. Everyone is so caught up in the reception that no one will notice us."

"I don't think too many zombies received engraved invitations to Lord Galm's party."

"There'll be quite a few humans there as well. Ones who are . . . drawn to the Bloodborn."

"I know what you mean. Shadows." Vampire groupies who get their rocks off by having their blood drained, or who hope to form a relationship with a vampire and become one of the Bloodborn. Or both. They're called Shadows because they stick close to whichever vampire claims them—and because over time the cumulative blood loss makes them thin, pale shadows of their former selves.

"If anyone takes note of your pallor, and the way you walk, they'll just think you're another Shadow." She smiled, almost shyly. "My Shadow."

I frowned. "What's wrong with the way I walk?"

"Never mind." She took my elbow, the strength of her grip surprising me even though it shouldn't have, and led me across the street toward the Cathedral. I tried very hard not to feel self-conscious about my slightly stiff-legged zombie gait.

A crimson carpet, appropriately enough, had been laid out for the occasion, and we walked across it, up the steps, and toward the open doorway. Above the entrance perched a clutch of snarling stone gargoyles, and as we came closer, I could have sworn that one of them moved the slightest bit. I tried to tell myself that it was my imagination, but I wasn't very convincing.

Whether they were just statues or something else, the gargoyles remained motionless after that, and then we were in.

Before us stretched a long stone corridor with torches burning in wall sconces. The flames were green-tinted—the same fire as that which burned in Phlegethon? I didn't know. But whatever the nature of the flame, it produced no smoke. No heat, either, as near as my dead nerves could tell. Still, I didn't want to get too close. No sense taking a chance on becoming zombie barbecue.

"We'll just take the corridor to the ballroom, and then keep on going," Devona whispered.

I nodded slightly. We were on her turf; all I could do was follow her lead.

As we continued, the mingled sounds of merriment—tinkling glasses, the buzz of conversation punctuated by an

41

occasional burst of laughter, the soft lyrical sound of a string quartet—grew louder. The couple before us, who were garbed in Roman togas as white as their alabaster skin, were greeted enthusiastically at the ballroom entrance by a large burly vampire dressed like a Scottish highlander.

The highlander said something I didn't catch, and the three of them broke into peals of laughter. But their merriment had a dark edge to it, and I was glad I hadn't overheard what had sparked it.

We reached the ballroom and kept going, passing the Romans and the highlander who were still chuckling over whatever black joke had amused them. And although I shouldn't have done it, was risking drawing attention to ourselves—or specifically to my non-vampiric, non-human, not-invited-to-the-party self—I couldn't resist taking a quick look into the ballroom. What can I say? A curious nature was one of the things which led me to become a cop in the first place.

The ballroom was gigantic, four stories high at least. The floor and walls were completely covered by a smooth, mirrored surface that reflected the greenish light from the wall sconces, a scattering of people whom I took to be human, and nothing else—despite the fact that the room was packed with men and woman garbed in all manner of historical dress, from ancient Greece to Victorian England.

I tried to catch a glimpse of myself in the wall mirror, but there were so many people milling about I couldn't. I did, however, see a hazy ghost image of a petite blonde for just a moment. Devona was half human. It only made sense she would cast half a reflection.

But as impressive as the gathering of Bloodborn royalty was in and of itself, one thing was more impressive still. In the center of the room stood a great marble fountain, and bubbling forth from it a thick shower of reddish-black liquid. I told myself the viscous fluid couldn't really be what it seemed; that it was merely a decorative effect of some sort achieved through Lord Galm's dark arts. I almost believed it, too.

And then we were past the ballroom and continuing down the corridor.

"I don't think anyone noticed us," Devona said, relieved.

"I hope you're right."

After a few dozen more feet we came to a winding stone staircase. Devona removed a torch from a sconce on the wall and started up the stairs. I held back a little. Maybe the torch wasn't lit with real fire, but zombie-flesh is dry, bloodless, and very flammable. I wasn't about to take any chances.

Devona led the way up: two, four, seven floors. I don't tire as I did when alive, but just to break the silence, I said, "I wonder if Lord Galm has ever considered installing an elevator."

"Most Bloodborn don't need to rely on stairs," she answered. "They have their travel forms. Besides, Father won't have anything to do with technology. He thinks it a decadence which promotes laziness of the mind and spirit."

"I didn't notice Lord Galm in the ballroom," I said.

"He's probably still meditating, marshaling his power for the Renewal Ceremony."

I thought I might take the opportunity to find out more about this ceremony—it struck me as awfully coincidental that one of Lord Galm's most powerful mystic objects should just happen to vanish so close to the Renewal Ceremony. But then we reached the ninth floor and Devona gestured that we should stop.

Devona stuck her head into the corridor, looked both

ways, and then motioned for me to follow. I did, but to the right I saw a window, and I couldn't resist stepping over to it and taking a quick peek outside.

The window was covered with thick iron bars, but that wasn't the only protection. I could hear, or rather almost hear, a hum in the air, like the ultrasonic whine of an alarm system.

"Don't stand too close," Devona said. "The wardspell on the window is a particularly deadly one."

"Thanks for the tip."

The borders of Necropolis form a perfect pentagram, and the points of the pentagram—connected by the flaming barrier of Phlegethon—are the strongholds of the five Darklords. This window faced outward from Necropolis and toward the Null Plains: a flat black featureless expanse which stretched to the horizon. A whole hell of a lot of Nothing.

I'd only seen the Null Plains a couple times before, but viewing them always gave me the creeps. There was something about the blackness that the human (or zombie) eye couldn't quite deal with, a subtle movement, nearly undetectable, like glacially slow tides of solid darkness sliding and swirling against one another.

I thought of crazy Carl and the headline of his idiotic "newspaper"—WATCHERS FROM OUTSIDE PLOT CITY'S DESTRUCTION—and I couldn't help shuddering. Looking out at the endless darkness, I could almost believe something was out there, watching, waiting . . .

"Not much to see," Devona said.

"Not much," I agreed, turning away from the window. There was nothing out there, certainly not any Watchers. Carl was a loon, and that was the end of it.

We continued down the corridor past a series of solid-looking wooden doors, each of which appeared to be exactly like the one before it, until we came to a door which didn't seem particularly special, but evidently was, for Devona stopped.

"This is it. The entrance to the Collection." She unzipped her leather jacket halfway to her waist to reveal an iron key hanging between her partially exposed breasts.

As she removed the key and the chain from which it dangled, I asked, "Is this the only key to the chamber?"

She nodded. "Not even Lord Galm has one. But then, he doesn't need a key. The door is spelled to open at his touch." She moved to insert the key in the lock—not having bothered to zip up her jacket (like I said, I pay attention to details)—but I grabbed her wrist before she could.

"Let me have a look first." I let go of her wrist and knelt down to examine the lock.

There aren't too many good things about being a zombie, but one of them is that, while my thought processes take a little longer than they used to, I'm able to focus my attention and concentrate like crazy. The dead aren't easily distracted.

The lock appeared to be made of the same iron as the key. The door handle rested directly above it. I looked closely for scratches, nicks, or dents—anything which might indicate the lock had been picked or forced. There were none.

I straightened. "Let's go in." I stepped aside, and Devona inserted the key. The lock turned with a metallic clack, she pushed open the door, and Lord Galm's great Collection was laid bare before us.

−FIVE−

And most impressive it was.

The stone walls were covered with weapons, from simple wooden spears and bows to highly polished swords and ornate jewel-encrusted daggers. There were broadaxes far too large for anyone possessed of merely human strength to wield, and a series of maces and morningstars, each covered with larger and crueler spikes than the last.

The floor was taken up by stone tables, daises, and columns upon which rested a variety of non-military objects: a tiny golden skull which glowed with a soft, gentle yellow light; an Egyptian scarab carved from jade, but which nevertheless moved, scratching away at the inner surface of the glass globe which imprisoned it; a stereopticon constructed entirely of what appeared to be spider silk, a stack of picture cards next to it, displaying what looked like Tarot images; and on and on. There were no placards, no labels to name the objects, but after nearly thirty years of tending the Collection, I doubted Devona needed any.

The Collection communicated an almost tangible sensation of antiquity, and for the first time I had an inkling of what it truly meant to be immortal.

"I'm surprised everything's out in the open like this," I said.

"They're protected by wardspells placed by Lord Galm himself."

"I don't much know about magic, but as I understand, certain spells have to be renewed from time to time." Like the preservative spells which, up until that point anyway, had kept me from crumbling into a pile of rotten hamburger. "Maybe some of these, specifically the one protecting the Dawnstone, are due for a recharge."

She shook her head. "My job is to oversee the Collection, which means that I primarily monitor the wardspells. Lord Galm saw to it that I was taught just enough spellcraft to check the wards, but not enough to actually tamper with them. The wardspells Lord Galm employs are powerful and intricate. It takes me over six hours to check them all. And the first thing I did when I realized the Dawnstone was missing was examine the ward which protected it. The spell was intact and not due to be recharged by Lord Galm for some time."

"Is it possible for someone with enough magical know-how to circumvent the wardspell?"

She thought about that for a minute.

"I suppose, but it's highly unlikely. Another Darklord might be able to do it, but then a Darklord could never enter the Cathedral without Lord Galm knowing."

It was my turn to think. "How about any of the visitors from Earth? Do any of them possess enough power and skill?"

"There are some who are almost as ancient as my father, and certainly as cunning," she admitted. "But Father keeps a very close eye on them when they're in Necropolis."

"Might he have brought one of them up here to show off his Collection and—"

"No," she interrupted. "Father is a private man, and not given to bragging."

"I see. It strikes me as odd that someone—" I couldn't bring myself to call Lord Galm a man—"who is so secretive and possessive about his Collection should entrust its care to another, no matter how worthy of that trust she might be."

"Father is very, very old, and his mind . . ." She paused. "After millennia of existence, time doesn't mean the same thing to him as it does to you and me. Not only would the constant examination of the wardspells waste hours which he could be spending on more important matters, quite frankly, months, perhaps years, might go by before he remembered to check the wards."

"So you got your job because your dad has a lousy memory."

She smiled ruefully. "Something like that."

I nodded. It was looking more and more like Lord Galm—despite Devona's assurance that he would never do so—had removed the Dawnstone for reasons of his own, reasons he had elected not to share with the guardian of his Collection. But I decided to continue my examination of the room anyway. After all, that's what she was paying me for, right?

"Show me where the Dawnstone was."

Devona led me through the maze of clutter that was Lord Galm's Collection until we came to a narrow stone column with nothing on it.

"It was here. Don't get closer than a foot or so," she warned. "The wardspell's still active."

"And we don't want to alert Lord Galm that we're here. Right." I stood as close as I could and took a look at the spot where the Dawnstone had rested. I didn't know what I thought I might see, but then I never did; that's why you look.

At first glance there appeared to be nothing special about the flat surface of the column. Just smooth gray stone, no cracks, no sign of age. The column might have been chiseled yesterday for all I could tell. Part of the wardspell's protective qualities?

Another thing about being dead: my patience has increased. When I was alive, I would've given the column a quick look or two, and then moved on. But now I scanned each inch thoroughly, and then I did it again. It was on my second pass over the column that I saw, in what from my vantage was the far righthand corner, a couple tiny specks of white powder.

I smiled. Score one for the dead man.

I pointed the specks out to Devona. "Know any vampires with dandruff?"

She ignored the joke—I don't blame her; it wasn't one of my better ones—and instead leaned forward and looked closely at the white grains.

After a bit, she straightened and said, "I have no idea what that is. Do you?"

"Maybe," I said, declining to elaborate. "There's no way we can reach it, is there? Not without setting off the wardspell's alarm."

She nodded.

"Figures. Well, if there are two specks, maybe there's more." I asked Devona to stand back, and then got down on my hands and knees—my zombie joints creaking in protest—and did my best impersonation of a bloodhound, crawling slowly across the floor, face only inches above the stone and searched. I had the patience, the ability to hyperfocus my attention, and I didn't breathe, so I didn't have to worry about accidentally blowing any specks away before I could find them.

It took some time, but I located five more grains, all of which I collected with a pair of tweezers and slipped into a small white envelope. I never was a Boy Scout, but I know enough to be prepared all the same. And the gods of evidence collection were in a beneficent mood that day, for I also stumbled across a hair.

I gripped it in my tweezers, stood, and showed it to Devona. It wasn't especially long, but longer than mine (which doesn't grow anymore; another of the few fringe benefits being a zombie: no trips to the barber). It was difficult to tell the color in the greenish light of the torch, but it appeared to be—

"Red," Devona pronounced.

"I think you're right. Lord Galm's?"

"He has brown hair; and his is much longer than this."

"Well, it's not yours. That is, unless you're not a natural blonde."

She smiled. "As half Bloodborn, I suppose I qualify as an unnatural blonde. But no, I don't color my hair."

I took another envelope out of my jacket and carefully placed the hair within. I didn't bother to seal it—no saliva—and tucked the envelope and tweezers away in a pocket.

"Know anyone with red hair who might somehow gain access?"

"Well . . . There's Varma, I suppose. But I don't see how he could possibly get in here."

"Who's Varma?"

"One of Lord Galm's bloodchildren—a human that's been fully transformed. He's one of Father's favorites, though why, I don't know. He's an irresponsible hedonist."

"That's a fine way to talk about your own brother." As soon as the words were out of my mouth, I knew they were the wrong thing to say: Devona's jaw tensed and her eyes flashed. Literally.

"He's not my brother!" she snapped. It might have been my imagination, but her canines seemed longer, sharper.

"In Bloodborn terms, we're considered the equivalent of cousins. Distant cousins at that."

I held up my hands in what I hoped was a placating gesture. "Okay. I'm not here to untangle the roots of your family tree anyway. I'm here to help you find out what happened to the Dawnstone."

She glared at me for a moment longer, and then, with a sigh, relaxed. "I'm sorry. It's just that half humans like me are looked down upon by the fully Bloodborn. To put it mildly. I'm not sure Father would ever have given me my position if I hadn't displayed a talent for magic. It's one of the few advantages of being half human: we tend to possess more aptitude for magic and psychic feats than the fully Bloodborn."

I understood then why her position and its attendant duties meant so much to her. It was a way for her to feel important, to be something more than just a mere half breed in the eyes of the fully Bloodborn—and most significantly, in the eyes of her father.

I understood how she felt, at least a little. I was a zombie—not human anymore, not even alive. I'd seen the looks of disgust, heard the jokes and taunts, especially when my latest batch of preservative spells started to wear off and I didn't look my best. I knew what it was like to feel less than everyone around you.

If she couldn't get the Dawnstone back, she'd consider herself a failure to the Bloodborn, to her father, and especially to herself.

I was determined to do my best to see that didn't happen, whether I kept my body from crumbling to dust or not.

"I didn't mean to snap at you like that," Devona said.

"Forget it. We've all got something that pushes our hot button."

"What about you?"

"With me, it's flies who mistake me for a nursery. Now let's go see if we can find Varma. I've got a few questions to ask him."

–SIX–

Devona wasn't too thrilled with what I had in mind. Truth to tell, neither was I. But we needed to talk to Varma, and in order to do that, we had to find him. And the most likely place to look was Lord Galm's party.

"You said yourself that Galm won't be there, that he'll be meditating to prepare himself for the Renewal Ceremony. And I can stay out in the corridor while you hunt for Varma in the ballroom. Then the three of us can go somewhere private and we'll see what your cousin has to say for himself."

She agreed, but she didn't look too happy about it.

We went back downstairs, and I took up a position in the corridor about fifty feet from the ballroom entrance.

"Good luck, Devona. Oh, and you, uh, might want to zip yourself up."

She looked down at her jacket, which was still open halfway to her waist. She smiled. "I suppose I should if I don't want to attract any more attention than necessary." She pulled the zipper tab upward, and then headed for the ballroom. Considering how tight her leather outfit was, I thought she would attract attention no matter what she did.

I crossed my arms and leaned against the wall and waited. I'd waited quite a bit during my two decades as a cop, and I was real good at it—and being dead made it even easier. I listened to the sounds of celebration wafting from the ballroom, stared at the opposite wall, and let one part of my mind wander, while another kept watch for Devona's return.

I don't know how much time passed, but eventually I became aware of someone approaching. I turned, expecting to see Devona with Varma hopefully in tow, but instead a middle-aged woman in an elaborate pre–French Revolution gown and a towering white wig was staggering down the corridor toward me. Her skin was chalk white, and I doubted it was because she powdered it. She bore a fake beauty mark in the shape of a tiny bat on her left cheek. Cute.

"Pardon, Monsieur, could you direct me to the—" That was as far as she got before doubling over and vomiting a gout of red-black liquid all over the corridor floor.

I was a sympathetic vomiter when alive; all I had to do was hear someone retch and my own gorge would start to rise. My zombiefication had cured me of that, but I was still uncomfortably aware the booze I had drank at Skully's while waiting for Honani to show up was still sitting undigested in my stomach. I knew I had to get rid of it soon, before it pickled my dead innards.

When she was finished, she straightened and wiped her mouth with a dainty hand. Her wig had gone slightly askew, but she didn't bother to right it. She smiled shyly at me.

"Forgive me, but I have such trouble resisting the temptation to overindulge at these affairs."

I was hoping that would be the end of it, and she would return to the party. But she stood looking at me expectantly, so I said, "No apologies necessary."

She looked into my eyes and I noticed a thin red line dimpling the flesh of her neck. From an encounter with Monsieur Guillotine? "Well, aren't you a gallant one?" She reached out and drew a long, blood-red fingernail lightly down my cheek. "And you're rather handsome, in a consumptive sort of way."

Some compliment. But I didn't say anything.

She smiled lopsidedly. "Did you know that the Bloodborn do not cast shadows? It's true. And I miss mine something awful. Perhaps you would be a gentleman and take its place for a while?"

Before I could answer, she linked her arm in mine, and started pulling me forward. Despite appearing middle-aged and being inebriated, she was still a vampire and strong as hell. I couldn't resist, not unless I wanted an arm torn off for the second time that day.

"I'd be honored," I said as she dragged me toward the ballroom. At least she'd mistaken me for a Shadow. I could only hope Lord Galm's other guests would do the same.

"Matthew, allow me to present the honorable Amadeo Karolek. Amadeo, this is my new Shadow, Matthew."

The male vampire, who was dressed in a coat of gold brocade, didn't bother to hide his disgust. "Charmed," he said in a voice which let me know he was anything but.

I almost offered my hand to shake, just to irritate him, but the way he glared at me, he'd most likely have crushed it, then torn it off.

"Excuse me, Calandre, but I see someone I really must say hello to." And then Amadeo collapsed into a pool of black water and flowed away across the floor.

Calandre—which meant lark, she'd told me—still had a death grip on my arm. But after introducing me to more than a dozen vampires, all of whom acted like I was some new species of giant maggot, I was considering sacrificing the limb, like an animal caught in a leg-hold trap, desperate to escape.

I knew next to nothing about Bloodborn etiquette, but from what I was able to observe as Calandre hauled me about the ballroom, Shadows were supposed to walk or stand at least three feet behind the vampires they belonged to, keep their heads down, and remain quiet. But Calandre, still drunk—or whatever the vampiric equivalent was of gorging on too much blood—was parading me around like I was her new lover. And the other vampires definitely did not like it. I had the impression her behavior was akin to that of a human woman going to a party and introducing everyone to her favorite vibrator.

So much for my keeping a low profile. I could only hope that Devona would eventually find me and come to my rescue, or that Calandre would tire of me and let me go.

Calandre licked her lips. "I'm dreadfully thirsty, Matthew." She smiled, displaying her incisors. "Dreadfully."

This was bad. If she bit into my flesh, she'd realize I wasn't alive. My blood had long ago turned to dust in my veins. It'd be like someone expecting a nice, refreshing drink of water suddenly getting instead a mouthful of chalk.

I was seriously contemplating spending the rest of my unlife as a one-armed zombie, when a statuesque woman in an Edwardian frockcoat walked up, her features scrunched into an expression of supreme distaste.

"Really, Calandre, this is too much, even for you!"

Calandre drew herself up haughtily, which wasn't easy since her wig looked as if it would topple off her head any moment. "I have no idea what you're talking about, Naraka, nor do I care. Now why don't you take your little penis-envy pageant elsewhere?"

Naraka made a sound deep in her throat, and I realized she was growling. This did not look good, especially since Calandre still had hold of me; I didn't relish the prospect of being caught in the middle of a catfight between two vampires.

"Ladies, please, there's no need for—"

"Silence, Shadow!" Naraka's hand flashed out and her nails, which had suddenly become claws, raked my left cheek.

"Really, Naraka, you didn't . . ." Calandre's voice trailed off, and I had a pretty good idea why. She had noticed that the deep scratches Naraka had inflicted on my face weren't bleeding.

"Father Dis," Naraka swore in disgust. "It's one thing to drag a human around as if he were one of us. But a zombie!"

"But I . . . He . . . I didn't . . ." In her surprise and confusion, Calandre released my arm, and I decided that, zombie-slow or not, I was going to make a run for it.

And then the torches along the ballroom walls dimmed, and the noise and music ceased as if a switch had been thrown. Everyone looked upward, even Calandre and Naraka, who seemed to have forgotten all about me. I didn't know what was happening, and I didn't care. I was just grateful for the distraction.

I started to edge away from Calandre and Naraka, but then I stopped. The atmosphere of the ballroom felt charged with energy, like before a violent storm breaks loose. It had to be a psychic and not physical sensation, or else I probably couldn't have perceived it, but whichever, it stopped me in my tracks and made me look up along with everyone else.

Darkness gathered along the mirrored surface of the ballroom walls, thickening and growing. And then the darkness exploded into a thousand shards which darted and whirled through the air, a cyclone of shadow. One of the black fragments dipped near my head, and I could see that what had been formless pieces of darkness had assumed the shape of large bats. Not actual three-dimensional animals, but instead shadowy silhouettes circling madly about the room.

And then the flock of shadow-bats drew close together directly above the gushing fountain of red, and coalesced into the form of a huge, well muscled man, who wore only a loincloth, boots, and a cape made out of black fur. His skin was white as ivory, and his body looked hard as marble. He had long brown hair, and an equally brown beard which spilled onto his chest. His eyes were frost-white and cold as glaciers.

I didn't need a formal introduction to tell me this was Lord Galm, progenitor of the Bloodborn and ruler of Gothtown—and, if I was lucky and Devona managed to persuade him to help me, my eventual savior.

As one, the assembled vampires fell to their knees and bowed their heads. "Our Lord," they chanted in unison.

I was about to kneel myself to keep from drawing the Darklord's attention, when I felt someone grab my arm and start dragging me backward. It was Devona—and she looked scared.

I didn't know what to do: stay and risk being exposed as a zombie and a party-crasher—thus earning Galm's wrath— or go with Devona and risk drawing the vampire lord's ire for not displaying the proper obeisance. In the end, simple fear won out and I turned and we both ran like hell for the exit.

I felt a freezing-cold sensation on the back of my neck, as if it were suddenly coated in ice. I didn't have to turn and look to know the Darklord was watching us. But for whatever reason, he did nothing, and we reached the corridor, turned left, and kept going.

As we ran, I thought it was a good thing I was dead. If I'd been alive, I would surely have needed a change of underwear.

★ ★ ★ ★ ★

We didn't stop running until we were a couple blocks from the Cathedral. Devona put her hands on her knees and gulped air—another sign that she was half human; a full-fledged vampire wouldn't have needed to breathe, let alone catch her breath. I just stood and waited for her to recover, not fatigued in the slightest, although I thought my left arm was a trifle looser than it had been.

"Will he send someone after us?" I asked Devona when her breathing had returned to normal.

She shook her head. "He's going to be too busy receiving guests for the next few hours. But I'm sure he'll tend to us later." She slumped back against the wall of a building and rubbed her forehead, clearly upset.

I laid a hand on her shoulder. "Perhaps Lord Galm will be more forgiving of our disrupting his entrance if we can recover the Dawnstone, or at least discover what happened to it."

She gave me a weak smile. "Perhaps. It's something to hope for anyway." She stood straight, took a deep breath, and did her best to regain her composure. And then she noticed the cuts on my face. "Oh, you're hurt!"

She reached a hand toward my wounds, but I took a step back. I didn't want her smooth, half-living hands touching my dead flesh, didn't want to see her possibly pull away in disgust.

"I'm a zombie; I can't be hurt. Don't worry, Papa Chatha will just take care of it the next time I see him." Or in a couple days I'd be gone, and a few scratches wouldn't matter anymore. I changed the subject. "Did you locate Varma?"

"No one had seen him. He's probably off celebrating in the Sprawl somewhere."

"Do you have any idea where he might be? Any favorite hangouts?"

"I know a couple places that he frequents. So we're off to the Sprawl, then?"

"Not just yet. First, we need to find out as much about the Dawnstone as we can."

"How are we supposed to do that? We can hardly ask Father, can we?"

"Maybe not. But I know someone else we can ask."

"Who?"

I smiled. "Do you have your library card on you?"

—SEVEN—

"You're not serious."

We stood before the Great Library, not that it looked all that great from outside, just a simple wooden building, more appropriate for a cobbler's or a baker's.

Devona's doubts had nothing to do with the Library's appearance. Everyone in Necropolis knew about that; no, what she didn't believe was what I'd said.

"You really expect to just walk up to the door, knock, and be let into the repository of not just the sum total of Bloodborn history but the accumulated knowledge of the entire Darkfolk?"

"No," I deadpanned (I'm good at that). "I've never had to knock before."

"Matthew," she said in the tone of an adult speaking to a willful, misled child, "no one just goes into the Great Library whenever he wants. That's not how it works."

So it was Matthew now. I wondered when in the last few hours we'd gotten on a first-name basis.

"Call me Matt. And yes, that's precisely how it works for me."

"Waldemar is very selective about who he allows inside the Library and when. And no one knows how he chooses who may enter. I've never been inside. Even Lord Galm cannot just drop by whenever he feels—"

She broke off when she saw me reach out and open the door. Her jaw dropped. "That's . . . impossible!"

"Are you sure Waldemar's reputation isn't just exaggerated?

Like I said, the door's always been open every time I've come here." Even Necropolis, a place where so many myths and legends are real, still has its share of tall tales.

"I don't . . ." Whatever she was going to say, she decided against it and finally just shook her head.

"C'mon, let's go." I held the door open and gestured for her to enter. She walked past me and stopped on the other side of the threshold and swayed dizzily.

I shut the door quickly and put a hand on her arm to steady her. "Sorry, I should have warned you. The shift in perspective hits you pretty hard the first time."

We stood inside a vast room, far larger than such a small building as the Library appeared to be from outside could possibly contain. And the room was filled with case after case, shelf upon shelf, of books, papers, parchments, and scrolls. And what the shelves couldn't hold were stacked on the floor, piled on top of cases, shoved into corners, jam-packed into every nook, cranny, and crevice available.

I didn't have a sense of smell anymore, but I could imagine the wonderful musty odor of ancient knowledge and thought that permeated the place. Breathing this air would be like breathing Time itself.

"So what do we do?" Devona asked in the hushed, respectful voice people only use in churches and libraries.

"We start wandering around. Eventually Waldemar will show up."

She looked skeptical, but she didn't say anything. After all, the front door had opened as I said it would. We started walking.

As big as the Great Library looks when you first enter, you don't really get a sense of how truly enormous it is until you start exploring. Room after room: some large, high-ceilinged, footsteps echoing against tile floors; some small, cramped, barely bigger than a closet, with hardly enough room to squeeze through the moldering books and papers jammed against the walls.

After a time, Devona asked, "Do you know where we are?"

"Of course," I answered, even though I had no idea. It didn't really matter, not here.

I don't know how long we wended through the maze of books and papers, but eventually we came to a circular room with a high domed ceiling fifty feet above the floor. The walls were lined with bookcases which rose nearly all the way to the ceiling, leaning against them at irregular intervals a half dozen long, rickety-looking ladders to provide access to the upper reaches of the shelves. In a regular library, the ladders might have had wheels. Here, they had tiny clawed lizard feet. They might have been for purely decorative purposes, but I doubted it.

"We're wasting time, Matthew," Devona said, exasperated. "Waldemar obviously doesn't wish to talk to us. Instead of wandering aimlessly through here, we should be trying to locate Varma."

"I understand how you feel, but the more we can learn about the Dawnstone, the more—"

I broke off as a soft rustling sound disturbed the Library's quiet. A sheaf of torn book pages blew into the room on what I imagine was a musty, antiquity-laden breeze, tumbling and scratching against each other like dry autumn leaves caught in a windstorm. The pages stopped in front of us, whirled about in a column, faster and faster, closer and closer, until they merged together and resolved into the form of a friendly faced, middle-aged man wearing granny glasses. He looked like Ben Franklin by way of Shakespeare's tailor.

He grinned and took my hand in both of his pale, pudgy ones and pumped vigorously. "Matthew, my boy! Delighted to see you again!"

"Good to see you too, Waldemar." I was about to introduce Devona when he released my hands and took hers, shaking them just as energetically.

"Devona Kanti—it's a privilege and a joy to finally meet you! And how is your esteemed father?"

Devona looked at Waldemar for a moment, his effusive greeting catching her off guard. "He's, uh, rather busy right now, actually."

"Of course, of course. It is the anniversary of the Descension, after all. The three hundred and seventy-third, to be precise." He paused and touched a finger to his lips. "Or is it three hundred and thirty-seven? Oh, well, it's one or the other. I think." Then he looked at me and brightened, as if he'd forgotten all about us and had just remembered.

"How may I be of service to you and your lovely companion, Matthew?"

Waldemar's befuddled scholar pose didn't fool me. I'd known him too long. He was a vampire as old as Lord Galm, perhaps older. And when I looked closely into his gray eyes, I sometimes got a sense of the ancient, vast intelligence at work between them. I had no doubt he'd be able to tell us what we needed to know.

"We'd like to learn about a mystic artifact called the Dawnstone."

Waldemar's finger returned to his lips, only this time to tap them thoughtfully. "Dawnstone, Dawnstone . . ." His eyes got a faraway look in them, and not for the first time after asking him a question, I had the impression that I had set a complicated process into motion, as if I'd asked a computer to divine the meaning of life and then balance my checkbook.

Waldemar began meandering about the room, muttering softly to himself, the words unintelligible, except for the occasional repetition of Dawnstone.

Devona looked at me as if to ask what we should do now. I shrugged and started after Waldemar.

"Dawnstone, Dawnstone, Dawnstone . . ." He pulled books off the shelves, seemingly at random, flipped them open, and barely glanced at their pages before putting them back. Once, I swore he checked a book, replaced it, and then immediately removed and looked at it once more before moving on.

Curious, I pulled the book in question off the shelf myself and opened it. I wasn't particularly surprised to find that the page I had chosen—all the pages, in fact—was blank.

I reshelved the volume and wondered if all the books, scrolls, and parchments in this room—maybe in the entire Library—were also blank.

As I watched Waldemar continue randomly searching his collection, I had the impression that he wasn't consulting books so much as sifting through the immense reaches of his unfathomably ancient mind, and that perhaps the Great Library itself was nothing more than a physical manifestation of his memories.

If Devona and I truly were standing somehow within Waldemar's memories made real, what might happen if his absent-mindedness wasn't an act after all, and he really did forget we were here? Would we vanish, just two more minor memories, no longer needed? I didn't want to think about it. I had all the existential dilemma I could handle just being a possibly soon-to-be-rotted-away-to-dust zombie, thank you very much.

"I have a number of interesting references regarding dawn," Waldemar said as he continued looking. "Some lovely bits of poetry, and quite a few more references dealing with stone, stone cutting, stone working . . . Especially fascinating is a song cycle from an ancient aboriginal people dealing with a man who wanted to mate with a boulder shaped like a woman. His chief difficulty lay in his inanimate paramour's lack of the requisite, ah, anatomy. He solved the problem by constructing a crude hammer and chisel and—"

"We just want to hear about the Dawnstone, Waldemar," I cut in. "Not to be rude, but we're in something of a hurry."

He looked a bit hurt, but thankfully didn't resume his story. Instead he took a volume which appeared to be bound in green scale from the shelf, flipped it open, and ran a finger along the righthand page. "Ah, yes, here it is! No wonder it took me so long to find it. The object in question is only mentioned in several obscure pre-Atlantean myths, and only once as the Dawnstone. Other names include the Eye of the Sun and—"

I must have been frowning because Waldemar looked at me, cleared his throat, and said, "So on and so forth. While the details of the myths vary somewhat, the basic story is the same. A loathsome demon carries off a beautiful young woman to a shadowy underworld with the intention of making her his bride. The maiden's paramour, a strong and clever hero, ascends into the heavens and steals one of the Sun's eyes. He takes it down into the underworld, and—after overcoming sundry obstacles—confronts the demon and unleashes the eye's light. The creature of darkness cannot withstand the Sun's all-powerful illumination and perishes. The hero escorts his love back to the surface world, and then returns the eye to its rightful owner, the Sun."

Waldemar snapped the book shut. "Quite an amusing little fable. It puts one in mind of Orpheus and Eurydice, doesn't it?"

"Is that all?" Devona asked, sounding like a kid who's opened all her Christmas presents and discovered that Santa only brought her underwear this year.

"I'm afraid so, my dear," Waldemar said. "But I have quite a selection of other myths dealing with similar themes. For instance, there's a story among the Native American Indians regarding—"

"Thanks, anyway, Waldemar," I said hurriedly before he could get too far into this latest digression. "But we really must be going."

"So soon? Ah well, if you must, you must, I suppose. You'll have to promise to stop back and see me again, though, Matt."

"I will," I said, knowing it was a promise I wouldn't be able to keep. "Same price as usual today?"

"Of course." And then Waldemar reached into my chest—or seemed to; I was never clear on that—and pulled forth a scrap of paper, leaving my flesh and the shirt that covered it unmarked.

I felt a wrench deep in my soul, and then a sense of loss which quickly began to fade.

"Father Dis!" Devona swore in surprise. "What . . . ?"

"Waldemar's standard price for information," I explained. "A page out of your life."

Waldemar held the page up to his face, adjusted his glasses, and quickly perused its contents. "Most interesting, most interesting indeed." He sniffed the paper like a blood-hound trying to catch a scent, and then in a single, swift motion crumpled the page and stuffed it into his mouth. He chewed greedily, noisily, a thin line of saliva rolling down his chin. Then he swallowed and grinned.

"Most delicious, Matthew. Thank you."

Devona had gone as pale as a full vampire. I took her by the arm, said goodbye to Waldemar, and led her out of the room with the domed ceiling, the master of the Great Library licking his fingers behind us as we left.

I knew it didn't matter which way we went. After a time, we found ourselves back at the entrance, and then outside once more.

"What happened in there?" Devona asked. "Waldemar didn't actually—"

"Devour a snatch of my life? He sure did. Most vampires live on blood. He subsists on memories."

"You mean you gave up one of your memories just for some information . . . to help me?"

I didn't want to tell her that it hardly mattered, seeing as how I'd be zombie guacamole in a couple days. So I just nodded.

"Which . . . which memory did you lose?"

"I don't know. I never do. Once they're gone, they're gone completely. It could have been something as boring as failing an algebra test in high school."

"Or something as important as the first time you fell in love."

"I suppose. But it doesn't matter now."

She thought for a moment. "How many times have you done this, Matthew? Given Waldemar one of your memories?"

Too damn many, I almost said, but then I realized it would cheapen what I had done in her eyes—cheapen me, too, for what kind of a man, living or dead, thinks so little of his own memories that he's willing to spend them like money?

"Only a couple," I lied.

"You shouldn't have," Devona said. "It's my case you're working on; I should've been the one to pay."

But you're not the one who may die soon, I thought. "The important thing is we've gained some vital information about the Dawnstone."

"Assuming what he told us was more than just an old, forgotten myth. And even if it was, I'm not sure we learned anything useful, certainly not anything worth the price you paid."

"We learned that the Dawnstone is probably the most potent weapon Necropolis has ever seen. For what could be more devastating in a world of shadows and darkness than a piece of the sun itself?"

–EIGHT–

We were walking through Gothtown, away from the Great Library, heading toward the Bridge of Nine Sorrows. Devona kept looking about nervously, as if she were expecting trouble.

"Worried that Lazlo's going to show up and run us over?" I asked, only half-jokingly. "Don't be. His frequency of appearances, like everything else about him, tends to be erratic. A month might go by before I see him again." Not that I might be here—or anywhere for that matter—in a month, but I decided not to mention that particular tidbit.

"It's not that," she said, shooting a quick glance over her shoulder. "I think we're being followed."

On TV and in the movies, cops always know when they're being tailed, as if they have a sixth sense or something. It's true that you do develop certain instincts after a while, but when you live in Necropolis, where quite a few of the residents possess the physical capabilities to sneak up on a fly, instincts don't do you a lot of good. Besides, Devona's half-vampire senses were much sharper than my dulled zombie ones; I decided to trust her.

I reached into one of the homemade inner pockets of my jacket and removed one of the little surprises I'd picked up before we left my apartment. I held it down at my side, and gestured with my other hand for Devona to stop. I quickly scanned the street, looking for cover, but there was nothing. We'd just have to fight in the open.

"Hey, deader! What you doing here in Bloodsville?" The

70

voice, a male's, came from out in the street, but no one was in sight.

"Maybe he's come to see how his betters live," came a second voice, this one female.

"Or maybe he's looking to upgrade." Another male. "Trade in his rotten zombie teeth for a nice new pair of shiny fangs."

Disembodied laughter echoed up and down the street.

"Who—" Devona started to ask, but I cut her off and pointed to the end of the street.

"Just watch," I said.

Moments later a roiling wall of crimson mist came wafting around the corner. It rolled forward, gathering momentum, completely filling the street. The mist stopped when it reached us, and quickly dissipated, as if scattered by wind. But the air was still.

Standing in front us were now three young (or at least young-seeming) vampires, two male, one female. Instead of wearing clothing, their bodies were wrapped in tangles of multicolored wire, coaxial cables, and circuitry. The girl had a pair of CDs dangling from her lobes like earrings. All three had clean-shaven skulls, and in their foreheads were embedded tiny silver crosses, the flesh around the holy objects swollen, cracked, and festering. They smiled, displaying their canines, the left incisors bright ruby red—the calling card of the Red Tide, one of the most vicious street gangs in Necropolis.

"How you two doing this Descension anni?" asked the girl, whose body couldn't have been more than fourteen, fifteen tops.

"Us, we're bored bloodless," said one of the males, who was tall, lean, and looked to be in his mid-twenties.

"Bored?" I said. "With all the celebrating going on? You

three ought to be in the Sprawl, living it up with the rest of the city."

The other male, short, stocky, body in its early thirties, spat a gob of blood-colored saliva onto the cobblestones. "Buncha lame-asses running around drunk in the streets. Not our kinda fun, is it, Narda?"

The girl gave a wicked, lopsided smile. "Not at all, Enan."

The lean male giggled, a high-pitched, crazy sound.

"What is your kind of fun?" I asked, though I had a damn good idea.

The girl, Narda, answered. "Thought maybe we'd take ourselves apart a zombie."

"See what it looks like inside," added Enan.

The still nameless male just kept giggling.

Narda looked at Devona and frowned. "What are you doing with this corpse, honey? Can't find yourself a real man?"

"Maybe she likes 'em dead," Enan said.

"Dead and limp," added the giggler.

"Why don't you just go on ahead and find a party somewhere, honey?" Narda said. "And leave the deader to us."

I'd had enough of this, and was about to step into the street and confront them when Devona said, "Do you have any idea who I am?" Her voice was shaky with barely contained fear.

"A dumb half-breed bloodcunt who ought to have better taste than to hang around with a pile of walking hamburger like him," Narda said contemptuously.

I signaled for Devona to be quiet, but she ignored me.

"I am Devona Kanti, daughter of Lord Galm and guardian of his Collection," she said haughtily, or at least as haughtily as she could while trembling.

72

I groaned. That was exactly the wrong thing to say.

"You're probably lyin', bitch," Narda said. "And if you aren't, you're just plain stupid. Red Tide don't give a damn about the mighty Lord Galm."

"Galm hates tech," Enan put in.

The giggler raised his forearm and made a fist. The wires around his arm quivered like hungry worms. "And Red Tide is wired, man."

"Wired solid," Narda finished.

Screw this, I thought, and raised my surprise and leveled it at the three undead gang bangers.

"You'll get the hell out of here if you know what's good for you," I said in my best I'm-a-cop-and-I'm-through-taking-shit voice.

They saw what I was holding and burst out laughing.

"A squirt gun?" Narda said, incredulous. "Deadboy, your brains must have rotted away to goo!" She turned to her two companions. "C'mon, let's each grab a limb and make a wish."

They started forward and I aimed my plastic green squirt gun at their heads and pumped the trigger three times in rapid succession. Three streams of liquid flew out of the nozzle, one for each vamp.

When the fluid struck them, their undead flesh sizzled and popped and steam rose into the air. I imagine it didn't smell too good, either. They screamed and fell to their knees, clutching their wounded faces in their hands.

"It's a mixture of holy water and garlic juice," I said. "And unless you want some more, you'll—" Before I could finish, Narda pointed toward me and a tentacle of wire and circuitry shot forth from her arm. The tangle wrapped around my gun arm and started squeezing. Sparks crackled where the wire connected with my arm, and I could hear my own flesh begin to fry. I knew I had to do something quick, before my dry zombie skin caught fire.

I dropped my gun, intending to catch it with my left hand and continue squirting, but my zombie reflexes were too slow and the plastic gun clattered to the street.

I started to bend down for it, but Narda yanked me forward violently. I fell face-first onto the cobblestones and got to listen to a few ribs break for good measure.

This wasn't going as well as I'd hoped.

More tendrils of wire uncoiled from Narda and came toward me, these seeking out my mouth. She intended to cook me from the inside.

I reached into my jacket with my left hand and tried to get hold of something else that might fend off the vampires, when they started shrieking anew. I looked up and saw that Devona had retrieved my gun and was squirting frantically, dousing the Red Tide members.

"For godsakes, be careful!" I warned. "You don't want to get any of that stuff on you!"

Narda retracted her wires, releasing me. She and the other two vamps didn't look so hot. Their faces were a mass of burns, and their combination hi-tech and magic body suits were starting to short circuit, throwing off a shower of miniature fireworks.

They staggered to their feet and stumbled off, howling in pain. At the end of the street, Narda turned, and fixed us with a hate-filled stare from her single remaining eye.

"Red Tide's gonna store this in permanent memory, fuckers! Bet on it!" And then she continued after the other two, leaving us alone on the streets of Gothtown. They were vampires; their injuries would heal eventually. But it was going to take some time.

I pushed myself to my feet with my left arm, and stepped

over to Devona. She still pointed the squirt gun in the direction the Red Tide vamps had gone, holding it in an iron grip.

"Why don't you give it back to me before you break it and do some serious damage to your hands?"

She looked at the gun as if realizing for the first time what she was holding and handed it over to me gingerly, like it was a live grenade.

I checked it, saw that it was almost empty, and then replaced it in my jacket pocket.

"Thanks for taking care of those three, Devona. You probably saved my unlife." At least for another day or two, I added mentally.

"I didn't think about it; I just grabbed the gun and started shooting." She sounded amazed, as if she'd surprised herself. "Where in Necropolis did you get holy water, anyway? It's extremely illegal. If Father Dis found out—" She stopped and looked at me in horror. "The Hidden Light! You're one of the Hidden Light!"

She started backing away and I held up a hand—my right hand—to calm her. It was a little hard to control, thanks to Narda sizzling my arm, but it still worked. "I'm not one of the Hidden Light. But they do supply me with certain items from time to time."

That didn't do much to reassure her. "They're a terrorist version of the Inquisition, Matthew: radical Christians completely dedicated to the destruction of Necropolis and the Darkfolk by any means necessary!"

"Look, I don't condone their actions. But they're the only way for me to get certain things, like the holy water that just helped save your butt."

"I don't care what your reasons are. People like them are one of the reasons my kind had to leave Earth in the first place. People like them—and like you." She looked at me like I was the lowest form of life imaginable.

"If you don't want my help anymore, just say so. Maybe you'll get lucky and the Dawnstone will just show up on its own. And if it doesn't, maybe Lord Galm will have mercy and kill you quickly." It was a rotten thing to say, and I wanted to take it back, but I didn't know how. I've never been real good at apologies.

She was silent for a few moments, and I could tell that she was considering walking away. But in the end her dedication to her job—and fear of her father—won out. I was glad; I needed Devona, needed her to intercede with her father on my behalf, get him to use his powers, or his influence with the other Lords or even Father Dis himself, to save my undead excuse for an existence. Not because I cared what happened to her, not because I was starting to care for her.

Honest.

"Where to now?" she asked, not bothering to hide the resentment in her voice.

"Back to the Sprawl, to find Varma. And, with any luck, the Dawnstone."

—NINE—

I wouldn't have been all that unhappy if Lazlo had shown up then, truth to tell. I wasn't looking forward to battling the crowds in the Sprawl again. But of course he didn't, and so we had no choice but to walk. There were few coaches for hire in Gothtown—and given Lord Galm's feelings about technology, certainly no cars.

To pass the time, and more importantly because it might have something to do with why the Dawnstone was stolen, I asked Devona to tell me everything she knew about the Renewal Ceremony.

"The river Phlegethon, the air we breathe, and in some ways the city itself are all maintained by the power of Umbriel. When the Darkfolk first came to this dimension, Father Dis and the five Lords created the shadowsun and set it above the Nightspire to sustain their people in their new home. But Umbriel isn't eternal; it needs to be recharged once a year."

"And thus the Renewal Ceremony," I said.

She nodded. "The five Lords conserve their powers for months and then, on the anniversary of the Descension—the only time of the year when the ceremony can be conducted—they gather in the Nightspire along with Father Dis to perform the rite which will revitalize Umbriel. Necropolis' most illustrious citizens are invited to witness the ceremony. I myself have never been so privileged. My rank among the Bloodborn is not sufficient to merit an invitation." She said this quietly, without self pity.

I pressed her for more details, but since she had never attended any of the ceremonies, she had nothing else to add. It was more than I had known before, but not much more.

"Do you think there's a connection between the theft of the Dawnstone and the Renewal Ceremony?" she asked.

"Maybe. The Darklords don't particularly like being equal; they're always trying to gain an advantage over each other. And from what Waldemar told us, it sounds like the Dawnstone would be a mighty big advantage—especially against a vampire."

Devona stopped walking, grabbed me by the arms, and turned me toward her. She might have only been a half vampire, but she was still strong as hell. "You think someone—perhaps Varma—is plotting to destroy my father?"

"Possibly."

"Then we must return to the Cathedral and warn him!" She let go of me and started to run, but it was my turn to grab her.

"I thought you didn't want Lord Galm to know about the Dawnstone before we at least had a chance to find out what happened to it."

"That was before you told me he might be in danger. Now let me go!"

"Listen to me for a minute: if someone does intend to kill Lord Galm, whoever it is won't try now. Think. You told me the Darklords conserve their power for months before the Renewal Ceremony—right?"

"Right."

"So who would be foolish enough to attack Galm at the height of his strength? No, the best time to kill him would be during the Ceremony, when he's distracted and spending his power to help recharge Umbriel. He's safe until then."

Devona didn't look completely convinced, but she stopped trying to tear away from me, which was good, because as strong as she was, she probably would've taken both of my arms with her when she left.

"Even if you did try to warn him, as busy as he is right now, would he even talk to you?"

"Perhaps not."

"And don't forget that there's a good chance he's angry with you right now for bringing a zombie to his pre-Ceremony celebration. Besides, what do you have to tell him, other than vague suspicions? The more we can learn, the greater the chance we can make him listen to us. Make him believe us. Look, how long do we have before the ceremony starts?"

She shrugged. "Hours, at least. We'll know it is near when the Deathknell of the Nightspire sounds."

"So we have time to try to find Varma."

She sighed. "I suppose."

"All right, then let's quit talking and start walking."

She nodded, but she didn't look happy about it.

We started in the direction of the bridge again, but immediately stopped. There before us was a midnight black coach hitched to two large ebony horses. And perched in the seat on top, a man in a top hat and cloak which looked as if they'd been fashioned out of solid darkness, a horsewhip cradled in his lap. He turned his face toward us, but I couldn't make out his shadowy, indistinct features. He inclined his head and touched the brim of his hat in greeting, but said nothing.

The coach had made no noise whatsoever pulling up, but either Devona hadn't noticed or it didn't bother her.

"Look, Matthew, perhaps we won't have to fight our way through the crowds after all." She stepped toward the coach, but I grabbed her elbow and pulled her back.

"That's Silent Jack's rig," I said harshly. "You don't want to ride with him."

She frowned at me. "Why not?"

"That's right; you said you didn't get out much. Let's just say that Jack has a thing for the ladies. And his fares are quite steep."

Jack's shadow-shrouded face remained pointed at us a moment more, then he turned forward, raised his whip, and cracked it soundlessly over the horses. They whinnied silently, displaying teeth as black as their hides, and then the rig vanished, winking out of existence as if it had never been.

"You know," Devona said in a shaky voice, "suddenly walking doesn't seem so bad after all."

We decided to check the clubs in the Sprawl which Varma frequented. There were quite a few, so we started with the first we came to: the Krimson Kiss. I'd never been inside before, but I'd heard a few things about it. I wasn't looking forward to finding out if they were true.

Like everyplace else in the Sprawl, the club was crowded, and there was a long line of less-than-patient would-be patrons standing outside. But we managed to shove our way to the front of the line only to be stopped at the door by an initially uncooperative vamp bouncer. But his attitude changed when he recognized Devona as the keeper of Lord Galm's Collection, and he let us go on in. The people who had been waiting in line were none too thrilled with the special treatment we received, and it looked like a small riot might result. We hurried inside before things could get uglier than they already were.

The atmosphere of the Krimson Kiss was even seedier than Skully's. Bare dirt floor, crude wooden tables and chairs, guttering candles shoved into beer bottles the only illumination. Vermen waiters scuttled from table to table, and I felt a wave of disgust. I never have been able to get used to the humanoid rodents. Maybe my mother was frightened by a Mousketeer when she was pregnant.

The clientele was a mix of vampires, lykes, and ghouls, with a scattering of demon kin and a few less identifiable beings. Some were watching a horror movie playing on big screen TV—I didn't recognize it, but it was one of those English ones, in color, with lots of blood—and laughing uproariously. But most were busy gorging themselves on the establishment's specialty—plates heaping with slabs of raw, wet meat and tankards brimming with blood, all provided by the Krimson Kiss's claim to fame: the Sweetmeat.

The ghastly thing filled a recessed pit in the center of the club, a grotesquely fat blob of pink, boneless flesh from which a dozen stunted, withered arms and legs jutted forth. Vermen waiters ringed the creature, cutting off hunks of its flesh and slapping them on serving trays, filling mugs from brass spigots surgically implanted in its sides, all as fast as the ravenous crowd could order them.

Once a verman sliced off some meat, he took a step to the right and cut another. By the time he had taken three more steps, the first cut he had made was already healed.

The Sweetmeat possessed a horrendous, toothless maw on its back, and a line of vermen were passing down metal buckets full of a grayish glop which they dumped into the obscenely gaping mouth. Bucket after bucket after bucket. No slowing, no end in sight.

"Lovely, isn't it?" I said sarcastically.

Devona didn't answer; she looked like she was too busy trying to keep from vomiting.

"Do you see Varma?"

She took her eyes off the Sweetmeat—and was more

than likely quite grateful for a reason to do so—and scanned the room.

"No."

"Then let's start asking around."

It would've been more effective if Devona and I had split up, but I was mindful of the fact that she didn't have much experience outside Gothtown—maybe even outside the Cathedral, I suspected—so I thought it best if we stuck together. I didn't see anyone I knew or better yet, who owed me a favor. But of the beings stuffing their faces, I did recognize a few from around the Sprawl before, so we began with them. Most told us to fuck off (if they even paused in their gluttony to speak to us at all), but a couple said that they were acquainted with Varma, that he came in here now and again for a tankard or three, but he hadn't been in for a couple weeks, far as they knew.

"You know who you should be asking," said a huge, burly man I suspected was a werebear. He turned and pointed to an obese ghoul sitting at a large table in the rear of the place. "Arval. He owns the joint."

I thanked the lyke and with Devona in tow, made my way to the ghoul's table. Given the way they eat, ghouls tend to run to fat, but this specimen was the largest I'd ever seen. His face was practically all jowl, his thick-fingered hands so swollen they resembled flippers. He was bald, as all ghouls are, male and female alike, and he had the same eyes—completely black, no white of any kind. His fleshy lips were ridged like a reptile's, and his mouth was lined with double rows of tiny piranha teeth, top and bottom.

Ghouls normally go naked, and Arvel was no exception. We were saved, however, from having to gaze upon the entirety of his body by a large drop cloth that was spread across his chest and belly, a cloth covered with bloodstains and gobbets of partially chewed meat.

Arvel was so huge that he had to sit in a specially constructed chair made of steel and bolted to the floor in front of a cherrywood table which had been cut in a half moon in order to accommodate the vast spill of the ghoul's stomach.

Vermen waiters tended him constantly, bringing him a steady stream of meat and blood which they shoved and poured into his mouth. Arvel chewed and swallowed, his flipper-hands resting on the tabletop, unneeded. I wondered how long it had been since he'd last lifted them. Quite some time, I suspected.

His moist black eyes were fixed on the big screen TV and the image of a buxom young English actress who was succumbing to the satanic charms of Christopher Lee's Dracula. He didn't take his gaze off the movie as we approached his table.

"Excuse me," I began.

"Shhh!" he admonished, a bit of bloody meat falling out of his mouth and sticking to one of his upper chins. "Forgive me, but this is the best part!"

Christopher Lee made his move and the girl swooned as Dracula put the bite on her.

Arval let out a wet, bubbling chuckle. "They always react so melodramatically when he bites them. A ghoul wouldn't waste precious eating time on such carnal preliminaries." He looked up and saw us for the first time. "Pardon me for speaking so crudely, Miss. I didn't realize a lady was present."

Devona didn't respond. Vampires and ghouls, despite their dietary similarities, don't get along too well. Vampires consider ghouls disgusting mistakes of Unnature, while ghouls view vampires as little more than walking leeches with an unholier-than-thou attitude. I tend to agree with both sides.

"What can I do for you two fine people this glorious

Descension Day?" Despite his appearance and physical
mannerisms, Arvel's voice was smooth and cultured, as if
he'd OD'd on *Masterpiece Theatre*. Even so, he didn't stop
his gluttony to talk to us, but rather continued speaking his
refined words through mouthfuls of meat and blood, spilling
liberal amounts onto the drop cloth as he conversed.

I introduced us, and his lamprey mouth twisted into a
delighted grin. "Your reputation precedes you, Mr. Adrion!
I've heard quite a bit about your exploits, but I never
thought I'd be fortunate enough to actually meet you!"

He clacked his teeth together twice, and a verman scurried
up.

"Bring chairs for my friends," he ordered, his tone cold,
completely devoid of feeling. When the rat-man had scam-
pered off, Arvel was once again the gracious host. "Ignatz
will be back momentarily. While we wait, would either of
you care for a beverage?" He smiled sheepishly, suddenly
embarrassed. "Forgive me, Mr. Adrion, I forgot that you
have no need of nourishment. But surely you won't pass up a
tankard, Ms. Kanti? We serve the best blood in Necropolis."

Devona didn't say anything at first. I don't know if it was
because she was too disgusted to answer, or whether she was
actually thinking it over. After all, she was a half vampire.

"No, thank you. I fed earlier."

"Pity. You don't know what you're missing." A verman
hurried up with a full tankard. Arvel opened his mouth and
the rodent poured the gore straight down his gullet. The
ghoul didn't even have to swallow.

Ignatz returned then, carrying a pair of the simple
wooden chairs that everyone else in the place but Arvel was
using. The rat-man set them down at the table, took a few
steps back, and waited for more orders, his whiskers
twitching nervously.

Devona looked at me and I nodded. I wasn't feeling especially sociable, but my years as a cop taught me that sometimes it's better to go along with the program if you want to loosen someone's tongue. We sat.

Arvel was brought another mouthful of meat followed by a mug of blood. As he devoured them, I said, "This is certainly an . . . interesting place you have here."

He belched loudly. "Pardon me. Yes, it's quite nice, isn't it? Though I dare say that has everything to do with my delectable Sweetmeat. Amazing what a little magic combined with genetic engineering can do, isn't it?" He shook his head, or rather, wobbled it from side to side a fraction. "I'll never understand why some of the Darklords are so against importing human technology from Earth."

I thought of the misbegotten thing trapped in Arvel's pit, constantly being bled and cut for his patrons. "I can think of a few reasons."

Arvel ignored the dig. "Tell me, Mr. Adrion, is it true what they say? That you're responsible for Lady Talaith's recent ill fortune?"

"I'd really rather not discuss it, if it's all the same to you."

More meat, more drink. "Ah, but there is something else you wish to discuss, no?" He licked a smear of red from his lower worm-lip. "*Quid quo pro*, Mr. Adrion. We ghouls have an ancient aphorism: You feed me, and I'll feed you." He smiled smugly. I wanted to punch him in the mouth, but I'd probably just have shredded my hand on those teeth of his.

"Yes, it's true. But it was a couple years ago, when I first came to Necropolis."

"Please, go on."

I sighed. "My partner and I were investigating a series of killings on Earth. There was no connection between the victims' age, race, gender, economic status, or location. The only similarity was in the way they were killed. Each victim showed no signs of having been in a struggle, and they had a small entry wound over the left temple, as if someone had drilled through their skulls. Autopsies revealed that a tiny segment of the frontal lobe was missing. But that in and of itself wouldn't kill them, and there were no other injuries."

"Sounds like quite a mystery," Arvel said as he chewed another in his endless mouthfuls of meat.

"It was. To make a long story short, through dogged detective work and more than a little luck, my partner and I tracked the killer down to a park near the lake. But just as we were about to catch him, the killer disappeared through a strange shimmer in the air."

"A portal," Arvel said.

I nodded. "Varvara's. My partner Dale and I followed, and found ourselves in the basement of the demon queen's lair. The killer was gone. It took a bit for us to acclimate to Necropolis—"

Arvel laughed. "I imagine it did!"

"But once we had our bearings, we continued to search for the killer. At first, we thought the warlock had ties to Varvara, but we learned Talaith had been using the demon queen's portal because hers had been damaged in a previous struggle with Lord Edrigu. When we learned the truth, we headed to Glamere, determined to bring the killer back to Earth to face justice."

"And what happened?" Arvel's black eyes were shining; he was hanging on to my every word as if he were a child being told a favorite bedtime story.

"Talaith had sent one of her warlocks to Earth to harvest brain tissue from mystically talented humans who were unaware of their powers. She'd hoped to create a sort of organic computer capable of boosting her own magical strength, which she dubbed the Overmind. Dale and I stopped her, in the process destroying her big brain. The resulting psychic feedback killed the warlock who'd gathered the tissue for Talaith." I was silent for a moment. "And it killed my partner, too."

Devona, who'd been listening as raptly as Arvel, put a hand on my shoulder. "I'm sorry for your loss, Matthew."

"Dale was a good man and a good cop, and he died in the line of duty." It was all the epitaph I could think to offer, but maybe it was enough.

"What happened to Talaith?" Arvel asked.

"She's a Darklord; her powers enabled her to withstand the blast, but considerably weakened. She's recovered some since then, but she's still not up to her full strength. Needless to say, I haven't been to Glamere many times since. And I make sure to watch my back when any Arcane are around."

Arvel smacked his lips. "A most . . . delicious story, Mr. Adrion. But you left out one salient detail: how you became a zombie."

"Remember how I said the murder victims showed no sign of injuries beyond that left by the extraction of their brain tissue? It's because the warlock threw a deathspell at them, stopped their hearts instantly. Talaith did the same to me—just as the Overmind exploded in a blast of psychic energy. Somehow, the deathspell and the Overmind's power combined and when I awoke, I discovered I was dead, but in a way still alive, too."

"Fascinating!" Arvel gushed. "I knew some of the details, of course, but I've never heard the full story. Tell me, how did you manage to destroy the Overmind?"

"Some other time, huh? My associate and I are in something of a hurry."

"Ah, another case full of danger and intrigue! You must let me know how it turns out!"

"I will," I said. It was an easy promise to make, since I knew there was a chance I might not be around to keep it. "Now if you could *quid quo pro* us right back?"

"I'll be happy to answer your questions; once I've finished attending to nature's call, that is."

I was about to ask if he needed any help getting up, but then I noticed the large metal washtub beneath his chair. Arvel clicked his teeth and Ignatz scuttled over and pulled a lever on the side of the ghoul's chair, releasing a trap door in the seat.

As the next few moments passed—along with a number of other things—I was more grateful than ever that I had no sense of smell.

-TEN-

As we left the Krimson Kiss, Devona looked like she was suffering from shellshock.

"Lord Galm is anything but a saint, and during my time at the Cathedral I've seen some pretty terrible things. But I have never experienced anything as sickening as that ghoul!"

"He's disgusting, no doubt about it. But he did give us some useful information."

Devona snorted, but whether because she didn't agree with me or because she was trying to get the stink out of her nostrils, I don't know.

"All he told us was that while Varma used to frequent the Krimson Kiss, he hasn't been around in the last few weeks."

"You're forgetting what he said about Varma being a heavy drug user."

"That's no surprise; I told you he was a hedonist. Besides, drugs don't affect Bloodborn physiology the same way they do the human body. Varma would need to take large doses to get even mild effects."

Necropolis has all the drugs you'd find on the streets of any city on Earth—marijuana, coke, crack, heroin—as well as quite a few locally produced specialties, such as tangleglow and mind dust.

"But that gives Varma a motive for stealing the Dawnstone beyond mere lust for power. He wouldn't be the first junkie to steal to support his habit. And don't forget the traces of powder we found in the Collection room. They could very well be drug residue of some sort."

Devona shook her head. "I told you, Bloodborn handle drugs differently than humans. We don't get addicted. I suppose it's because the need for blood supersedes all other needs."

"Maybe," I allowed. "We'll just have to ask Varma when we find him, won't we?"

We checked a couple more places including, as Father Dis is my witness, a country vampire bar named Westerna's. I'll never forget the sight of vampires in cowboy hats, jeans, and boots line dancing.

Finally, we had penetrated to the heart of the Sprawl, and one of the hottest of its hot spots: the Broken Cross. From the outside, it looks like any trendy Earth night club: all chrome, glass, and glitter. The only difference is the day-glow neon sign above the entrance; it looks like the sixties' peace symbol, only without the circle. An upside down and broken cross.

The street outside the club was completely jammed with people who wanted in. Half a block away was the closest we could get. I steered us toward a fluorescent street light, and we took up a position alongside it.

"Now what?" Devona asked.

I reached into one of my jacket pockets and brought forth two of the most dangerous weapons in my entire arsenal—dangerous to me, that is—a string of firecrackers and a lighter. I handed them to Devona.

"Would you do the honors? Zombies and fire don't exactly mix."

She frowned, unsure of what I was up to, but she did as I asked and lit the firecrackers.

"Quick, throw them as close to the entrance as you can!" I instructed.

She heaved the firecrackers over the heads of the crowd and, thanks to her half-vampire strength, they fell within five feet of the entrance.

I cupped my hands to my mouth and shouted, "The Hidden Light! They're attacking!"

And the pop-pop-pop of firecrackers exploding began. The sound wasn't very impressive, but then it didn't have to be, given what I'd just yelled. People screamed, shrieked, bellowed, and howled in fear, probably believing incendiary grenades were going off in their midst, or perhaps a hail of silver bullets rained down upon them. Whatever they thought, they had a single common desire: escape.

"Grab hold of the pole and don't let go!" I told Devona. We held tight as a panicking mass of Darkfolk and humans rushed past, nearly sweeping us away. We got battered pretty good, but we managed to hold on, if only barely.

Several minutes later, the street was clear.

Devona scowled at me. "That wasn't nice."

"Tell you what, you find me a blackboard, and I'll write, 'I'll never fake a terrorist attack again' a thousand times— after we find the Dawnstone." I started across the empty street and Devona followed, although she didn't look at all happy about it.

Inside, the party was going strong. Either word of the faux Hidden Light assault hadn't filtered into the club, or everyone was too high or drunk to care. I suspected the latter.

Techno-rave music throbbed and pulsed, and laser lights flashed in erratic patterns. Beings of all sorts gyrated wildly on the dance floor, looking more like they were engaging in foreplay or ritualistic warfare—perhaps both—rather than dancing. Above their heads played out a holoshow depicting various scenes of torture. It looked as if MTV had produced a special on the Inquisition.

Devona leaned close to my ear and shouted in order to be heard over the racket. "How are we supposed to find Varma in this chaos?"

She had a point; we could barely move to circulate, and even if we could get around, the music was so loud, people would have a hard time hearing our questions. But we didn't need to make the rounds of the club. Not if Shrike—

I spotted him by the VR booths. I took Devona's arm and steered her over.

Despite his true age, which I had no way of knowing, he resembled a skinny boy in his teens. His hair was a wild tangle of black the same shade as his deliberately ragged T-shirt and pre-torn jeans. As always, he had a cigarette in his mouth and as he exhaled, he became transparent, solidifying again only when he took his next puff.

He saw us approaching and grinned, displaying his vampire teeth.

"Matt!" He had to shout to be heard over the din. "What the hell are you doing here? This isn't exactly your kind of scene." Then he looked at Devona, ran his gaze along her body from foot to head, and back again. "Your taste in friends is definitely improving, my man."

"Shrike, this is Devona Kanti," I said loudly. "Devona, Shrike."

"Lord Galm's kid? Cool." He took a battered pack of cigarettes out of his back pocket and held it out to Devona. "Want one?"

Devona shook her head. "No thanks."

I noticed the brand: Coffin Nails.

I nodded toward the pack. "The name's a cute touch."

He grinned again. "I like to think so," and then put the pack back in his pocket.

I don't know why he carries the pack around. In all the time I've known him, I've never seen his cigarette burn down, no matter how many drags he takes on it.

"What's up, Matt? You gotta be working a case. I can't imagine any other reason why you'd be here." He leaned toward Devona as if about to confide a secret. "The man's sense of fun is as dead as the rest of him." Then he looked at me and frowned. "Say, you all right, Matt? You're not looking too fresh, if you know what I mean." He pointed to the wounds on my face.

If I was alive, I could've run my fingers over my cuts to check their condition. As it was, I'd just have to wait until I came across a mirror. But from Shrike's comment, I doubted they looked very good. Injuries don't hurt zombies, but they do tend to start rotting before the rest of the body.

"You're not looking all that hot yourself, kid."

Shrike grinned. He always got a huge kick out of my calling him kid. Probably because he was a hell of a lot older than he looked.

He put an arm around my shoulder and addressed Devona. "If it wasn't for this guy, I wouldn't be here today. Hell, I wouldn't be anywhere today! I love this guy!" and then he planted a loud, wet kiss on my cheek.

"Get off of me, you lunatic," I said good-naturedly as I shoved him away.

Devona laughed. "Another favor?" she asked me.

I nodded. "Shrike got himself into trouble with the madam over at the House of Dark Delights a while back."

"One of their girls accused me of making her Bloodborn without her permission. I was innocent, but it took Matthew to prove it. Good thing, too. Madam Benedetta was so mad, she'd sicced a Soulsucker on me." He took a long drag on his cigarette, his hand shaking slightly. "I still get nervous when I think about it."

Me too. Defeating a Soulsucker isn't easy. I still have a few psychic scars from that one.

"So what can I do you for, Matt?" Shrike said, cheerful again. "You name it, you got it."

I removed one of the evidence envelopes from my jacket and handed it to him. "Know what this stuff is?"

He opened the envelope, stuck his finger inside, and brought out a couple of the white grains I'd gathered in Lord Galm's Collection chamber. He smelled them, then took his omnipresent cigarette out of his mouth and gingerly touched his finger to his tongue.

His reaction was immediate. "Jesus Christ, Matt!" As soon as the holy name had passed his lips, his mouth burst into flame.

I grabbed a beer out of the claw of a demon at a nearby table and splashed Shrike in the face, hoping to douse the fire. It worked: the flames died, leaving Shrike's lips charred and his tongue blackened.

"I've told you before, kid, you've got to be careful what you say when you're upset!"

The demon had risen from his chair, and was coming toward me, carapace turning battle-angry red. I tossed a couple darkgems at him (Her? It? Who could tell?) to pay for another beer and that ended the matter.

"Do oo know what dis stuff is?" Shrike said as best he could with his ravaged mouth.

"No, that's why I asked."

He looked around to see if anyone was listening, then leaned forward. "It's veinburn." He leaned back. "Ashully, it's prolly a good thin I swore. Maybe burned ou' the shit 'efore it got inna my shystem."

"C'mon, Shrike, it was only a couple grains."

He took a puff on his cigarette, and while his mouth didn't heal all the way, it improved noticeably. I bet the Surgeon General would've been surprised to see that.

"It doesn't take much to get you hooked." His speech was a little clearer, too. "Where'd you get it?"

"Never mind. Is it new? I've never heard of it before."

"New and nasty. It's really strong and very addictive—even for Bloodborn."

Bingo. Sometimes I love being a detec—doing favors for people. "Who produces it?"

"I don't know. But I wouldn't be surprised if the Dominari have a piece of it."

"Me neither. Got another question for you."

"Shoot." His mouth was almost completely healed, just singed a little around the edges now.

"You seen a vampire named Varma tonight?"

"Varma? You mean the one who's Lord Galm's bloodchild, right? Yeah, sure. He was out on the dance floor last I saw him. That was probably, oh, an hour ago, maybe less."

"Think you could make a quick circuit of the club for me, see if he's still here?"

"Sure. Be back in a minute." He took a deep drag on his cigarette, became solid, and blew out a long stream of gray-white smoke, turning transparent as it left his lungs and then fading altogether until he was gone. The smoke he'd blown out wafted purposefully toward the dance floor.

"That's his travel form?" Devona asked. "Interesting."

"Yeah, Shrike's got his own style, that's for sure."

She leaned close to me in order to be better heard over the music. "I've been thinking. I have an idea of how Varma might have been able to get into the Collection chamber and past the wardspell on the Dawnstone."

"Go on."

"Even though Varma isn't biologically Lord Galm's child, the transference of blood necessary to turn a human into a vampire makes him Galm's son in a metaphysical sense. It's possible that since the door to the chamber and the wardspell both are keyed to recognize and permit access only to Lord Galm, they could be made to recognize someone who shares the same blood—provided this someone had the right magical help."

"Are you sure?"

"Remember, I'm no mage; I was taught only enough magic to monitor the spells on the Collection chamber. But from what I understand, it might be possible."

The way things were going, the Dawnstone would be back in Lord Galm's Collection before he returned from the Renewal Ceremony. Devona would hang on to her position and her dignity, and maybe, just maybe, she could convince her father to help me stave off my dissolution.

I should've known better. Life—and death—is never so easy.

"Matthew Adrion?"

I turned around. "Yes?"

Before me stood a tall brunette in a red mini dress. She might have been pretty if her features hadn't been so sharp, her expression severe. Her eyebrows met in the middle. A sure sign she was a lyke.

"My name is Thokk. Honani and I were littermates."

Her dress ripped away as she began to change.

—ELEVEN—

Thokk was a mixblood, like Honani, but where he'd turned out a patchwork mess, whoever engineered her had done the job right. She was primarily lupine—the most common wildform for lykes—but her stomach was hairless and scaled, resembling a snake's, and her gray fur held a greenish tint. Her eyes were reptilian as well, cold and staring, and when she opened her canine jaws, long, curved fangs sprang forward, glistening with venom.

"You killed Honani, zombie." Her barely intelligible voice was a deep growl with a slight hiss to it.

I was aware of people abandoning their tables, having decided that being in my proximity at the moment wasn't conducive to their continued good health.

"Technically speaking, he's not dead," I pointed out. "His body's still alive." I was uncomfortably aware that I still was carrying the soul jar containing Honani's spirit in one of my jacket pockets.

She pulled her head back and in a single liquid motion, jerked forward and spit a stream of venom into my eyes. If I'd been alive, the venom probably would've started me shrieking, perhaps cause me to fall to the floor in agony and Thokk would've moved in to finish me off. But I felt nothing and calmly wiped the venom out of my eyes. My vision was a trifle blurry, but it was nothing I couldn't deal with.

"What good is the body if the soul is gone?" She swayed back and forth, her torso undulating bonelessly.

"According to some folks, zombies don't have souls, and

I feel just fine," I countered. "Besides, Honani's body does have a soul. It just happens to be a new one."

For a second I considered offering to give her the soul jar which contained her brother's spirit, thinking it might placate her. But then I realized she'd probably attempt to return it to its original body, supplanting Kyra. I couldn't allow that.

"Your littermate was a killer, Thokk, and he got what he deserved. End of story. Now why don't you leave, unless you'd like some of the same?"

She hissed and came at me.

I reached around to the small of my back and pulled a gun—a real one this time—from where I'd had it tucked in my pants. It was loaded with silver bullets, but one would be all I needed to take care of Thokk. I aimed and started to squeeze the trigger—

But I was too slow. Thokk's arm lashed out and she smacked the gun out of my hand, sending it tumbling through the air toward the suddenly deserted dance floor.

I reached into my jacket, but Thokk was on me before I could pull forth anything from my dwindling supply of surprises, slamming into me and coiling her python-supple arms around my midsection, pinning my arms to my sides. She lifted me off the floor and began squeezing.

I felt pressure, but no pain. I couldn't breathe, but all that meant to me was that I couldn't pull in any air to make my voice work. Still, I was concerned. If she snapped my spine, I'd survive, but I'd be unable to walk. After I was immobilized, it would be a simple matter for her to take my head in her hands and crush my skull. And once my brain was destroyed, no amount of preservative spells, no matter how powerful, could restore me.

I used to complain a lot when I was a cop. But right then busting junkies and typing reports looked pretty damn good.

98

I was wracking my dead excuse for a brain, trying to get it to come up with a brilliant plan that would, if not defeat Thokk, at least get me out of her clutches. But it was like my head was filled with molasses—and frozen molasses at that.

Thokk chuckled, the sound almost like a snake's rattle, and opened her mouth wide. I doubted she was going to try to eat me; most lykes can't stand the taste of dead meat, unless they have scavenger wildforms. More likely she intended to get a solid grip on my head with her teeth and then rip it off my shoulders.

I watched helplessly as her mouth descended, and then she stopped, stiffened, and shrieked. Her arms uncoiled, dumping me to the floor, and I saw what was happening. Devona had leaped onto the lyke's back and was tearing into the beast's neck with her own teeth. Thokk's arms curled over her shoulder, grabbed Devona, yanked her off, and threw her forward—into me, just as I was starting to rise.

We went down in a tangle of undead and half-undead limbs. Thokk advanced on us, the ragged neck wound Devona had inflicted already healing.

With vampiric grace and speed, Devona disengaged herself from me and stood before Thokk, fingers touching her temples.

"Stop," she said in an even, measured voice.

Thokk hesitated.

"Leave this place now," Devona continued. "Go."

Thokk stopped. She lowered her hands to her sides and actually seemed about to turn away, and then she reared back and spat venom into Devona's face. Devona screamed and frantically began wiping at the poison, trying to get it out of her eyes.

Thokk knocked her aside easily and came stomping toward me once more. But I'd had enough time to fish a small metal box out of my jacket. I flipped open the lid, stood, and flung the contents at Thokk's muzzle.

Her eyes teared up instantly and she began wheezing.

"Powdered wolfsbane," I said. "Never leave the grave without it."

Her eyes began swelling shut and her wheezing took on a more desperate, labored tone. Her throat was closing. I allowed myself to feel smug. All lykes are allergic to wolfsbane to some degree, some more so than others. But it appeared Thokk—

I stopped my self-congratulating in mid-thought. Thokk's breathing became easier and the swelling around her eyes lessened. Her mixblood physiology was counteracting the effects of the wolfsbane. Like I said, whoever designed her had done it right.

I had nothing left in my bag—or rather jacket—of tricks that would stop her. I glanced toward the dance floor. I doubted I could reach to my gun before Thokk recovered. But I had to try.

I started toward the dance floor, running as best I could in the slow, stiff-legged way we zombies have. If it took Thokk just a few more moments to throw off the effects of the wolfsbane . . .

Claws raked the right side of my head, knocking me to the floor.

"I'm going to shred you to gobbets for that," Thokk said, her voice hoarse and thick with mucus. "Very, very slowly."

I rolled over to look up at her. After all, dead or not, a man should look his fate straight in the eye.

She lifted her clawed hands to strike, disturbing a cloud of smoke hovering over her head. And then the smoke darted toward her mouth and curled down her throat.

Thokk howled in agony, and thrashed about as if her

every nerve was on fire. She coughed up a gout of blood and crashed to the floor, rolling back and forth, her limbs flailing spastically. But finally her exertions slowed and then ceased altogether.

A moment later tendrils of smoke wafted from her mouth and coalesced into the form of Shrike, his ever-present cigarette the last thing to solidify.

He took a drag and exhaled. "Did you know you can do a lot of damage by partially solidifying inside someone?"

"Do tell." I hauled my undead carcass to its feet. "Is she dead?"

"Nah, not even the kind of hurt I put on her can kill a lyke. But I bet she's not gonna be moving too fast for a few weeks. Unless, of course, someone does something about her first." He nodded toward my gun.

It was tempting. Thokk had tried to kill me, and would no doubt try again when she recovered. And it wasn't like anyone would try to stop me. But that wasn't the way I operated.

I shook my head. "Why don't you retrieve the gun while I see to Devona?" Without waiting for Shrike to reply, I turned and headed back toward my client—I mean, the person who I was doing a favor for.

She knelt on the floor, her face cradled in her hands.

"Are you okay?"

"Not exactly. I'm blind."

I helped her stand and kept a hand on her elbow to steady her. She took her hands away from her face, but she kept her eyes shut tight.

She took in a hiss of breath. "Dis, but it hurts!"

I didn't know what to say. I'd been human for most of my existence, and in that time I'd known my share of pain. You'd think I'd remember what it was like to hurt. And I do, sort of, but the memory's hazy, indistinct, like a memory of a memory. I suppose a lot of people would've been grateful for that. But it made me feel cut off from Devona, distant, as if we were at the moment inhabiting two vastly different worlds, and there was no bridging the gap between them.

Shrike came up, holding my gun gingerly by the butt with two fingers—like lycanthropes, vampires aren't especially fond of silver. He was carrying a glass in the other hand: a glass filled with thick red liquid. He handed me the gun, then offered the glass to Devona, saying, "Drink; it'll help."

Her nostrils flared as she picked up the scent of blood. She reached out and Shrike placed the glass in her hand. She brought it to her lips, then hesitated.

At first I couldn't figure out why she wouldn't drink. And then it hit me. Being half human, while a negative to most Bloodborn, was important to Devona, maybe even a secret source of pride. And humans didn't drink blood. "Go on," I said. "Shrike's right, it'll help."

She hesitated a second more, then drank. Slowly at first, but then with increasing enthusiasm, gulping down the last few swallows.

She shuddered as if she'd just downed a glassful of hard liquor and couldn't stand the taste. A few moments went by, during which a couple lykes came forward and hauled Thokk out of the club, probably to take her back to the Wyldwood so she could convalesce. Or maybe just to clear the dance floor. Soon the noise level in the club returned to normal and people were back on the floor, dancing. No one bothered to wipe up the blood Thokk had vomited. Perhaps they thought it added to the decor.

Devona gingerly opened her eyes. She blinked a few times, then smiled. "Much better."

Like lykes, vampires heal fast, but only if they've fed recently. Otherwise their wounds don't heal any faster than a human's.

I tucked the gun into the back of my pants once more, then turned to Shrike. "Thanks for taking care of the lyke. I owe you one, kid."

"Hardly. I've got a few hundred more favors to do for you before we're even." Shrike grinned. "Besides, it was fun."

"That kind of fun I can do without, thank you." I turned back to Devona. "And thank you for jumping into the fray too."

"What for? All I did was manage to get myself blinded."

"If you hadn't attacked when you did, she probably would've squeezed me in two. And what was that other thing you tried? It looked like you were casting a spell on her or something."

Devona looked embarrassed. "Remember when you asked about my travel form, and I told you I had other talents? I possess some minor psychic abilities, as half Bloodborn often do. Not that they did anyone much good today. All I did was make her hesitate."

"When you're fighting for your life, sometimes that's enough."

"That's nice of you to say, but I still—" She broke off and frowned. "Matthew, are you missing an ear?"

Shrike snapped his fingers. "Almost forgot!" He reached into the pocket of his jeans and brought out a grayish-colored ear. "Found this on the floor, not too far from your gun. Thokk must've torn it off you sometime during the fight."

I brushed my hair back and felt the open dry wound where my right ear had been. "Probably happened when she knocked me down the last time." I took my ear from Shrike and, without any place better to put it, stuck it in one of my jacket's handy pockets.

"Won't you lose it if you don't get it reattached right away?" Devona asked, concerned.

"Maybe not. An ear isn't all that complicated, not like an arm. It'll keep longer." I had no idea if that was true or not, but I didn't have time to bother with one ear, not when I had the survival of the rest of my body to worry about.

That reminded me of why we'd come to the Broken Cross in the first place.

"Shrike, did you spot Varma?"

"In all the excitement, I forgot you were looking for him. Yeah, I found him. He was sitting alone at a table in the back, looking like he was higher than Umbriel." He turned and pointed. "Right over—" Pointed to an empty table. "He was there just a minute ago, I swear to Christ! OW!"

I sighed as Shrike's mouth sizzled. He'd never learn.

Varma had probably cut out when Thokk attacked. I doubt he recognized me, but he surely did Devona. He didn't have much of a head start on us, though.

"How are you feeling?" I asked Devona.

"Well enough; let's go."

I thanked Shrike again, but he was too busy frantically slapping his tongue in an attempt to extinguish the flames. Devona and I headed for the table Varma had until only recently occupied—the one next to the door marked EXIT.

The door opened onto a trash-strewn alley.

"Which way?" Devona asked.

I pointed left. "But there's no need to hurry. Not anymore."

Lying face down on the ground not twenty feet away, surrounded by a massive pool of blood, was the body of a redheaded male.

Varma.

-TWELVE-

I was pretty sure he was dead, but I looked to Devona—and her heightened senses—for confirmation. She nodded. Her face was drawn, her eyes moist with tears. I was surprised; I'd thought there was no love lost between Devona and her "cousin."

I moved forward to examine the body, trying not to step in blood, unable to avoid it. He was thin, and shorter than I'd imagined. I realized that somehow I'd expected him to resemble Galm, even though he wasn't the Darklord's biological child. He was dressed in the white silken weave of spidermesh, a fashion popular in Necropolis at the time, and one with partially technological origins—a rebellion against his bloodsire? Or just the latest in a series of trends he'd followed over the centuries? Or maybe he'd just liked the way it felt; Devona had said he was a hedonist.

From the back, there appeared to be no marks on the body to account for so much blood. I put my hands under him, intending to roll him over, but my damaged right arm refused to cooperate. I had no choice but to ask Devona to help me.

She did so, fighting tears, but when Varma's blood-smeared face was revealed, she lost the battle and sobbed.

His skin was bone-white, dry, and brittle like the cast-off husk of a cicada. He stared lifelessly, eyes wide, whites completely red, pupils dilated so much they were practically nonexistent. His skin was white as polished bone. Dry, cracked lips had pulled away from his teeth to reveal sickly gray gum. The inside of his desiccated mouth was caked with blood-soaked clumps of whitish powder. Veinburn.

No sign of a wound on his front, either. I looked more closely.

"He overdosed on veinburn, didn't he?" Devona asked as she wiped tears from her eyes. "When one of the Bloodborn's blood supply is contaminated beyond the power of his system to cleanse it, his body casts it out—all of it—and unless he can replenish it within moments, he dies."

"I didn't know vampires could die of bloodloss. Interesting."

She looked at me as if I had just slapped her. When she spoke, I thought she might yell at me, though I had no idea why she would want to. But all she said was, "It's very rare."

"Shrike said veinburn was an extremely powerful drug. but I'm not sure Varma did this to himself."

"What do you mean?"

"The veinburn in his mouth. You said a vampire's blood is poisoned, he has to get rid of it. I assume it would be vomited out."

Devona's expression became steely, and she wiped away the last of her tears. "Primarily."

"Then why is there veinburn left in his mouth? Wouldn't the blood have washed it away?"

Devona glared at me. She was obviously upset with me, but I still didn't know why. "Perhaps it had been in his stomach and became lodged there, perhaps after he fell forward onto his face."

"Maybe, but then why is it still partially white? With all the blood Varma brought up, the veinburn should be completely soaked. And there are these." I turned Varma's forearm so Devona could see the five tiny puckered marks arranged in a half circle.

"They look like needle marks," she said.

"They sure do, don't they?"

"So perhaps Varma injected the veinburn."

"Then why is there some caked in his mouth? And where's the needle? There isn't one lying around, and spidermesh is skin tight; no room for pockets. Not that Varma needed them. I assume that as the bloodchild of a Darklord, he could charge whatever he wanted to Galm's account—when he just didn't get things handed to him free, that is." I shook my head. "In my experience, addicts don't usually vary how they ingest drugs. There's more than one reason they're called drug habits."

I ran a finger over one of the marks. Why, I don't know; it wasn't like I could feel it. "And these are fresh. All of them."

"That merely means that Varma died before they could begin to heal."

"Which means he died fast. And that he injected quite a bit of veinburn into himself at one time. Literally one time, for if he'd given himself five shots with one needle, the first mark would've started to heal before the last was made."

Devona's eyes widened in comprehension. "Unless it had been some time since Varma had fed, the first mark might very well have been fully healed before he made the fifth."

I glanced at the pool of ichor surrounding us. "I think it's safe to say it hasn't been too awfully long since his last meal."

Devona's lips tightened, but she didn't respond.

"So if the first mark is as fresh as the last, that means Varma was injected by five different needles at the same time. And I doubt even the bloodchild of a Darklord is talented enough to do that, and then make the needles disappear the instant before he dies. No, Varma was killed. Probably to keep him from revealing what happened to the Dawnstone." I looked up and down the alley. "No tracks. Whoever injected him took off before he started puking." Too bad; I could've used an easy-to-follow set of bloody footprints just then.

I stood. "Damn it!" I swore in frustration. Or rather my muted zombie version of the emotion. With Varma dead, and no clues as to who killed him, I didn't know what to do next.

And then I saw a tiny black shape I hadn't noticed before scuttle quickly away along the surface of the alley wall. A roach. Or something so close to a roach as to make no difference.

I knew then what we could do—if I was willing to risk it, that is. But given Papa Chatha's prognosis for my survival, what choice did I have?

Time to pay Gregor a visit.

"C'mon, Devona. We need to talk to someone."

"Talk—Matthew, Varma's dead. We have to take care of him."

"Take care . . . what are you talking about? He's dead; for real this time. There's nothing we can do for him now."

"We can not leave him lying in an alley like discarded refuse," she said tightly.

"Well, we can't very well take him with us. Even in Necropolis, carrying a bloody corpse around attracts attention. Besides, you didn't seem to care very much for him when I made the mistake of calling him your brother. You actually appeared quite offended."

"Varma was not especially kind to me, it's true. But he

was related to me, after a fashion. He was family. And besides, you just don't leave a person to rot in an alley when
he dies—it just isn't right!"

"Now I know you don't get out of the Cathedral much.
Most of the people in this city would do just that and not
think twice about it. Hell, I doubt they'd even think once
about it."

"I'm not most people. But I guess you are, eh?"

"What are you insinuating?"

"I can't believe how cold you are, Matthew. The way
you talked about your partner dying like you were talking
about the weather . . . the way you didn't blink an eye when
we found Varma . . . examined him as if he were just a piece
a meat. He was alive and now he's dead, Matthew. Doesn't
that mean anything to you? Doesn't it do anything to you?"

"I'm a zombie, Devona. And zombies don't feel—"

"Normal zombies don't think, either; they only do what
their masters tell them too. But you think just fine. If you
don't feel anything, perhaps it doesn't have anything to do
with your being a zombie. Perhaps that's who Matthew
Adrion really is—a man who was dead inside long before he
died on the outside."

She pushed past me and ran out of the alley. I just stood
and watched her go, her words having hurt me in a way I
didn't think I could be hurt anymore. I told myself I'd only
been doing my job, had been focused on trying to help
Devona and prevent my final end.

Maybe she was right, maybe I should have, could have,
felt more. But Christ, I was a cop for twenty years, and in
that time I saw more dead bodies than I can remember.
You had to become numb eventually to survive, to get
through the day without flipping your lid, climbing up a
water tower, and taking potshots at pedestrians. All cops

knew it; it was part of the price you paid when you signed on to serve and protect.

But human beings aren't machines: they can't turn off their emotions at work and then turn them on once they get home. So they get into the habit of leaving them off all the time. That's why so many cops are divorced. Or substance abusers. Or end up suicides.

Maybe Devona was right; maybe I had been a zombie long before I got to Necropolis.

I looked down at Varma, and tried to feel something—sadness, pity, disgust . . . But I didn't feel anything. I hadn't known Varma. But I did know Devona.

I bent down and, as best I could with my bum right arm, lifted Varma over my shoulder and carried him out of the alley.

Devona didn't say anything when I caught up with her. We walked in silence, making our way through the crowds in the street as best we could. I had been wrong about one thing: no one paid any attention to us. Since it was the Descension celebration, I guess everyone assumed that we were escorting a friend who'd ingested a little too much fun. That, or they had ingested a little too much and didn't give a damn about much of anything anymore except remaining upright.

I didn't know what Devona expected us to do with the body. If we took Varma back to the Cathedral—to Lord Galm—that would be the end of our investigation. Galm would learn of the Dawnstone's theft, punish Devona (and perhaps blame her for not informing him about the Dawnstone earlier so that he could have taken steps to prevent his son's death), and in a day or two I'd be a pile of Kellogg's Zombie Flakes. Unless Lord Galm in his anger decided to destroy Devona and me on the spot.

Preoccupied with these cheery thoughts, I almost didn't notice when Devona held up a hand for me to stop. She pointed to a hulking gray figure stomping unimpeded down the street as if the crowd didn't exist.

"Sentinel!" she called out. "Sentinel!"

The faceless—and for that matter earless—golem stopped, and then turned in our direction. It regarded us for several seconds before heading toward us with its stiff-legged Frankenstein gait, parting the crowd before it like the Moses of ambulatory clay.

It stopped and regarded us with whatever sensory apparatus it possessed. It looked like every other Sentinel I'd ever seen, save that this one had a faint line about nine inches long down the middle of its chest. Probably a souvenir left by one of Necropolis' more powerful (and foolish) denizens resisting arrest.

"My friend and I found this man," she indicated Varma, "in the alley behind the Broken Cross. We believe he died of a drug overdose."

The Sentinel stood impassively for a moment, then pointed with a thick finger at the ground. The message was clear; I set Varma down. The Sentinel bent forward from the waist as if hinged, and examined the body. At least, I assumed it examined the body. I had no real way of telling for certain.

When it was satisfied, the Sentinel straightened and pointed down the street. Again, the message was unmistakable. We were free to go.

If I'd been alive, I'd have probably had to release a nervously held breath. There had been a good chance that the Sentinel might've wanted to take us to the Nightspire for questioning. Maybe there was too much going on during the Descension festival for it to bother. Even in Necropolis, where the police force had been mystically manufactured, there weren't enough cops to go around.

I nodded, one cop to another, and we got the hell out of there before the Sentinel could change its mind. When we were halfway down the street, I looked back to see that the Sentinel had slung Varma's body over its shoulder and was moving off in the opposite direction—toward the Nightspire.

"The Sentinels will eventually identify Varma, and then inform Lord Galm," Devona said. "And Father will claim the body and see that it's laid to rest." She sounded relieved.

"Then you intend to continue searching for the Dawnstone?"

"Of course. Whatever gave you the idea I wanted to stop?"

Human, vampire, or a combination of the two—sometimes women just didn't make any sense to me.

"Oh, and Matthew? Thanks." She smiled gratefully.

It was one of the best smiles I'd ever been favored with. "Sure. And now we need to find a way to—"

I was interrupted by the loud blat-blat-blat of some idiot leaning on a car horn.

Across the street, parked halfway on the sidewalk, was a cab.

"Hey!" Lazlo shouted. "You two need a ride?"

—THIRTEEN—

"Are you out of your worm-eaten mind?" Lazlo shouted as he swerved to avoid a being that resembled a pair of giant Siamese frogs.

"I've gone through Glamere a few times since my run-in with Talaith," I said. "And you've taken me on nearly every occasion. And we got through okay."

"That's because of my finely honed driving skills and a hell of a lot of luck." Lazlo roared across the Bridge of Nine Sorrows, taking us from the Sprawl and into Gothtown. "But luck doesn't hold forever, Matt—and you've used more than your fair share over the last couple years."

"Life's a gamble, Lazlo." Especially when you might only have a day or two of it left. "The case I'm working on is stalled, and I need Gregor to give it a jump start. Besides, if you think about it, this is the safest time for me to cross Glamere. Talaith is undoubtedly conserving her strength for the Renewal Ceremony. She won't have the time—or the energy—to worry about me."

"Maybe," the demon allowed, "but if your bones end up hanging on the wall of Talaith's stronghold, don't say I didn't warn you."

"Duly noted." I sat back against the seat and turned to Devona. "Maybe you should think about letting us drop you off before we get to Glamere. If Talaith detects my presence, things will get very ugly, very fast."

"I understand the risk involved, but I still want to go. It's my problem we're trying to solve, after all. And I've never been to Glamere or the Boneyard. Besides,"—she paused—"I think we make an effective team."

I smiled. "I think you're right."

We didn't say much more after that, just sat, gripped the armrests, and prayed that Lazlo wouldn't drive us headlong into a building. After a time, we drew near the Bridge of Shattered Dreams, the entrance to Glamere. As we drove across, I hoped its name wouldn't turn out to be prophetic.

Glamere is home to the Arcane, the magic workers of Necropolis, but it resembles nothing so much as an extremely large medieval village nestled in a bucolic countryside. The buildings range from simple huts and shacks to wood and stone houses with thatched roofs. Nearly every house has a garden full of herbs, flowers, and plants, some recognizable, most not. And some which sway and undulate as if they are more than simply exotic-looking vegetables. Emblazoned on the outside of each building, sometimes in crude soot-drawn lines, sometimes in elaborately painted colors, are an infinite array of hex signs. I couldn't decipher any of them, so I asked Devona.

"I only recognize those that serve as wardspells," she said. "As to the rest, your guess is as good as mine."

The roads were unpaved, but smooth, so we made good time. We often saw fires in the distance, probably surrounded by chanting witches and warlocks celebrating the Descension in their own pagan way. Besides producing most of the city's spells, potions, and magic devices, Glamere was also the primary farming center, and on a normal day we might have run into (literally, with Lazlo driving) ox-drawn carts full of produce or herds of animals being brought in from pasture. But this was Descension Day, and thankfully the roads were deserted.

If I'd been alive I would have been holding my breath

ever since we'd driven across the bridge. But we were halfway across Glamere—or at least I thought we were; it's hard to judge distance since there are no road markers or prominent landmarks—and nothing had happened yet. I actually allowed myself to start thinking this was going to be the easiest part of the case yet.

Stupid of me.

Lightning flashed across the sky, startling me. Not because I'm afraid of storms, but because Necropolis normally doesn't have weather. No sun (save Umbriel's eternal shadowlight), no heat, no rain, no snow—nothing except wind, and never very strong at that. No, this lightning wasn't natural. And that could only mean one thing.

"Talaith's aware of us," I said. Thunder rumbled from somewhere off in the distance, probably originating from Woodhome, Talaith's stronghold.

"How?" Devona asked. "She should be husbanding her power for the ceremony!"

"Maybe she doesn't care," Lazlo said. "And by the way, Matt, I told you so."

"Get exorcised. How much farther do we have to go until we reach the Boneyard?" Darklords do not directly use their powers in another Lord's domain—not unless they want serious trouble from Father Dis. I knew if we could make it to Lord Edrigu's lands before Talaith attacked, we would be safe. Hopefully.

"Too far," Lazlo answered. He stomped on the pedal, and the cab, which had already been doing what seemed to me close to the speed of sound, accelerated.

Go as fast as you like, Adrion, said a smug, slimy voice in my head. *It won't do you any good.*

More lightning. And the thunder which followed was closer this time.

You're mad, Talaith, I thought back. *You can't afford to waste your energy like this. The Renewal Ceremony is approaching. And Father Dis won't be too pleased if you're too weak to fulfill your part in it.*

I'm touched by your concern, she thought mockingly. *You'll be relieved to know that I'm not using a single iota of my own power. My loyal subjects are thoughtfully allowing me to borrow theirs.*

I realized the significance of all the fires we'd seen. The Arcane weren't celebrating; they were conducting a rite to transfer power to their Lady.

A series of lightning flashes this time, much closer, and the crack of thunder sounded almost immediately.

How'd you know we were coming? I doubt you've been wasting power constantly scrying for me—you don't have it to spare. Not in your present condition.

I sensed her anger at my taunt. *I always conduct an augury using a mourning dove before every Descension Day to determine how things will go. This year, the bird's entrails told me that you would be passing through tonight. And so I prepared.* Glee and anticipation suffused her thoughts. *With the help of my people, I'm going to destroy you once and for all, Matthew Adrion, and your friends along with you. What do you think of that?*

Lightning crashed outside the cab, thunder cracked, rattling the windows. A driving rain began to fall. Lazlo hit the wipers.

What if I told you that I'm due to decompose in another day or so anyway? Why bother wasting mystic energy, even if it isn't your own, to destroy me if I'll be gone in a handful of hours?

Talaith didn't respond right away, and the rain slackened, but didn't let up entirely.

I sense you're telling the truth. And in that case letting you go would be the sensible thing to do. But I don't want to be sensible; I want revenge.

The rain picked up, coming down so hard that visibility was near zero, but Lazlo didn't let up on the gas. The lightning and thunder were constant now.

Instead of destroying you, perhaps I'll try to merely incapacitate you. That way you'll get to see your friends perish, and afterward I can bring you to Woodhome and have the pleasure of watching you rot away to nothing. Yes, that sounds quite lovely.

And then I felt her foul presence depart my mind. If I could have, I would've taken my brain out and given it a good scrubbing to get rid of the mental aftertaste of Talaith's thoughts.

"Uh, guys, we have a problem."

"No shit we have a problem!" Lazlo shouted over the riotous thunder. "I can barely see two feet in front of us, and these so-called roads are rapidly turning into mud!"

I filled them in on my mental tête-à-tête with the mistress of the Arcane.

"An augury!" Lazlo said in surprise. "Those went out with evil eyes and love potions!"

"This is no time to discuss fashion trends in magic," I said. "We have to figure a way out of this."

The cab fishtailed wildly, and for a moment I thought the perilous combination of tire rubber and mud had rendered any talk of escape moot. But Lazlo regained control of his vehicle and did something I'd never seen him do before: slow down on purpose.

I turned to Devona. "Is there anything you can do? Any spells you know, any psychic techniques?"

"I told you, my magical skills are rudimentary at best, and I've had no real psychic training; my abilities are primarily instinctual. I doubt they'd amount to much against a

Darklord, but I'm willing to try."

She closed her eyes and deepened her breathing, her hands resting loosely in her lap. But after only a few moments, she opened her eyes and slapped the seat in frustration. "It's no good—I can't concentrate past the noise of the storm and the cab's bouncing around!"

"If you don't like it, lady, feel free to climb up here and take a turn behind the wheel yourself!" Lazlo snapped.

I wracked my dull zombie brain, furiously trying to get its rusty wheels turning. It didn't matter if Talaith got me: I'd already died once and was due to expire again in a day or so anyway. But I'd be damned if the witch was going to take Lazlo and Devona too.

Think, dammit, think! What did I know about the Darklords?

"Matt?" Lazlo said in a worried voice. "If you've got any brilliant ideas, now's the time to share them." He pointed at the sky beyond the windshield. There, highlighted against black clouds, was the figure of an angel with wings of lightning. But this was a dark angel with wild raven hair, hate-filled eyes, and lips twisted in cruel laughter that boomed louder than thunder. Talaith, or at least a reasonable facsimile, getting ready to swoop down for the kill.

Darklords, Darklords, Darklords . . . I knew they constantly strove against one another—within the boundaries set by Father Dis, that is. They spied on and schemed against one another, tried to outdo the others' accomplishments and win favor in the eyes of Dis. They ruled their individual sections of Necropolis' pentagram and the inhabitants thereof absolutely, though some of the Lords were more involved in their subjects' lives than others. Still, it was considered an act of great transgression for a Darklord to interfere with another's domain and its subjects.

I knew the four remaining Darklords had to be aware of what Talaith was doing—the sheer power she was expending (even if it was borrowed) would stand out like an atomic bomb detonating at a July Fourth celebration. In fact, they were likely keeping close watch on the situation, if for no other reason than to make certain Talaith wasn't somehow gearing up for an attack on them.

I looked out the windshield. Talaith's avatar had left her position in the sky and was swooping down toward us, dark glee and anticipation blazing on her face.

And then I had an idea: I lived in the Sprawl. That made me a subject of Varvara, didn't it? If called upon, might she intervene to save one of her subjects? No, I decided. Varvara liked me well enough, but we weren't friends. What she liked about me—about anything, for that matter—was the amusement value I offered as a zombie ex-cop trying to survive in Necropolis. But I doubted she'd find a run-in with Talaith fun. Especially not when the witch queen was filled with the combined mystic power of her subjects. Varvara might miss me when I was gone, or she might get a kick out of my demise, but she wouldn't help me.

The angel closed on our cab. She plucked a bolt of lightning from her wings and it shaped itself into a sword crackling with electricity. As she neared, she shrieked like a banshee experiencing labor pains, lifted the glowing yellow-white sword, and, as she reached the cab, swung.

But Lazlo was ready for her. Just as she brought the sword around, he jerked the steering wheel to the left and hit the gas. A sizzling sound filled the interior of the cab and then we were spinning out of control. I grabbed Devona because I hoped my zombie body might absorb some of the impact—neither of us were wearing seatbelts because Lazlo's cab doesn't have them. He tore them out because, as he once explained to me, they "show a real lack of confidence in the driver"—and together we bounced around the back seat as Lazlo swore mightily and struggled to regain control over his machine.

But it was no good; the car tipped, bounced, and rolled five times before finally crunching to a stop. The cab—what was left of it—was resting on its hood in the middle of a rain-soaked field. I still had hold of Devona.

"You okay?" I shouted above the still rollicking storm.

"I think so. Plenty of aches, but I don't think anything's broken."

"Lazlo?"

He moaned and I thought he'd been hurt. But then he said, "My cab! What did that bitch do to my beautiful cab?"

If any of us had been human, or in Devona's case all the way human, we most likely would've been killed. As it was, it looked like we were going to survive long enough for Talaith to kill us in person.

I kicked out the safety glass of the shattered rear window, which wasn't easy since my left leg didn't work quite right anymore, and pushed Devona through the opening. I yelled for Lazlo to get out of the car, then crawled after Devona.

Getting up wasn't easy with my latest injury, but once I was up, I could stand okay. Devona pointed to the cab's passenger-side tires: they were nothing but melted globs on the rims.

So Talaith's avatar had gotten in a shot after all. I suppose the air was filled with the greasy-oily stink of burning rubber, though my dead zombie nose couldn't detect it. The rest of the cab didn't look much better than the tires.

The driver's door burst off and flew into the field. Lazlo climbed out, took one look at what Talaith had done to his beloved cab, and began sobbing.

I looked up, trying to locate the avatar. The angel of lightning was high above us, circling like a vulture, cackling like a madwoman. Talaith was enjoying drawing this out and would make it last as long as she could. Good; that gave us at least a little time.

I quickly explained to Devona my idea about the Darklords watching.

"If they are, then that means Father is watching too," she said. "And he knows I'm here and in danger. But if that's the case, why hasn't he done anything?" She looked up into the sky. "Father!" she cried. "Father, help us!" But nothing happened.

Maybe I'd been wrong about the Darklords watching. Or maybe they were, but Galm was constrained by one of Father Dis' edicts, or maybe he just couldn't afford to expend any of his power so close to the Renewal Ceremony, even to save the life of his own daughter. Or maybe his reasons were political. From what I understood, Galm and Talaith, while not the best of friends by any means, had about as cordial a relationship as any two Darklords can.

But I knew a Lord who Talaith wasn't on such good terms with—a Lord she'd planned to attack with the Overmind before my partner and I destroyed it.

Talaith's avatar stopped circling and began descending for another go at us.

I raised my hands to the heavens. "Lord Edrigu! Hear me! You are Master of the Dead; I am a zombie! Will you allow Talaith to insult you by attacking one of your own subjects? I ask you to help us, if for no other reason than to spite her!"

I waited. At first there was no sign my plea had been heard, but then the air near us shimmered and a black coach appeared.

It was Silent Jack's.

–FOURTEEN–

We didn't have time to think about it.

"C'mon!" I shouted, grabbing both Devona's and Lazlo's arms and pulling them toward Jack's coach.

"I'm not gonna ride in no ghost hack!" Lazlo protested. "I'm a real cabby! Besides, I'm not gonna leave my car. I'm—"

The avatar shrieked, furious at Jack's sudden appearance. She leveled her sword and a bolt of lightning crashed to the ground less than three yards from where we stood.

"—gonna shut my mouth and get inside," Lazlo finished.

The door of the coach sprung open of its own accord, and we climbed in: Devona first, Lazlo second, me last. I pulled the door closed after us, and it shut with a muffled click. The interior of the coach was dark and the wood looked . . . insubstantial, somehow, as if you could put your finger through it if you pressed hard enough. But what else could you expect from a ghost coach? At least it was solid enough to keep the rain out.

I thumped on the roof to get the driver's attention. "Let's go, Jack!"

Silent Jack, true to his name, didn't reply. His whip cracked soundlessly, his ebony horses let out a pair of inaudible whinnies, and we began to move. But the horses didn't pull us, at least not in the usual way. The entire coach, horses, slid forward as if on a conveyer belt, slowly at first, but with increasing speed. There was no bouncing or juddering; the ride was eerily smooth.

122

I pushed aside the curtain over the rear window and saw Talaith's avatar pursuing us, eyes blazing bright with anger and frustration, sparks shooting off her wings. She poured on the speed, but inch by inch, we began to outdistance her.

Damn you, Adrion! a furious voice thundered in my head. *This isn't over!*

It is for now, I responded, and settled back in my seat. I'd survived another encounter with the mistress of Glamere. I looked up at the ceiling and thought of Jack sitting atop the coach, driving the horses onward in silence. We'd gotten away, but, I wondered, at what price?

The coach neared the border between Glamere and the Boneyard, but instead of heading for the Bridge of Lost Souls, it aimed straight for Phlegethon. Before we could protest, the coach had passed through the wrought iron fence at the side of the road—somehow allowing us to pass through as well—and continued through the air as if the road had never ended, bearing us easily across the river of green fire. I wonder if any Lesk, the giant serpents that plied the flaming waters of the river, were looking up, disappointed we hadn't fallen in.

The avatar no longer pursued us. Either Talaith had run out of borrowed power, or she had decided there was no point in continuing to give chase. I didn't care which; I was just grateful.

As soon as we reached the other side, we were in Lord Edrigu's domain, and the coach glided to a stop.

"It wasn't as much fun as a car," Lazlo said, "but I have to admit it was a pretty decent ride." He tried to open the door, but it wouldn't budge. "Hey, it's locked!" Lazlo gripped the handle tighter and shook it for all he was worth, but the door remained closed. "What gives?"

"I believe it's time to settle the matter of our fare," Devona said.

I remembered the rumors about Silent Jack, about how much he liked the ladies. And from the look on Devona's face, she was thinking the same thing.

"I'll get this one, Jack," I said loudly.

The door sprung open.

"Matt, no!" Devona protested. "You shouldn't pay for all three of us!"

"She's right," Lazlo agreed. "We all three rode; we all should pay."

I shook my head. "I'm the one who requested Lord Edrigu's assistance, so I'll be the one to settle the tab. Now go ahead and get out, both of you."

Devona refused, so I looked to Lazlo. The demon sighed. "All right, Matt; if that's the way you want it. Let's go, Miss." He took Devona's hand and pulled her struggling from the coach. As strong as Devona was, Lazlo was stronger. As soon as they were both out, the door snicked shut once more, and Silent Jack appeared on the seat opposite me.

He held out a gloved hand, but I was fairly certain he wasn't asking for darkgems.

"Name your price, Jack."

He put his hand in his lap, held it out again, and then pointed to me. The message was clear—he wanted me to hold out my hand. I extended my left hand palm up. Jack reached out and with his index finger traced a letter on my palm: the letter E. When he removed his finger, my flesh puckered and scar tissue formed, creating the letter. E for Edrigu. What did it mean?

I started to pull back my hand, but Jack gripped my

wrist, and with his other hand got hold of my pinkie and
yanked. There was a snapping, tearing sound, and my
finger came loose in his hand. He inserted the finger in his
vest pocket, tipped his hat to me, and then vanished.

The door opened.

I climbed out and stood next to Devona and Lazlo. We
watched as Silent Jack—who sat once more atop the
coach—and his rig faded from sight.

"What was his price?" Devona asked.

I showed them the mark on my palm.

"What do you think it means?" I asked.

"I'm not certain," Devona said. "Perhaps merely that
you are in Lord Edrigu's debt. Or perhaps that you now
have yourself a new master."

A master. I couldn't deal with all the implications of
what that might mean. I'd always been my own man, even
when I was on the force in Cleveland. And now I had a
master?

Edrigu was Lord of the Dead—had he . . . I took a quick
inventory. No, my face was still scratched, my ear still
missing, right arm and left leg still damaged. Edrigu hadn't
bothered to repair me, which meant that I was still in the
process of decomposing for the final time. It didn't make
any sense. Why would Edigru have Jack put his mark on me
if he wasn't going to bother preserving me?

And then I felt an echo of a chill run along my dead
spine. What if Edrigu wasn't interested in my undead body?
What if he wanted my soul?

Well, if that was the price I had to pay to save my
friends, it was worth it. But I wasn't about to give up on
Devona's case or on trying to find a way to keep my body
intact. Lord Edrigu might have a lien on my soul, but that
didn't mean I had to make it easy for him to collect.

Devona noticed my finger was missing. I told her what had happened to it.

"I don't understand," she said, puzzled. "Why would Jack take your finger if you'd already paid Lord Edrigu's price?"

"For his tip," Lazlo said, "what else?"

Bereft of transportation, we had no choice but to walk. However, this wasn't a problem in the Boneyard, even during the Descension celebration. The streets were deserted, save for the occasional shade that drifted across our path. Everything was in a state of arrested decay: the roadways buckled and bulged, bricks cracked and crumbling; the buildings covered with dead, dry ivy, shutters hanging by one hinge, roofs full of holes or collapsed entirely; the trees and bushes lining the streets twisted, gray, and barren. And, according to Devona and Lazlo, the air was still, stagnant, and stale.

We caught glimpses of movement out of the corner of our eyes, flashes of darting wraith-like shapes that disappeared when you tried to look at them directly. I seemed to be more aware of them than either Devona or Lazlo, maybe because I was dead myself. Not for the first time I wondered just how many spirits inhabited the Boneyard. If we could see them clearly, would we find the streets full of people, perhaps celebrating the Descension along with the rest of the city? Were we even now walking among—walking through—throngs of laughing, shouting merrymakers, oblivious to their presence?

Eventually, we came to an open field containing the bent, broken, and rusted hulks of hundreds of cars. A junkyard. It made sense, I suppose. After all, this section of the city was reserved for the dead, right? And what was a junkyard other than a cemetery for machines?

Lazlo stopped and stared, a beatific expression on his hideous face. He looked like a demon who had died and, much to his surprise, gone to heaven.

"Look." He pointed to a crumpled hunk of yellow metal that had once been a taxicab and grinned. "I thought I'd never see it again."

"Surely you don't think that's yours," Devona said.

"Look at the tires on the passenger side," I said. "They've been melted."

She shook her head. "It's not possible."

"Maybe this is where cars go when they die," Lazlo said in wonder.

"Or maybe it's part of the deal I made with Lord Edrigu. Whichever, it sure looks like your cab."

"I'm gonna check it out, see if anything's salvageable. Maybe, with enough work, I can even get it running again. You guys go on ahead." He started forward.

"We can't just leave you here," I said.

He stopped. "Why not? What can happen to me in the Boneyard? Everything's dead here."

I thought of the E emblazoned on my palm. "This is Necropolis, Lazlo. Just because something's dead doesn't mean it isn't dangerous."

He chuckled. "You worry too much."

"We almost died in Glamere," Devona pointed out.

"We didn't, though, did we?" Lazlo countered. "But my cab did. Maybe now I have a chance to get it back. You two take care, and good luck." And with that he walked toward the wreckage of his pride and joy and began surveying the damage.

"Let's go, Devona."

"But—"

"Lazlo's cab is his whole life. And you've seen him drive. Once he starts, he doesn't slow down, and he doesn't listen to anyone telling him to stop. He's like that about everything. He'll probably mess around with the cab for a few hours, realize it's no use, mourn his loss, and then head on back to the Sprawl. Eventually, he'll either find another cab, or he'll be forced to go into a new line of work and the pedestrians of Necropolis will be able to breathe a little easier."

Devona looked at Lazlo—who was walking around the wreckage of his cab, shaking his head and muttering—one last time, and then together we continued down the street toward Gregor's.

—FIFTEEN—

The streets in the Boneyard had no names, and there were no particular landmarks, just block after block of decay and dissolution, so finding Gregor's place wasn't easy. But eventually, I recognized a broken beam here and a shattered wall there, and soon we stood before the ruins of a stone building: roof collapsed, walls fallen, columns broken and time-worn.

"This is it," I pronounced. "Good thing Gregor has the columns, or I'd never be able to find this place."

"Who is Gregor, precisely?"

"Gregor is probably Necropolis' best kept secret. He's an information broker on a par with Waldemar. But whereas Waldemar specializes in the past, Gregor deals in the present." I smiled. "If he doesn't know something, it's because it hasn't happened yet."

"Then why didn't we come here in the first place?"

"Because to do so we had to go through either Glamere or the Wyldwood. It's suicide for anyone but a lyke to travel the Wyldwood—and you experienced Talaith's hospitality. Gregor may be the best source of information in the city, but he's not exactly the most accessible."

"I understand." She surveyed the ruins. "How do we get in?"

I led the way up the cracked and broken steps and we walked carefully through the rubble of Gregor's building until we came to a shiny black rectangle set into the ground.

"It's me, Gregor. And I brought a friend."

Nothing happened for a moment, and then the rectangle parted as the tiny black shapes which comprised it scurried off.

Devona took in a hiss of air. "Insects!"

"Gregor's little friends—and his informants."

As the roach-like bugs retreated, they revealed stone stairs leading down into the earth.

"Try not to make any sudden moves," I told Devona. "Gregor and his friends tend to be on the skittish side."

I took out a pocket flashlight, thumbed the switch to low, and shined its beam down the steps, sending more insects fleeing, thousands of hair-thin segmented legs whispering across stone. Gregor didn't keep his underground lair lit, so the flashlight was a necessity for me—one which he tolerated. And even though I had no reason to fear Gregor, none that I could name, anyway, I always felt better visiting him with flashlight in hand.

We started down into the darkness, roaches scuttling away from the steps and walls as we descended. I'd been here only a handful of times since coming to Necropolis, but I'd never gotten used to seeing so many of Gregor's friends in one place. My dead nerve endings didn't work anymore, but I still felt itchy when I visited.

When we reached the bottom of the steps, Devona turned around.

"The insects have closed up behind us." Her voice was steady, but I detected a hint of nervousness beneath her words.

"They always do that; don't worry about it."

We were in a large, empty basement which, save for a small patch of gray stone around us where I was pointing the flashlight, seemed cloaked in tangible darkness.

"Is this place . . . filled with them too?" Devona asked me in a whisper.

"Try not to think about it," I whispered back, and then in a normal voice said, "Thank you for seeing us, Gregor."

From the darkness where the opposite wall would be, a faint clicking sound emerged.

"Always a pleasure, Matthew." The voice was soft and the words rustled like insect carapaces sliding against one another. "Ms. Kanti, it's quite an honor to meet you."

"The honor is all mine." As a half vampire, Devona's eyesight was far better than mine, and I was sure she could see through the basement's gloom to Gregor.

"Please, both of you, come closer. But keep your flashlight pointed downward, if you don't mind."

"Not at all," I replied, and we walked forward, the carpet of insects which blanketed the floor flowing out of our path like living oil. We stopped about nine feet from the gigantic insect huddled against the basement wall. He leaned back like a humanoid, though his body wasn't really built for it: he looked as if he might topple over any second. I wondered, as I had before, whether this was a natural position for him, or if he assumed it to seem more humanlike. If the latter, the attempt was a dismal failure.

Gregor was a gigantic version of the far smaller insects which served as his spies throughout the city. Somewhat like a roach, but his head was too large, his legs too many, and his eyes . . . they didn't resemble a human's, but then they didn't look all that much like an insect's, either. They looked more like obsidian gems set into the hard shell of his carapace.

A constant stream of the smaller Gregors ran up his body, over his head, and touched their antennae to the tips of his far larger feelers. They then scuttled back down as another took their place, and then another, and another. The flow of information from his spies never stopped, even when he was involved in a conversation.

"You'll have to excuse me if I seem a bit distracted today," Gregor said. "But the Descension celebration is the busiest time of the year for us—so much happens around the city—and the sheer tidal wave of information my children bring me can be a bit overwhelming at times. Please bear with me."

"No problem," I said. "So I don't waste your time or ours, Gregor, why don't you tell us how much you know about why we've come? I assume you at least know a little. After all, I did see one of your children in my apartment when I first spoke with Ms. Kanti, and I saw another in the alley where we found Varma's body."

Gregor made a high-pitched chittering sound which I thought might be laughter. "Very observant, Matthew. Suffice it to say I have a fair grasp of your basic situation."

I knew that was all we would get out of him on the subject. Gregor never gave away more information than he had to.

"I'd like to ask you a few questions."

"Of course you do. Why else would you be here?" More chittering. Then he folded his legs across his abdomen—a sign he was preparing to listen closely.

"First off, do you know who stole the Dawnstone?"

"Regrettably, no. My children have a very difficult time penetrating the Darklords' strongholds. Their protections are too strong, too intricate."

"Are you aware of anyone trying to fence the Dawnstone?"

"Again, no."

I was certain Gregor's children had every fence in town "bugged." If he didn't know of anyone trying to sell the Dawnstone, then no one had.

"Do you know who killed Varma?"

"My child happened late upon the scene, but arrived within enough time to see three members of the Red Tide departing."

The Red Tide. And three of them. When it came to believing in coincidences, I was an atheist. "Are you aware we had a run-in with some Red Tiders?"

"I am."

"Were the three who left the alley the same three who attacked us?"

"As I said, my child only saw them leave the alley, but I believe it was them, yes."

It was beginning to look like our encounter with the gang members in Gothtown hadn't been just random bad luck after all.

"Do you know where they went?"

"Alas, no. My children lost them in the confusion of the festival."

"What do you know about veinburn?"

"It's a relatively new drug, very powerful, created by a fusion of magic and science. It's effective on all of Necropolis' species, with the exception of the completely dead, such as zombies and ghosts." He paused. "Since you're the city's only self-willed zombie, I have no idea whether it would affect you or not. It would be interesting to find out, wouldn't it?"

"After what happened to Varma, I think I'll just say no, if you don't mind. Who's making the stuff?"

"The Dominari are distributing veinburn. But the drug itself is made by the Arcane."

Arcane? That meant—"Talaith."

Gregor's head bobbled, his version of a nod, I suspect. "And the plants which are used to make veinburn are cultivated in Glamere."

"That's surprising," Devona said. "I wouldn't have

expected Talaith to use technology. The Arcane have always made it a point of pride that they practice pure, natural magic."

"Times change," I said. "And the Darklords will do anything to gain an advantage over each other—including abandoning their principles. Assuming they ever had any in the first place." I suddenly recalled who Devona's father was. "No offense."

"None taken. You're right; even Father might be persuaded to set aside his hatred of technology if he thought it was to his advantage." She thought a moment. "Could the Hidden Light be mixed up in this somehow? After all, they manage to smuggle holy items into Necropolis. Perhaps they also bring in technology."

I answered before Gregor could. "Doubtful. The members of the Hidden Light are capable of a lot of things, but working closely with Darkfolk isn't one of them. They have a deep aversion to associating with those of a supernatural persuasion."

"Then why do they deal with you?" she asked.

"Because I was killed while foiling one of Talaith's plots. They view me not as a monster so much as a victim of a Darklord's evil." I turned to Gregor. "What do you think? Could the Hidden Light be in on this?"

"I must concur with your assessment, Matthew," he said. "The Hidden Light has always worked alone in the past."

That settled, I returned to my original line of questioning. "Do you know where the Dominari have their lab set up?"

"Somewhere in the Sprawl, I believe, but the exact location is unknown to me." Gregor's mandibles clicked together once, twice, an action I think was intended to substitute for a smile. "The Dominari may not be Darklords, but their protective spells are still quite formidable."

"I don't suppose you know who Varma's veinburn connection was."

"Actually, I do, or at least, I have a suspicion. The only veinburn dealer I'm aware of is a demon named Morfran who works out of the Sprawl."

I frowned. "Only one dealer? That doesn't make any sense. It's not like the Dominari to work on so small a scale."

"I have the impression they've been field-testing veinburn," Gregor said, "trying to get the formula just right."

"I suppose." Still, it didn't sound like the Dominari's style. Like the criminal organizations back on Earth, they always went for the money, and they weren't exactly known for their patience. "Can you think of anyone in particular who would gain from stealing the Dawnstone?"

"You're asking me to theorize. You know how much I dislike doing so in the absence of facts. But if I were to hazard a guess, I would say someone who wished to harm Lord Galm—or perhaps even Father Dis. And in all likelihood, that would be another Darklord."

"Talaith," Devona said. "Relations between my father and Talaith might be cordial at the moment, but they haven't always been so. And if Talaith is behind the creation of veinburn—"

"She could have gotten Varma hooked on the stuff, and used his addiction as leverage to get him to steal the Dawnstone for her," I finished. "It certainly seems to fit. No wonder she was ready for us when we tried to cross her domain. Augury, my dead ass. One of her people probably saw us asking around about Varma in the Sprawl and alerted her that we were investigating the Dawnstone's theft and figured there was a good chance we'd consult Gregor."

"And the Red Tide?" Devona asked. "They came after us after we'd visited Waldemar—long before anyone could've been aware of what we were doing."

"Maybe she's got an informant in the Cathedral, then, someone who saw us there."

"Why the Red Tide, then? They hardly seem like the type to work for Talaith."

"Darkgems are darkgems, no matter who pays them to you. And the Red Tide's tech can't come cheap, not when it has to be imported from Earth."

Around us, Gregor's children began getting restless. A sign, I knew, that Gregor himself was becoming bored and was eager to move on to another topic.

"Anything else?" he asked.

"Not that I can think of," I answered.

"Then on to the matter of payment." If there's such a thing as an insect version of a purr, Gregor's words were it.

Before I could respond, Devona stepped in front of me and said, "I'll pay."

"No you won't," I said.

She turned to me, her face set in a determined expression. "You paid Waldemar's price, Lord Edrigu's, and Silent Jack's. It's my turn."

"I could afford to pay them, Devona. I . . . Papa Chatha gave me some bad news. My body can no longer be preserved by magic. I'll be gone in a couple days, maybe less."

Gregor didn't react; he'd probably already known. But Devona came forward and took my hand.

"I thought your skin looked a little grayer than when we first met, but I told myself it was just my imagination. It wasn't, though, was it?"

I shook my head.

"And you're spending the time you have left helping me." She sounded bemused, as if she couldn't quite bring herself to believe it.

I felt a need to tell her the truth. "My motives aren't unselfish. I was hoping that if we recovered the Dawnstone, you would intercede with Lord Galm on my behalf and ask him to help me make Papa a liar."

"So you haven't given up."

I smiled. "It's not in my nature."

"Then the prices you paid—a page from your life, bearing Edrigu's mark, losing your finger—you paid them even though you still intend to continue living. Uh, existing."

"Yes."

She nodded, as if in understanding, but of what I had no idea. She released my hand and turned back to face Gregor. "I shall pay this time."

"Actually," Gregor said, his antennae quivering as if he could barely contain himself, "since the information I've provided may benefit both of you—Devona, by helping recover the Dawnstone, and Matthew, by providing a chance to avoid discorporation—you must both pay."

"What?" Devona nearly shouted, setting Gregor's children to rustling nervously. "That isn't fair!"

Gregor leaned forward, and although nothing else in his attitude changed, I sensed a hint of menace in the motion. "This is my home. Here, I decide what is and isn't fair."

From behind us came a soft whispering, like a distant wave breaking on the beach. I turned to see Gregor's children had left the ceiling and the walls and were massing behind us.

I put a hand on Devona's shoulder. "It's okay. Information is the only coin he deals in."

"Quite so," Gregor affirmed.

Devona sighed. "Very well, then."

I looked behind us; the mound of Gregor's children was growing smaller as they returned to their previous places.

"Ms. Kanti, you shall pay first." Gregor settled back once more. "As Matthew told you, all that interests me is information. But as I mentioned earlier, there are some places in Necropolis—only a few, mind you—where my children have a difficult time venturing. Among these places, as I indicated, is the Cathedral. I want you to escort one of my children into Lord Galm's stronghold and then, after a period of precisely one month, escort it out again. You need do nothing else to pay your debt to me."

Devona considered briefly, and then said, "Agreed."

"Excellent." Gregor did or said nothing more, but one of his insects detached itself from the others and scurried up Devona's leg, over her waist and chest, along her neck, across her jawline, and then darted into her ear.

She screamed in pain and clapped her hand to the side of her head. Blood trickled out from between her fingers. She swayed, then fell to her knees.

I went to her and gently pulled her hand away from her ear. I saw no sign of the insect and, thanks to her half-vampire physiology, the wound of its passage was already healing.

"I apologize. I should have made clear what I meant by escort." Gregor chittered softly.

"If you've hurt her—"

"No need for dramatics, Matthew. My child must be hidden inside Ms. Kanti in order to be able to penetrate Lord Galm's wardspells. Despite the initial . . . unpleasantness of the process, she will not be harmed by hosting my child, and when a month is over, it shall depart and Ms. Kanti's body will heal the minor damage caused by its leavetaking." He rubbed four of his legs together, maybe in anticipation of soon gaining access to a place so long denied him.

"I'm all right, Matt," Devona said, sounding a bit shaky but otherwise unhurt. I helped her to stand. "It feels . . . odd," she said. "But that's all."

"All right, Gregor," I said. "My turn. Let me guess: you want me to carry one of your little spies too, so in case I do rot away to dust, I can ferry it over to the afterlife with me."

More chittering. "Hardly. You have only to answer one simple question for me, Matthew: how do you feel about being a zombie?"

— SIXTEEN —

"I don't know what you mean."

"Come now, Matthew, it's a simple enough question. How do you feel about being a zombie?"

"Why do you want to know?"

Gregor chittered loudly. "Why do I want to know anything? Because it is there to be known, because I do not already know. Because by knowing, I can perhaps come to understand."

"Understand what?"

"Everything, of course. But to answer your initial question more specifically, I wish to know because you are one of a kind, the only self-willed zombie in Necropolis, perhaps the only one that has ever existed. And unlike normal zombies, you are aware and can provide valuable insight into your state of existence."

"I'd like to help you, Gregor, but I don't experience emotions the way I did when I was alive. I'm not sure I have any feelings about being a zombie."

Gregor's mandibles clacked together slowly—tik-tik-tik-tik—a gesture and sound which I'd come to know as a sign that the big bug was losing patience.

"You forget to whom you are speaking, Matthew. My children have watched you many times since your arrival in Necropolis. You pretend to help people solely for monetary compensation in order that you might purchase preservative spells. But the lengths you go to in order to help them, the risks you take, indicate a man who is interested in far more than just collecting a paycheck."

"When I take on a job, I do it to the best of my abilities. That's how I am."

"And is that why you chose to help Lyra? She was a spirit, Matthew, and unable to pay you."

"Not true; I got to keep Honani's soul."

"Which you did not know would happen when you decided to aid Lyra. You helped her because you felt sorry for her and because her death filled you with righteous anger and you wanted to make her killer pay. You cannot deny it."

Gregor was right, I couldn't. "So?"

"So that proves you still feel, Matthew. Now answer my question and discharge your debt to me."

I looked at Devona and thought of what she had said to me in the alley where we'd discovered Varma's body. *If you don't feel anything, perhaps it doesn't have anything to do with your being a zombie. Perhaps that's who Matthew Adrion really is—a man who was dead inside long before he died on the outside.* Had she been right? Was that really who and what I was?

I heard the soft whisper of Gregor's children gathering behind.

"Matt—" Devona said warningly.

"How do I feel, Gregor? Even in Necropolis I'm an oddity—a freak in a city of freaks—the only walking dead man with a mind of his own. And that mind is trapped in a body that's little more than a numb piece of meat. I can't feel warm or cold, can't feel the wind on my face. Can't smell, can't taste. I'm cut off from the world around me, on the outside of life, looking in and trying to remember what it was like to be a man, to be Matthew Adrion, instead of just a pale memory of him.

"And now my undead body's preparing to betray me,

getting ready to fall apart like so much overcooked chicken slipping off the bone. And despite my hope that Lord Galm might have the power to help me, and that he might deign to do so if I can help Devona recover the Dawnstone before I rot away completely, I'm still scared that none of it's going to help, that my body will cease to be and my spirit—" I showed the E on my palm to Gregor. "I suppose Lord Edrigu will get that."

I lowered my hand. "You want to know how it feels to be me, Gregor? Right now, it well and truly sucks. Satisfied?"

Gregor slumped against the wall, legs curled across his abdomen and stroking it slowly with a faint rustling sound as of a mass of dry twigs being rubbed together. His attitude was that of a someone who has just had a very large and very good meal. Or just had great sex. "Extremely. Thank you, Matthew. And good luck on your dual quests to locate the Dawnstone and discover a way to avoid your impending dissolution. I truly hope you succeed. Necropolis is a far more interesting place with you inhabiting it."

I felt humiliated at having been forced to bare my soul for Gregor's amusement, and that Devona had been a witness. "I hope your next visitor is a very big can of sentient bug spray."

I turned to go, and Devona followed. Together, we walked up the temporarily insect-free stairs, Gregor's chittering laughter following us all the way.

We walked through the dilapidated streets of the Boneyard in silence for a time after that. The wraith images of the domain's inhabitants seemed to be sharper now, maybe because we'd moved further into the Boneyard, or maybe we were just getting used to them. A few tried to talk with us, but they made no sound, at least none we could hear, and after several moments of attempting to communicate by gesture, they gave up and drifted away.

When Devona finally spoke, she said, "What do we do now?" No mention of my embarrassing little scene back in Gregor's basement, for which I was quite grateful.

"We have several possible avenues of investigation at this point. We could try to find Morfran, the demon veinburn dealer; we could try to locate the drug lab the Arcane and the Dominari have set up in the Sprawl; or we could try to learn who hired the Red Tide vampires that killed Varma and tried to kill us."

As if on cue, a crimson mist rolled forth from a nearby sewer grate.

"No need to bust your rotting ass looking for us, zombie," Narda's voice drifted forth from the vermilion cloud. "Red Tide's right here."

The fog dissipated to reveal Narda, Enan, and the Giggler.

Enan raised his right hand. The fingers blurred and shifted, becoming five large hypodermic needles, the points glistening with liquid veinburn. He grinned. "Time to plug and play, Deadboy."

— SEVENTEEN —

The vampiric trio looked the worse for wear since last I'd seen them, but not as much as I'd expected. There were still traces of burns on their faces and hands, but the worst injuries had been covered by patches of what appeared to be blue rubber that seemed to have bonded to their skin. Narda's missing eye hadn't regenerated; rather, in its place was a camera lens which protruded several inches from the socket. Their tech bodysuits, which had been short-circuiting as they fled from us in Gothtown, had been repaired, but sloppily—exposed wires, mismatched parts, metallic glops from hurried soldering. The suits sparked here and there, and the power hum was overloud and sounded a bit strained. I imagined the air contained the faint hot metal and plastic smell of machinery working too hard.

"The Boneyard isn't exactly your normal stomping grounds," I said. "How'd you find us?"

"We want to find someone, they're good as found," Narda said.

"Can't hide from the Tide," Enan added.

The Giggler giggled.

"What's with the blue gunk?" I asked. "New fashion statement?"

"Plaskin," Enan said. "Helps burns heal faster. But they still hurt like a bitch." He gnashed his fangs, and his eyes blazed with anger. "But not as much as you're gonna hurt before we're done with you."

The Giggler lived up to his nickname once again, and I

decided now was not the time to point out that my body was incapable of feeling pain. It would just make them more determined—and inventive.

"I'd have thought you'd be used to pain by now," I said. "After all, don't the crosses embedded in your foreheads hurt?"

"Sure they do," Narda said. "Shows Red Tide's got tough hardware. Shows Red Tide's not afraid of anything."

The Giggler let forth another peal of his high-pitched, girlish laughter. I bent down and picked up half of a broken brick from the worn and cracked street.

The Red Tide vampires laughed.

"What do you think you're gonna do with that?" Enan asked.

"This." Throwing isn't easy as slow as I am, but I've had plenty of practice. With a wind-up and then a half-throw, half-lurch, I hurled the makeshift missile as hard as I could at the Giggler's forehead. It struck the cross set into his flesh, driving it inward. The Giggler screamed and clawed at his forehead, but it was no good. The cross's corrosive effect on vampire flesh and bone, aided by the impact of my brick, had buried the holy object in his brain. Steam curled forth from the wound, and then rays of pure white light shot out of his eyes, ears, nostrils, and mouth. The light winked out and Giggler now had nothing but open ruins where his sensory organs had been. He stiffened and fell forward onto the broken pavement. I was confident he was dead, but I half expected him to start giggling again anyway.

For a moment, Narda and Enan stared in stunned amazement at the body of their fallen comrade—long enough to allow me to pull out my garlic and holy water squirt gun, which was mostly empty. But before I could start pumping the plastic trigger, Narda pointed toward

145

Devona and tendrils of wire curled forth to encircle the latter's arm.

"Put the gun down, Deadboy, or little Miss Leather here'll get a few million volts. Enough to fry her up good."

Vampires, for all their strengths, have a surprising number of weaknesses. Beyond the ones everyone knows about—sunlight, holy objects, wooden stakes—are others such as silver and fire. Vampires aren't as flammable as zombies by any means, but fire can kill them.

I dropped the squirt gun to the ground with a plastic clatter.

"Kick it away."

I did.

Enan grinned. "Now we're gonna have ourselves a little fun. Put your hands above your head, zombie, and step toward me slowly. Make any funny moves, and Narda turns your friend into charcoal. Got it?"

I nodded and did as he ordered.

"Stick out your arm," he commanded.

I did; I knew what was coming. "Veinburn won't work on me. I'm dead. All the way dead, not like you overgrown mosquitoes."

"Then you won't mind if I do this!" Enan plunged his needle fingers into the unfeeling flesh of my forearm. After a few moments, Enan yanked his hand away—tearing five ragged holes in my gray skin in the process—and the needles thickened into fingers once more.

"Well?" he asked. "How's it feel, deader?"

"I told you, I'm not—" I broke off, my body beginning to shake all over. I collapsed to the pavement not far from the Giggler's corpse, flipping and flopping like a fish tossed live into a frying pan.

"I'll be damned again!" Narda crowed. "This shit's even

stronger than they said it is! Look at him go!"

"I bet that's the best he's felt in a loooooong time!" Enan laughed.

My exertions became so severe that I rolled over onto my stomach, and when I came around on my back again, I'd drawn my revolver from my pants and leveled it at Narda's head. If I'd still been a cop, I'd have given her a warning. But I wasn't a cop anymore.

Two silver bullets apiece later, Narda and Enan had joined the Giggler on the ground. I stood, walked over to the bodies, reloaded, and pumped another couple rounds into their hearts, just to be sure.

Devona had untangled herself from Narda's wire. "I take it the veinburn didn't affect you. Nice acting job."

"What can I say? I was in drama club in high school." I examined the patches of plaskin on the forms of the dead vampires. I wondered if the substance might help fend off my decay, but I decided it probably wouldn't. The plaskin likely only worked on living tissue. No loss; I don't look good in blue anyway.

Devona looked at the remains of the Red Tide members. "Makes it rather difficult to question them, doesn't it? Their being dead and all."

"You complaining?"

She smiled. "Not in the slightest. But it does narrow our options."

"The Red Tide have to get their technology somewhere. The only Darklord enamored of technology is Varvara, although if what Gregor said is true, Talaith has started dabbling in it. But Talaith wouldn't have the connections to supply the kind of equipment the Red Tide uses."

"Does Varvara?"

"Certainly, but none of this strikes me as her style.

Varvara's charming, fun, and she'd betray her best friend in a heartbeat if there was a laugh in it. But the Red Tide are too déclassé for her. My money's on the Dominari. They have the connections to import and supply technology to the Red Tide and from what Gregor told us, they're involved in the manufacturing and testing of veinburn, which Enan possessed in abundance."

I put my gun away and shook my arm; it felt heavy and swollen. "Stupid vamps. Not only doesn't this stuff work on me, you'd think they'd have realized I'd need a functioning circulatory system to distribute it throughout my body."

"What will happen to the veinburn?"

"It'll just sit in my arm until I have it removed. Papa Chatha can do it for me. If I'm still around in a few days." As soon as I said the words, I regretted them. It was one thing to think those kind of morbid comments, another to say them.

"Oh, Matt, I wish you had told me earlier."

"We just met not that long ago, Devona. My situation has no bearing on your problem or on our efforts to resolve it." I paused. "Besides, I didn't want you worrying about me."

"That's sweet." And then she did something that surprised the hell out of me. She leaned forward and gave me a kiss on the cheek. I hadn't been kissed since I'd died, hadn't even really been touched—in a non-violent way, that is—by another human being. Well, half a human being in this case.

I didn't know how to react, so I didn't. Just stood there and looked at her. Pretty smooth, huh?

"I want you to know something, Matt. No matter whether we find the Dawnstone or not, I intend to ask my father to help you."

Now I really didn't know what to say. But Devona didn't

wait for a reply. "I assume we're off to the Sprawl again?"

I nodded. "To locate either Morfran or the drug lab." I smiled. "And I promise not to kill anyone else before we've had a chance to talk with them."

You know the old punchline? You can't get there from here. Well, Necropolis can be like that, unless like some of the Bloodborn, you possess the ability to fly. The only way to move from one Darklord's domain to another is via one of the five bridges, which means the only way you can travel Necropolis is in a circle. To get back to the Sprawl, we had to either go through Glamere once more—definitely not an option—or pass through the Wyldwood, domain of Lord Amon, ruler of the lycanthropes.

When I brought up this point to Devona, she said, "Couldn't we take a shortcut across the grounds of the Nightspire?"

The Nightspire rests on a small island in the middle of the pentagram that is Necropolis. This island is surrounded by the fiery waters of Phlegethon, the same waters which enclose the city and separate the five domains from each other. But in addition to the main bridges, there is a second set of smaller ones which connect each section of the city to the Nightspire. Devona's suggestion made sense on the surface. It would make our journey to the Sprawl far simpler and less deadly if we could walk from the Boneyard to the Nightspire, pass the bridge leading to the Wyldwood and take the one which led to the Sprawl.

"Unfortunately, it isn't that simple. During my time here, I've helped a number of people. And I've had occasion to travel a good bit of the city. I had the same idea as you a while back and tried to cross over one of the bridges to the Nightspire."

"What happened?"

"It didn't work. Powerful winds buffeted me, nearly knocking me into the river. When I retreated, the winds ceased. I later learned from Gregor that the wind, which he said was caused by the invisible Furies which guard the Nightspire, repels all who attempt to cross—not including the Darklords, of course—unless they are accompanied by one of Dis' representatives."

"So that's out then," Devona said. "And we can't risk another encounter with Lady Talaith."

"I'd rather not," I admitted.

"Which leaves only the Wyldwood."

"Talk about Scylla and Charybdis."

Her eyebrows rose. "I didn't realize you were so well read."

"Yeah, well, when you don't sleep, eat or go to the bathroom anymore, you have a lot of extra time for reading. Let's go. And on the way, maybe you can talk me out of it."

-EIGHTEEN-

We crossed the Bridge of Silent Screams and entered the dense tangle of forest that was the Wyldwood. We picked our way carefully through the underbrush, searching for a path and trying not to make too much noise lest we attract the attention of any lykes that might be nearby. Lykes were chaotic enough outside their domain, but here they were reputed to be totally wild, killing on sight any who dared attempt to cross their land. Like I said, Devona and I made our way very carefully.

Despite the thickness of the forest, we could still see well enough. Some strange quality of Umbriel's shadowy light? Or maybe Lord Amon's magic was responsible. Whichever, I was grateful. Otherwise, I would have been totally dependent on Devona's vampire vision to lead me—and I don't like being dependent.

Still, being able to see didn't help us navigate. I'd been a city boy all my life and death, and Devona had spent most of her existence within the Cathedral and the surrounding environs of Gothtown. Neither of us was exactly a skilled outdoorsman. Devona had to climb gracefully and easily up trees a number of times to check the position of Umbriel and get a fix on our location.

After one such check, she climbed down from the large oak she'd gone up and said, "As near as I can tell, we've been going in circles."

"What a surprise." I would've killed for a compass, but I'm not certain one would work in Necropolis' dimension anyway. I thought for a moment, trying to get my dead brain to cough up what little woodlore it knew. "Maybe we should start marking trees as we go, so at least we don't—"

Devona put a finger to her lips to shush me, and then she touched her ear. I listened, but I didn't hear anything— not that that meant anything. Devona's half-vampire hearing was far superior to mine. I listened again, and this time I heard it: a soft rustling of leaves, not very far away and coming closer.

A lyke? I mouthed.

She sniffed the air, frowned, and then nodded, but she didn't seem all that certain. I wondered why, but knew now was not the time to ask. Something was coming, and whatever it was, I doubted it was the Welcome Wagon. We headed off through the brush in the opposite direction of the rustling, trying to be as silent as we could, but being two city dwellers, failing miserably.

The rustling became a crashing as something loud bounded toward us. I pulled my pistol out and rested my finger easily on the trigger. I only had five silver bullets left—not nearly enough to get us through the Wyldwood, but I couldn't worry about that now. Whatever it was came around our left and then approached from in front, slowing as it neared.

I aimed my weapon at the spot in the brush where I judged the lyke would appear and waited.

A few seconds later the leaves parted and I tightened my finger on the trigger. But then I stopped. For out of the underbrush stepped a six-foot-tall white rabbit with yellow eyes.

"Don't tell me," I said. "You're late for a very important date."

The hare scowled. "Real funny. But if she's Alice, then

what the hell are you?" The voice was masculine, if a bit on the high side.

"I'm the guy who's got a gun full of silver bullets pointed at your chest. Please tell me you're not a carnivorous bunny."

His large amber eyes fixed on my pistol, but his voice remained steady enough. "Who ever heard of such a thing?"

"This is Necropolis, pal. A meat-eating rabbit would actually be rather mundane here."

"Good point. But no, I'm not a predator." He opened his mouth and displayed flat rabbit teeth. And then his form blurred and shifted until before us stood a thin, but still rabbity-looking young man in his mid-twenties, with an unruly shock of white hair and wearing nothing but a pair of overalls.

"Where did the pants come from?" I asked, curious. "I mean, you weren't wearing them before, and now here they are."

He shook his head as if I'd just asked the stupidest question imaginable. "Magic. A far better question is where did you two come from?"

I lowered my gun, but I didn't put it away. I wasn't ready to trust Bugs just yet. "The Boneyard."

He looked me over. "That I could've guessed." He wrinkled his nose. "And smelled."

"Sorry, but they don't make deodorant for zombies." I gave him an extremely truncated version of who Devona and I were and what we were doing here.

"You'd have been better off taking your chances with Lady Talaith. The Wyldwood is never a safe place for outsiders, but it's even more dangerous now."

"Why?" Devona asked.

The wererabbit opened his mouth to reply, but was cut

153

off by the sound of horns echoing in the distance. Hunting horns.

"That's why. Today Lord Amon is conducting the Wild Hunt."

I sighed. "Of course he is." Why, I wondered to myself, are these things never easy?

The lyke, whose name turned out to be Arleigh ("It means 'from the hare's meadow,' " he said proudly), led us through the forest and to a vast stretch of pasture where cattle grazed contentedly beneath Umbriel's shadowlight.

"Here in the Wyldwood, we produce most of Necropolis' meat and blood—real blood, not that synthetic glop Varvara's factories have started churning out," Arleigh said. "Non-preds like me do, that is. The carnies tend to be too impulsive. They usually end up killing and eating the animals themselves."

"You're a farmer?" Devona asked.

Arleigh nodded. "Most herbs like me are."

"So you lykes have a caste system?" I asked. "Doesn't seem fair."

Arleigh shrugged his lean, bony shoulders. "It suits my nature, and I enjoy the work. What's wrong with that?"

I thought of my own work as a "doer of favors." In reality, I had to admit to myself, I was really still just a cop. My nature, I suppose. "Nothing wrong at all."

I noticed Devona was frowning, and I wondered what she was thinking about. Her own work as tender of Lord Galm's Collection, maybe?

"We're safe along the pastureland," Arleigh said. "The Hunt's conducted in the wilder part of the forest, using animals Lord Amon has specially bred at his Lodge." He lowered his voice. "I've heard it said that this year, he's using animals that have been . . . augmented."

"What, you mean through technology?"

He nodded.

"I guess it's everywhere," I said. I wondered how long it would be before Waldemar installed computers in the Great Library and Gregor set up Necropolis' version of the Internet.

"Unfortunately," Arleigh said, "the pastureland doesn't extend all the way to the Bridge of Forgotten Pleasures."

"Let me guess," I said. "The way we need to go is directly through the section of the Wyldwood where the Hunt's being conducted."

Arleigh nodded, and I sighed again. Never easy.

Arleigh offered to help us through the Wyldwood and I, distrusting soul that I am, wanted to know why. He puzzled over my question for a few moments before finally smiling apologetically. "The only reason I can give you is because it's the right thing to do."

I didn't buy it, but then twenty years as a cop and two as a zombie had made me cynical. Maybe the lyke was just following his nature again. Whatever his reason for aiding us, we couldn't afford to turn him down.

Arleigh led us through the Wyldwood's pasturelands, but even though he assured us we were safe here, I kept my gun out. Just in case. Before long, however, we had to leave the pastureland and return to the forest. Arleigh thought he'd be able to lead us past the Hunt, but I could tell by the nervous way the lyke kept sniffing the air and looking around that he wasn't as confident as he would've liked us to believe.

We periodically heard the hunting horns, sometimes closer, sometimes farther. Arleigh told us not to worry overmuch about the horns, for sound traveled in deceptive ways in the forest.

Eventually, we reached a small clearing, and Arleigh said he needed to stop a moment and get his bearings. He crouched down, his nose shifted back to a rabbit's, whiskers and all, and he sniffed the ground.

A horn blasted, sounding close by. It was followed by the noise of something large and heavy crashing through the underbrush directly toward us. Arleigh stood, rabbit nose quivering in fear.

"We need to get out of here!" I told him. "Which way?"

But he only stood, transfixed, staring in the direction of whatever was approaching, and trembled. I grabbed his arm and shook him a couple times, but I couldn't break him out of his terror-induced trance. I figured to hell with him, then.

"C'mon, Devona, we have to—"

Before I could finish my sentence, an animal unlike any I had ever seen before bounded into the clearing. It looked something like a muscular ostrich, only with a thick neck and a large, cruelly hooked beak. No doubt one of the "augmented" animals the Hunt pursued. The bird skidded to a stop upon seeing us. It cocked its head and examined us, probably trying to determine if we were a threat or not.

Evidently, the answer was not, for it let forth a loud angry SQUAWK! and came charging at us, snapping its hook-beak.

I only had five silver bullets left, and I hated to waste them on the lyke's prey, but I couldn't let the giant bird attack us either. I aimed for the thing's throat, but before I could fire, a spear whizzed through the air and sunk into the creature's back with a meaty-moist THUK! The bird screeched in pain and pitched forward, where it lay writhing in the grass.

A huge wolfman stepped into the clearing, powerfully built, lupine head held high in a regal fashion. Lord Amon, I presumed. He was followed closely by a half dozen other lykes of various predator species, one of which—a humanoid bobcat—carried an antler horn slung over his shoulder by a leather strap. I was impressed by how silent the lykes had been—they hadn't made a sound.

I didn't need Arleigh to tell us we had stumbled across the Wild Hunt.

The bird, though bleeding profusely, was still very much alive, squawking and thrashing its powerful legs. The wolfman walked up to the animal and regarded it for a moment. I expected him to finish it off, but instead the wolf-headed humanoid padded over to us. I thought he might do any number of things, all of them involving his teeth and claws and our flesh, but he stopped in front of us and then did something I didn't anticipate and couldn't have imagined: he fell to one knee.

"I have downed the bird, my Lord. Would you do me the honor of dispatching it?"

At first, for some crazy reason, I thought the lyke was addressing me. But then Arleigh replied, "You have done well, Rolf. Rise and claim the honor for yourself." The wererabbit's voice was no longer high-pitched, but low and resonant.

The wolfman stood and grinned. "Thank you, my Lord." Then he turned and loped toward the bird and, with a single savage bite and twist of his jaws, broke the animal's neck. He ripped off a hunk of meat, and walked away from the kill to devour it. The other lykes waited until Rolf was eating before rushing to the dead bird, snarling, yipping, and biting as they fought for the best of the remaining meat.

"My people have never been much for table manners," Arleigh said.

Devona and I turned toward him, but the rabbity man was gone; in his place stood a broad-shouldered, ruddy-faced man in full fox-hunting regalia—little black hat, red jacket, white jodhpurs, shiny black boots, even a riding crop held in one black leather-gloved hand. But despite his transformation, the being still possessed the same yellow eyes.

"Allow me to introduce myself," he said with a touch of English accent. "I am Amon, Lord of the Wyldwood." He smiled, displaying a mouthful of sharp teeth. "So nice of you to drop by."

— NINETEEN —

"Forgive my little deception, but once I became aware of you, I thought it best to investigate. And the guise of Arleigh seemed a perfect way to do so."

"And what did you learn?" I asked. It appeared Amon wasn't limited to one wildform as were his subjects—which made sense seeing as how he was Lord of the shapeshifters. Still, I was more than a little angry at myself for being fooled so easily. The yellow eyes should have been a tip-off. Who'd ever seen a rabbit with yellow eyes?

"The only important thing: that you're not a threat sent by one of my fellow Lords. This time of year, we Darklords tend to be busy with certain preparations. So busy that we're more vulnerable than usual to each others' machinations." He smiled. "I myself have set in motion several plots against my peers over the centuries, most of them around the anniversary of the Descension. Unfortunately, none bore much fruit. We tend to be too evenly matched. Still, the fun is in the game, is it not?"

"I'm not a Darklord, so I wouldn't know," I said. Devona gave me a warning look, but I ignored her. The English gentleman act was getting on my nerves. "And speaking of preparations, shouldn't you be conserving your energy for the Renewal Ceremony? I'm surprised you're out hunting instead of meditating or something."

The English fox hunter guise melted away to be replaced by that of a pith-helmeted, khaki-clothed big-game hunter, complete with elephant gun. The English accent disappeared, too, to be replaced by gravely American. "We each prepare in our own way. Galm meditates, Talaith engages in rites with her people, Edrigu communes with the spirit world, and Varvara throws a lavish party. I have been marshaling my power for weeks now. Today I prepare my mind and soul by engaging in the activity which is at the very core of my being—the Hunt."

I nodded to the ravaged corpse of the huge bird. "It didn't look like you were doing much hunting to me."

Amon ignored the dig. "My sons and daughters always accompany me. This was Rolf's kill."

I looked at the lykes of varied species scattered about the clearing, all of whom were hunkered down, greedily devouring their shares of meat. "Nice family," I said dryly.

Frank Buck gave way to a yellow-eyed Daniel Boone, dressed in the requisite buckskin clothing and coonskin cap. "What they lack in manners, they make up for in enthusiasm."

"You're a busy monster, so let's cut to the chase," I said. "What do you intend to do with us?"

"The story we told Arleigh—told you—is true," Devona added. "We're just trying to get back to the Sprawl. We're on an errand of great concern to my father, Lord Galm."

"You provided few details, though I could sense what you told me was indeed the truth."

I wondered how Amon could be so sure of that. Because of his heightened lycanthrope senses, which functioned as an organic lie detector? Or maybe through other abilities he possessed as a Darklord? Whichever, he did seem to believe us, which was the important thing.

Devona started to talk but Amon, who had become a tall, lean, spear-wielding African tribesman, silenced her with a gesture. "Details are unnecessary. Regardless of whether your errand is of major or minor importance, if your failure to complete it will inconvenience Galm, that's reason enough for me to keep you from continuing your journey."

I still held my pistol at my side. I wondered if silver would prove effective against Amon, who was obviously much more than an ordinary lyke. The way things were going, it looked like I'd find out soon enough.

"But I have another reason to detain you. Two, actually. And their names are Honani and Thokk."

I groaned inwardly and was uncomfortably aware of the soul jar containing Honani's spirit—which now seemed suddenly very heavy—still resting in my jacket pocket.

"Mr. Adrion, you are responsible for Honani's body being taken over by another, and for the grievous injuries inflicted on his sister when she tried to seek justice."

"Vengeance," I corrected.

Amon, now a Native American brave, shrugged. "A mere difference in terminology. Honani and Thokk are mixbloods, lycanthropes who have turned to science to alter their natural abilities. As such, they are outcasts among my people."

I gestured toward the nearly picked clean carcass of Big Bird. "You don't seem completely adverse to science."

"It has its uses," Amon admitted. "Provided it isn't taken too far. Still, even though they possess corrupted genes, mixbloods are still lycanthropes. Still family. You have transgressed against two of my subjects. As Lord of the Wyldwood, I have a responsibility to my people to see that justice is done." He smiled. "Or, if you prefer, vengeance."

I preferred neither in this case, but I kept my mouth shut.

Rolf had finished eating and walked over to us. "These

two aren't worthy of your attention, Father." He licked blood off his muzzle. "Especially the zombie. Allow me to slay them for you so that you might not dirty your hands."

Amon, now a shaggy caveman holding an animal's jaw-bone in one of his thick-knuckled hands, affectionately cuffed his child. "You've had your fun, Rolf. Now it is your father's turn."

Rolf bowed his head and stepped back.

I wondered what the odds were of my squeezing off a shot at Amon before one or more of his children fell upon me. Not good, I decided.

Then I had an idea. I raised my left hand and displayed the mark upon my palm. "My master, Lord Edrigu, will be displeased if anything should happen to us."

Amon looked at the mark for a moment and then burst out laughing. "That symbol merely means that Edrigu has laid a claim on your soul, zombie. I'm sure he'd be happy to collect it earlier than anticipated."

"Then what of my father?" Devona said in her best haughty-regal voice. "I am not just his daughter; I am also the keeper of his Collection. He would be furious if any harm were to come to me or my companion."

She sounded convincing enough, but I could tell by the uncertain look in her eyes that she wasn't sure that Lord Galm would be all that upset if his half-breed daughter died in the Wyldwood. I felt sorry for her then. What would it be like to have known a father for over seventy years, to have taken care of his Collection for nearly thirty, to have worked hard for him in hope of some simple recognition and still not know whether he cared if you lived or died?

Maybe Amon sensed her uncertainty as well, for after a moment's thought, he said, "You have aided in an assault on one of my subjects and trespassed on my domain. Galm cannot gainsay my right to justice."

Amon shimmered and was now a beer-gutted, flannel-shirted, John Deere-capped, shotgun-toting hunter, complete with chewing tobacco juice dribbling down his stubbled chin.

"But as it's the anniversary of the Descension and we are in the middle of the Wild Hunt, I shall make you a proposition." He turned his head and spit a brown stream into the grass. "Several miles from here is a small glen. You will be taken there and set free. All you need do is reach the other side, and I shall let you continue on your way to the Sprawl and will seek no further action against you for what happened to Honani and Thokk."

"And the catch is?" I asked.

Amon smiled, displaying tobacco-stained fangs. "I shall be hunting you."

"You have been given a great honor," Rolf said. He and his feral siblings escorted us through the forest, Rolf leading, the others enclosing us in a circle.

"Yeah, it's a dream come true," I replied.

He snarled and his clawed hands tensed. I'm sure he would've taken my head off if we hadn't been his father's prey. Before we'd set out, Rolf had taken my pistol from me and now carried it in his left hand. Lykes are highly allergic to silver, but my bullets were safely encased within the gun, allowing him to hold it without harm. Still, I thought I could detect a slight swelling of his hand. I was surprised and puzzled that the lykes hadn't gotten rid of my gun as soon as they'd taken it from me. But when we reached the glen, I understood why.

"The hunt shall begin as soon as we depart," Rolf said solemnly. "My father, in deference to your weakness, shall give you a head start." His sharp-toothed smile reminded me of Amon. "How much of a head start, however, you shall not know." He pointed a clawed finger toward the other side of the glen. "The rules are simple. Reach the other side and your lives will be spared. Fail to do so, and you die."

He dropped my gun to the ground. "Once we are gone, you may pick up your weapon and begin." Before we could ask any questions, Rolf and the others bounded away into the forest, moving through the underbrush with silent, liquid grace.

I retrieved my gun and checked the cylinder. Five silver bullets.

"It seems Lord Amon doesn't believe in hunting defenseless prey," Devona said.

"Or that he isn't as vulnerable to silver as an ordinary lyke." I clicked the cylinder closed. "Let's get moving; the clock's ticking."

As soon as we stepped into the glen, it became night. I don't mean the perpetual dusk created by the diffuse shadowlight of Umbriel; I mean honest-to-God night, with stars and everything. Despite our situation, I was so surprised that I stopped and stared overhead. They were the first stars I had seen in two years, and they were beautiful.

For an instant I had the dizzying sensation that we had somehow stepped through an unseen door between Necropolis and Earth—that I was home.

"Are those stars?" Devona asked, her voice soft with wonder. "I've heard about them, but I've never actually seen any before. They're lovely—and so far away. They make me feel small, and yet somehow big at the same time. Does that make any sense?"

"It makes perfect sense. But they can't be real stars.

What we're looking at is most likely nothing more than an illusion, a distraction designed to slow us down."

"You're right, of course. I'll lead the way; my night vision is better than yours." She took my hand and pulled me forward.

"And keep a nose out for Amon. We don't know what form he'll be wearing when he attacks, but it has to have a scent."

"Right."

We ran. The grass was slick with dew, and the sound of crickets chirping filled the air. I knew it was all just special effects supplied courtesy of Lord Amon, but a wave of homesickness hit me hard, and I thought that if I had to die for good, I could pick far worse places in Necropolis.

We continued forward, Devona's gaze fixed unwaveringly on the opposite treeline, her heightened senses alive and alert; I held my gun at the ready, my comparatively weak vision and hearing working overtime, cop instincts on full.

Moments that felt more like hours passed, and no sign of the master of the Wyldwood.

"Why is Amon even bothering to stalk us?" Devona said in frustration. "He's a Darklord, one of the six most powerful beings in the city, including Father Dis. How can we possibly provide him with a real challenge?"

"I don't know much about Amon, but I've heard it said he gets as much pleasure from hunting down and swatting flies as he does from stalking big game. To him, the hunt is everything."

Devona started to reply, but then she suddenly squatted down, yanking me along with her so hard I felt something pull in my arm. I heard rather than felt something large pass through the air above us, approximately where our heads had been. A shrill cry of frustration and then the flapping of wings as whatever it was began gaining altitude for another run.

"Looks like our head start's over," I muttered, scanning the night sky for Amon. I looked for a black patch against the stars, but whichever shape Amon was wearing, he was moving too fast for me to locate him. And then I heard something large whistling through the air and Devona screamed.

The starlight didn't provide much illumination, but it was enough for me to see that Devona was struggling with a large bird—an eagle or maybe a condor; it was difficult to tell in the dark. Whichever the particular raptor, I knew it really was Amon. I raised my gun, but didn't dare fire for fear of hitting Devona.

"Throw him off you so I can get a shot!" I shouted.

Devona grabbed the bird by the wings and hurled him forward. It was dark, the bird was moving fast, and my reflexes are not nearly as good as they were when I was alive. But I didn't worry about any of that. I squinted my left eye, aimed, and squeezed off a shot.

The bird shrieked and hit the ground with a heavy thump. I held my gun on it, waiting for it to stir, but it didn't move. Without taking my eyes off it, I asked Devona if she was all right.

"A few cuts on my face, a couple fairly deep. Messy, but otherwise I'm unharmed. I should heal before too long."

The bird remained motionless, but I didn't lower my gun an inch; I knew better. "He was probably going for your eyes. Makes sense, since you're the only one of us who can see in the dark."

"Is he dead?" she asked.

"What do you think?"

"I think a Darklord doesn't die this easily."

"I think you're right." I moved toward the bird slowly, keeping my gun trained on it the entire time. It didn't so much as move a feather as I approached and stood over it.

"What kind is it?" I asked.

"An eagle, I believe," Devona answered. "I've only seen them in books, though."

I carefully toed the eagle, the slight pressure of my shoe making a dry, crinkling sound. And then the body of the eagle collapsed into dust. I bent down, intending to get a closer look, but within seconds, the dust too was gone.

"Perhaps we got lucky," Devona suggested.

"I don't believe in luck." I stood. "We'd better—" My sentence was cut off as a snarling piece of darkness detached itself from the night and slammed into me, knocking me to the ground, spitting and clawing. Ivory fangs glinted in the starlight as the panther buried its teeth in the undead flesh of my neck.

But as sudden and hard as the impact had been, I still had hold of my gun. As the big cat worried my neck, I calmly raised my pistol to its head, pressed the muzzle against its black fur, and fired.

The panther fell limp.

"Devona, could you help haul this thing off me?" I asked. "It's pretty heavy. Oh, and be careful. Its teeth are still lodged in my neck."

Together we got the panther off with the minimal amount of additional damage to my already ravaged neck. Devona then helped me to my feet, and I noticed that my head was slightly canted to the left. I tried to hold it upright, but it wouldn't stay. One more repair to add to the list for Papa Chatha—if I found a way to survive past the next couple days.

"Matthew, your neck . . ." Devona sounded concerned

and, although she was trying to hide it, mildly disgusted. She knew intellectually that I was a zombie, but I think this was the first time she'd really understood what that meant.

"It may look bad, but believe me, I'm okay. Now let's check out Sylvester here." I kicked the kitty corpse as I had the eagle's, with the same result: it collapsed into dust.

"Amon must be cheating," Devona said indignantly, "sending other lycanthropes in his place."

"I don't think so. Lykes don't disintegrate like this when they're killed. I think we have been fighting Amon, but he's a far different kind of shapechanger than his subjects. When we shoot him, we kill the shape he's wearing at the time—not him."

"You mean he discards his shape, leaves it behind?"

"Like a snake shedding his skin. He'll keep coming at us in different forms until I've used up my three remaining silver bullets. And then he'll have us."

"Not if we can get to the other side of the glen first," Devona said.

"I've been meaning to talk to you about that. We ran for a while before Amon attacked, right?"

"Yes, I'd estimate for perhaps five minutes."

"Me too. And in that time, we should've been able to cover a significant amount of ground, right?"

She nodded warily.

I pointed in the direction we had come, toward the line of trees where Rolf had left us—trees that were only a few feet away. "Then how come we haven't moved?"

—TWENTY—

"No wonder Amon steered us to this glen," Devona said. "It's enchanted."

"I hate Darklords. I really do."

"I don't know if we've been running in place, running in circles, running in a straight line through warped space, or have been standing still and just think we've been running."

As an experiment, I stepped back to the treeline—keeping an eye out for Amon's next attack, of course. I didn't seem to have any trouble getting there. I even reached out and touched the trunk of an elm. I looked back and saw Devona standing several feet away.

"Start walking."

She did, and it was the oddest thing. On one hand, she appeared to be walking away from me, but on the other, she seemed to stay in place. It was as two different films were being played at once on the same screen.

"Keep walking, but look back over your shoulder," I called. "And tell me what you see."

"All right." A pause. "This is strange; I appear to be moving away from you, but at the same time you seem to be almost right next to me."

"Okay, stop walking."

My vision lurched, and I experienced a dizzying moment of vertigo that might very well have nauseated me if I still had a working stomach. The far-off image of Devona was gone, and only the close-up Devona remained.

I returned to her side. "Well that didn't help any." I

scanned the sky and ground for any sign of Amon, but there was none. Maybe he had to recover, build up his strength again from having been shot twice. Or maybe he was just enjoying our confusion over the nature of his glen.

"No, it helped a great deal," she said. "The effect we experienced is similar to that of certain wardspells which operate by making someone believe he is walking toward the object warded, when in reality he cannot approach it."

"So how do we break the spell?"

"I said this spell is similar; I didn't say it was the same. We're talking about a spell laid by a Darklord. Even if I had the mystical ability to circumvent the normal version of this spell—and remember, my father made certain I was trained only in the monitoring of wardspells, not the laying or breaking of them—I couldn't begin to touch the enchantment on this glen."

"Just because Amon cast this spell doesn't mean it can't be broken. The Darklords can't afford to waste much power on such trifles as this, can they? They have the Renewal Ceremony to think about, let alone trying to defend themselves from each other. Maybe you didn't receive any formal training in getting around wardspells, but that doesn't mean you can't extrapolate from what you did learn. And if a person knows how a lock works, he stands a good chance of picking it."

"But I'm not a magicworker," Devona protested. "I'm a curator, and I suppose really little more than a glorified security guard."

I sighed. "Look, I'd like to do this gently, but we don't have time. What you are, Devona, is a half-breed vampire who gets her entire sense of self worth from basically dusting another man's treasures. Because of the way you were brought up and the attitude of other vampires toward your mixed heritage, you feel that being the keeper of your father's Collection is all you can do, that there isn't any more to you.

"But in the short time I've known you, I've seen much more. I've seen a woman who when faced with danger doesn't run, doesn't back away—she fights. I've seen a woman who when faced with a problem doesn't give up— she keeps working at it until she finds a solution. I've seen a woman who's intelligent and caring . . . and," I said softly, "who sees the man inside me, the man I thought had died along with his body.

"I've seen a woman who, having ventured beyond her tightly circumscribed life, is starting to find out who she really is and what she's truly capable of. Well, it's time to find out some more, Devona. It's time to find a way out of here."

I didn't know how she'd react: tell me to go to hell, start crying, or haul off and belt me. Maybe all three. But she just looked at me for a long moment, her expression blank, eyes unreadable in the dark. And then she nodded.

"Let's start walking again. I need to examine the spell while it's functioning." She headed off without waiting for my reply.

I smiled as I hurried after her. Wholly human or not, she was some woman.

While we walked and walked and got nowhere, Amon came at us again, this time in the more classic form of a large gray wolf. He managed to take a hunk out of my right leg before I dispatched him, or rather, his shape.

Two bullets left.

"I have an idea," Devona said not long after Amon's wolf facade had disintegrated. "I'm not sure it'll work, though."

171

"We're rapidly running out of ammunition. Anything's worth a try at this point."

"I don't have the mystical training to break the spell, but I do think I understand how it's constructed. As its basis, it's really very simple, a mere matter of aligning psycho-thaumaturgic energy structures in a constantly rotating—"

"In simple English, please, for the magically challenged among us."

She grinned. "Sorry. Basically, the spell works by constantly assaulting our minds with false sensory input. The trick to overcoming such a spell is to block out the false input so that our senses can detect reality once more."

"Sounds like quite a trick."

"It is. But I think I know how we might accomplish it. Remember I said that as half Bloodborn I possess a certain amount of psychic ability? While I haven't been trained in its use, I believe I may be able to sense in which direction the Sprawl lies by focusing on the combined mental energy of all the celebrants there. Ordinarily, I might not be able to accomplish such a feat, but this time of year there are so many people crowding the streets of the Sprawl and the emotional atmosphere is so charged, that even with my un-tutored powers I should be able to get a fix on it. And once I know where the Sprawl is—"

"You'll be able to shut out the glen's spell and lead us across," I finished. Earlier, I'd been wishing for a compass. Now it looked like Devona had found us a psychic equivalent.

"There's a problem, though."

"Only one?"

"You'll still be affected by the spell."

"Why is that a problem? You can guide me."

"And if Amon attacks and we become separated?"

172

"You can use your powers to locate me."

"I don't know if I can maintain my fix on the Sprawl and locate you at the same time. And even if I could, Amon might take the opportunity to finish one or both of us off while I'm looking for you." She shook her head. "No, it would be better if we both were able to home in on the Sprawl."

"That would be nice, but I'm afraid a set of psychic powers wasn't included in my zombie membership kit."

"You don't need powers of your own; we can link minds. That way you'll be able to sense what I sense."

"Link minds?" I tried to imagine what it would be like to have my mind joined with someone else's, but I couldn't. The closest I could come to was some sort of psychic equivalent to two-way radio, and somehow I doubted it would be like that.

She must have sensed my reluctance because she hurried to add, "I really believe it's the only way."

It wasn't like we had a lot of options to choose from. "Have you ever linked with anyone before?"

She looked down at the ground, and when she answered, she sounded embarrassed. "I've had a few Shadows of my own over the years. And I've linked with some of them."

She said "Shadows" but the word I heard was "lovers." I don't know why it bothered me—we were both adults, and Devona was older than I, in her seventies chronologically. And for that matter, I was a zombie, for chrissakes. I had no business being jealous. But I was.

"Are you sure it'll work on me? However my brain functions, I'm sure it's not the same as a living man's."

"I don't know if it will work, Matthew. We'll just have to try."

I didn't like the idea of anyone invading my mind, no matter who it was. But it didn't look like I had a choice.

"Okay. But we'd better hurry before Amon attacks again."

Without another word, Devona reached out with both hands and placed her fingers lightly on the sides of my head. I wondered what her touch felt like.

Nothing happened at first, and I was afraid that my zombie mind wasn't capable of linking with a living one, when all of a sudden a warm, bright light flashed behind my eyes. And then I felt Devona inside me.

There are moments in every person's life when they feel close to someone else. It could be something as simple as a shared look, a moment when you exchange glances and know that each of you understands the other perfectly. Or it could be a joke that you share, one that always makes the two of you break up even though no one else around you ever seems to get it. Holding hands while walking at sunset; running your fingers slowly, gently along each other's skin after making love; hugging each other tight, bawling like babies as your hearts are breaking.

Being linked with Devona was all of these things and more.

It had been so long since I had felt this close to another person—no, I had never felt this close to another person: not any of my friends, not my ex-wife, not even my partner Dale. And I didn't know whether to feel joy at this sharing of souls with Devona, or sadness because I had never allowed myself to experience it before.

And then I looked to the far side of the glen, and although it didn't appear any different than before, somehow I could tell that it wasn't very far away at all. Only a few minutes' run at most.

Race you, Devona said in my mind.

Not with the hunk Amon took out of my leg, I responded. *How about a fast walk?*

You're on, she thought playfully, and we set off. Together.

I expected Amon to attack just as we reached the other side, but he didn't. We stepped out of the glen, through the trees, and then the night sky and stars vanished, to be replaced once more by Umbriel and the featureless gray-black sky it hung in.

And there, not more than fifty feet away, lay the Bridge of Forgotten Pleasures, the crossing point from the Wyldwood to the Sprawl. We'd done it.

Without thinking about it, Devona and I hugged each other. Linked as we were, the gesture was automatic and completely natural, a physicalization, however imperfect, of the closeness that we shared.

And then the link dissolved and one became two again.

Devona stepped back. "I'm sorry. I was so excited to see the bridge, I lost concentration."

"That's okay. The link had served its purpose anyway." I had never felt more alone in my existence. I felt like half of my soul had been ripped away. And yet, an echo of Devona remained inside me, the merest trace, like a memory of shared laughter, or a kiss that lingers on the lips long after your lover has departed.

I reached out and took Devona's hand. "Let's get out of here before Amon comes after us." I led her toward the bridge.

"But he said we'd be free if we made it across the glen."

A guttural voice sounded behind us. "I lied."

I whirled around to see a massive yellow-eyed grizzly bear standing on all fours at the edge of the glen. Amon roared and charged. I raised my gun to fire, but before I could pull the trigger, the bear was upon us.

175

—TWENTY-ONE—

With a powerful blow of his huge paw, Amon knocked the revolver out of my hand. It flew through the air, struck the ground, and discharged. It would have been nice if the bullet had happened to strike Amon, but it went flying off into the trees, wasted.

One bullet left.

Devona leaped onto the bear's back and grabbed double handfuls of its coarse brown fur. She then bared her fangs and sank them into the beast's back, using them like knives, slashing and tearing at Amon's ursine flesh.

Amon bellowed in pain and reared up on his hind legs. He tried to shake Devona off, but she clung to his back as if she were the world's largest and most determined tick. Amon then tottered toward the bridge in the stumpy-legged gait bears have when walking erect.

I ran—well, given the state of my chewed up right leg, I half ran, half hobbled—toward my gun. I retrieved it, and galumphed toward the Bridge of Forgotten Pleasures.

Amon had crossed onto the bridge, and technically Devona and he were no longer in his domain. But he didn't show any sign of stopping his attack, and I didn't expect him to.

Devona continued ripping away at Amon's flesh. Her face was covered with blood, and she looked as savage and wild as the bear she battled. It was hard to reconcile this Devona with the one I'd so recently been linked to. But I didn't have time to worry about such things. Amon had backed up against the rail and his form began to shimmer and change.

So far he had only come at us in one shape at a time, and although that had never been spelled out as part of the deal, I'd assumed it was. Looked like I was wrong.

His interim form resembled a blurry amoeba, and Devona was having a tough time holding on. In a flash, I understood what he was going to do: he intended Devona to lose her grip on his fluid transitional form and fall into Phlegethon. If the river's mystic green flame didn't kill her, the Lesk which swam within it surely would.

"Devona, jump!" I shouted as I raised my gun and fired.

The last silver bullet struck Amon in the chest—or rather where his chest would have been if he'd been solid—just as Devona launched herself up and over the Lord of the Wyldwood. Devona landed easily on the bridge as the amoebic Darklord pitched backward over the rail and soundlessly (for he had no mouth at the moment) plummeted down toward Phlegethon's fiery green embrace.

I tucked my empty gun against the small of my back and hurried over to Devona. She was covered with blood, and it was impossible to tell if any of it were hers.

"Are you okay?"

She wiped a smear of blood from her mouth and nodded. "Do you think it's over?"

"It's possible Amon is more vulnerable in his transitional state and the last silver bullet did him in."

"Do you believe that?"

"I believe Darklords are very hard to kill. Let's get out of here before—"

A gigantic reptilian head rose up before us, fiery green water trickling down its black-scaled hide.

"Too late, zombie." The voice of Amon's English hunter

guise, the one that annoyed me so much, boomed out of the Lesk's serpentine mouth. I'd never seen a Lesk close up before, had seen little more than the black lines of their backs as they plied the waters of Phlegethon. The creature was far larger than I had imagined, and looked something like a snake encased in black armor. Its brow was spiked, and it had a row of bony serrated triangles running down its back. And of course it possessed feral yellow eyes—eyes full of fury and hunger.

"Let us go, Amon," I shouted. "We played by the rules of your challenge and beat you, fair and square!"

Amon laughed, a harsh, brittle sound, as of a thousand bones breaking.

"The Hunt has only a single rule, little man: victory belongs to the strongest and swiftest." He hissed and his jaws opened wide in preparation to devour us.

"What of Honani, Darklord?" I yelled.

Amon paused and narrowed his basketball-sized eyes.

I reached into my jacket and removed the soul jar. "This container is what I used to draw Honani's spirit from his body. Honani remains inside. All I have to do to release him is pry open the lid." I gripped the lid in my fingers. "If I do, his spirit will be set free to wander Necropolis for eternity. Or maybe he'll end up in the Boneyard as one of Edrigu's servants."

Amon's head swayed slowly back and forth as he regarded me.

"You told us earlier that despite being a mixblood, Honani was still one of your subjects—one of the family, as you put it." I gave the jar a shake. "Well, here he is, Amon. Are you going to abandon him just because his body now belongs to another?"

Amon hissed softly. "How do I know you're telling the truth?"

"How did you know it when you pretended to be Arleigh?" I countered.

Amon considered. "Very well," he said at last. "Place the jar on the bridge and you may go."

"Nothing personal, but I'd rather keep it with us until we reach the other side, if it's all the same to you."

Amon laughed again, and I was surprised to hear no malice in it. "Go on, then!"

We backed toward the Sprawl side of the bridge, keeping our eyes on Amon the entire way. When we reached the far side, Amon touched his serpent's nose to the bridge and flowed into his English hunter body.

I set the jar on the bridge and Amon gave me a little salute. "Well played, Mr. Adrion. Well played, indeed. I think it's safe to say that this has been the most enjoyable Wild Hunt in some time."

"I'm glad you liked it," I said wryly. And Devona and I turned and hurried into the Sprawl before the Lord of the lycanthropes could change his mind.

From now on Amon would have to add a corollary to his rule: sometimes victory doesn't go to the strongest or swiftest; sometimes it goes to a desperate dead man with deep pockets.

Devona and I sat in the small first-floor lounge of the House of Dark Delights. She sipped a blood and vodka, and I had an untouched rum and coke in front of me. I don't know why I bother to buy drinks. Probably helps me remember what it was like to be alive, I guess.

The House of Dark Delights is the most popular bordello in Necropolis, and the Descension celebration is its busiest time of the year; there were so many customers coming and going, the place seemed more like an international (or perhaps

I should say interdimensional) airport. Normally Madam Benedetta, hard-nosed businesswoman that she is, would never have let a couple of non-customers take up valuable table space in her lounge—especially not today. But word had gotten around about what I had done for Lyra, who up until she'd encountered Honani had been one of Benedetta's girls, and who I'd discovered had recently rejoined the fold in a quite different capacity. Because of this, Benedetta had been only too glad to let Devona and me have a table for as long as we wanted, no questions asked.

Devona glanced at the clock above the bar. Necropolis follows the standard twenty-four-hour day of Earth, not that it means very much when you live beneath Umbriel's perpetual dusk and you don't need to sleep.

"We've been here almost an hour," she said. "Perhaps Morfran's already left." The facial lacerations Amon had given her were completely healed by now, thanks to time and several glasses of drinks mixed with blood.

"We'd have seen him." All of the House's customers had to pass through the lounge in order to get to and leave the rooms. Benedetta didn't make nearly as much money on booze and drugs as she did sex, but she wanted to squeeze as many darkgems out of her customers as she could before sending them back into the streets, so she made certain her clientele had two opportunities to sit down and have a couple drinks. And, after hoisting a few, if they decided they'd rested up enough and were ready for another go, why, they could just head right back on through the lounge, and hire themselves some more fun.

I'd heard it said that Madam Benedetta is as wealthy as any Darklord. I wouldn't doubt it.

"Perhaps he left through a rear exit," Devona said.

"There is no rear exit. Benedetta had it bricked over years ago to stop deadbeat customers sneaking out without paying." Rumor had it that several such customers had been present—and bound in chains—when the bricks were laid. "Just try to relax."

"Shrike was probably wrong, and Morfran's not even here."

After beating a hasty retreat from the Wyldwood, we returned to the Broken Cross and Shrike had asked around about Morfran for us. We'd learned that he was demon kin of a particularly rare insectine subspecies who mated only during a three-week period every year. This was the middle of week two for Morfran.

It seemed he'd come into quite a bit of money recently (I didn't have to ask how) and that he'd been spending a good portion of his funds at the House of Dark Delights. From what Shrike had learned, Morfran came here for several hours every day.

"I bribed one of the girls to check for us, remember? He's upstairs all right." With three girls: one lyke, one Bloodborn, and one demon kin. I couldn't begin to imagine the geometric and metamorphic possibilities.

"She probably lied just to get her hands on your gems," Devona snapped.

I looked at her for a moment. "If I didn't know better, I'd swear you were jealous."

Devona laughed a little too loudly. "Right. As if I would be jealous of a cheap little werecat. Doesn't she realize that six breasts is just overkill?"

I smiled. "You're right; you don't sound a bit jealous."

She smiled back. "All right, I admit it, I am."

"I don't think you have to worry about anyone snatching me away. I'm not exactly the best-looking guy in the place at the moment." Cuts on my face, burnt arm, missing ear and pinkie, chewed-up leg, tilted head, and skin getting grayer by the minute—not to mention the state of my suit. I'd never been a male model, but I'd definitely seen better days.

She reached over and took my hand. "It's not the outside I see when I look at you. Especially after what happened in the glen."

All I could feel of Devona's touch was the slight pressure of her fingers against my skin. But it was enough.

"So you felt it too?"

She nodded. "It was the most intense experience of any kind I've ever had."

"I thought you said you'd linked with men before."

"I have, but it was never like that. Those men were Shadows in more ways than one, Matthew. Shallow, hollow men who just wanted me for my body, or because I was Bloodborn and exotic, or because they thought I could make them Bloodborn too. But you—you're special, Matthew. I don't think you realize just how much."

"Devona . . ." I didn't know what to say. We had only known each other for less than a day, but after what had happened in the glen, after joining souls as we'd done, it was like we'd known each other for years. No, forever. But I couldn't let this go on, no matter how much I wanted it to, and believe me, I did.

"What kind of relationship can you have with a zombie? I'm not exactly fully functional, if you know what I mean."

"I don't care about that, Matthew. We don't need physical love, not when we can link."

"Even so, I think it would be best for now if we just tried to concentrate our attention on the job at hand."

Her eyes grew cold and hurt and she tried to pull away, but I held her hand tight.

"I'm not rejecting you, Devona. I want to make that clear. I probably should, to be honest, but I can't. But I do think we shouldn't go forward with this until I know for certain that I'm going to . . . I guess 'live' isn't the right word. Survive, I guess. Unless your father can help me, I'll be gone soon."

"Then we can have that time together, Matthew."

I shook my head. "I won't do that to you, Devona. I can't. We know how we feel about each other—know it in a way that two people who haven't been linked never could. Right now that has to be enough. If I'm lucky, in a couple days, I'll still be here, and then we can continue this conversation where it left off. I promise."

A crimson tear pooled at the corner of her right eye. "And if you aren't lucky?"

I grinned. "Would you smack me if I said we'll always have the glen?"

She laughed, for real this time.

And that was all, because just then Morfran walked into the lounge.

— TWENTY-TWO —

Morfran came swaggering into the lounge like he was cock of the walk. Or in his case, gigantic walking stick of the walk. He was a twig-thin insectine demon, with a carapace resembling fluorescent-red Formica. He had a triangular face something like a praying mantis, with huge eyes like those of a too-precious moppet in a black-velvet painting.

As he scuttled past our table, I said, "Morfran!"

The demon stopped and swiveled his head back to look at me. His expression—assuming his bug face was even capable of making one—was unreadable.

"It's me, Matt. You remember, I was one of your customers, back when I was alive."

A few seconds ticked by, then he said, "Oh, yes" in a voice which sounded like a bunch of bees trapped in an empty coffee can.

His voice was almost as difficult to read as his face, but I thought he sounded a trifle unsure, as if he knew he didn't remember me, but thought maybe he should. Exactly the response I wanted.

"Why don't you sit down and have a drink with us, for old times' sake?"

His head cocked quickly to one side, then to the other, then back once more, as if he were an insect version of a metronome.

"I don't know. There is much I should be doing."

"I've heard you're quite the ladies' man," Devona virtually purred. "Three at one time, they say."

Given his physiognomy, it was impossible for Morfran to puff himself up with pride, but that's what it looked like.

"Nothing personal, Morfran," I said, good-naturedly but with plenty of skepticism, "but three at a time? C'mon!"

"Yes, three at a time." He sounded aggrieved. "Not only that, but once a day for nearly two weeks now."

"Really!" Devona said, leaning toward him and flashing more than a hint of cleavage. "Quite impressive!"

Even without the necessary equipment for facial expression, Morfran still gave the impression of leering at Devona's chest.

"I don't know . . ." I said doubtfully.

Morfran skittered up to our table and, since his body structure wouldn't allow him to take a seat, at least not comfortably, he stood. "Are you doubting my word, Mark?"

"Matt," I corrected. I signaled one of the lounge's waitresses—by coincidence the werecat I'd bribed earlier—and pointed to Morfran. She nodded and padded over to the bar, her tail swishing slowly back and forth, to get him a drink. I noticed Devona glaring at me, and I quickly returned my gaze to Morfran. "I'm not doubting you; I'm just saying that guys exaggerate sometimes, that's all."

"I am not exaggerating. It is the nature of my subspecies to be sexually prolific during this time of the year. It is our mating season."

I tried to imagine just how something so . . . alien could manage to have sexual congress with one humanoid female, let alone three. But try as I might, I just couldn't do it.

The cute little werecat brought over Morfran's drink, set it in front of the demon, and gave me a wink before departing with more tail swishing. I really wished she hadn't winked. I had a feeling I'd be hearing about that later on.

"You mean the rest of the year you don't . . . Well, that

explains it, then." I lifted my glass, and Devona did likewise. "Here's to you, Morfran; you're a bonafide sex machine."

"Only for three weeks out of the year," he said, but he seemed pleased nonetheless. He leaned his head over his drink and a needle-thin organ extended out of his small mouth and dipped into the booze. He drank greedily, with great slurping sips. Within moments, his glass was empty.

"Whoa! You must really have worked up a thirst back there!"

Morfran's body shivered. His equivalent of a laugh, I think. "One does tend to expend a great deal of fluid during mating."

I was glad my stomach was dead; if it wasn't, it would've turned right then.

Morfran's eyes narrowed. "I must admit that I don't remember you as clearly as I would like, Mark. You said you were a customer of mine when you were alive? I certainly hope my wares were not the cause of your demise." More shivering.

"Actually, I have a confession to make: we've never met before."

Head cocking again, very fast now, right-left, right-left.

"We've come here to ask you a few questions. About veinburn. And about a vampire named Varma."

Sometimes the direct approach works; sometimes it doesn't. This was one of the latter times. Morfran's carapace turned completely brown—the same color as the table and floor, I noticed—he whirled about, and his twig legs became a blur as he fled for the exit.

"I told you he'd run," Devona said.

"You were right." Neither of us bothered to get up and give pursuit. There was no need.

A few moments later, Morfran was carried back to our

table, squirming, legs flailing madly, carapace rapidly changing colors from red to yellow to brown.

"He almost got past me," the large lyke who had captured him said. "I guess I still haven't gotten the hang of this body yet."

"You did great for your first day on the job, Lyra. Now if you could just hold him still for a moment while I explain a few things to him?"

Madam Benedetta's newest—and strongest—bouncer smiled sweetly, the effect somewhat spoiled by Honani's jagged mixblood teeth. I'd told her about what had happened at the edge of the Wyldwood with the soul that had previously occupied her current body, but she hadn't seemed too concerned about it. Still, I made a mental note to talk with Madam Benedetta before I decomposed. With her wealth and devotion to her staff, I hoped she could arrange for some way to protect Lyra from Lord Amon, should it come to that.

Lyra squeezed Morfran and the demon's carapace creaked alarmingly.

"Careful, Lyra. We don't want to reduce him to kindling now."

"Oops. Sorry." She eased up a little. The demon struggled a bit more, until it became obvious he wasn't going anywhere, and then he finally gave up and just hung motionless in Lyra's massive arms.

"Okay, here's the situation, Morfran. Before the waitress brought your drink over, I spiked it with one of the potions Madam Benedetta keeps on hand. A place like this often has need of certain magical potions. Some work to induce a state of sexual readiness in someone whose spirit may be willing but whose flesh needs a little more help to get going. Other potions work just the opposite: they suppress sexual functioning. Benedetta uses these for clients who refuse to pay their tabs or for those who mistreat the staff." I wished Honani hadn't been too proud to accept the aid of one of Benedetta's potions when he'd visited Lyra. If he had taken one, she'd probably still be alive and in her own body.

"To put it simply, Morfran, you can't get it up anymore—or whatever it is males of your species do. And you won't be able to until you receive the antidote. If you cooperate and answer a few questions, I'll make sure you get it. If not, you'll miss out on the final week of your mating season." I'd learned from Shrike that Morfran's subspecies of demon was mindlessly driven to copulate during its mating season. And Benedetta's potion was a cruel one: it removed sexual functioning, but actually increased desire, making it all the more effective when it came to convincing delinquent customers to make good on outstanding debts.

Morfran's carapace edged toward black now. "It doesn't matter. I have quite a bit of money; I can easily afford to purchase an antidote from a witch."

"You could try. But Benedetta pays the witch who makes her potions a great deal to ensure they aren't easily neutralized. It's true you might find someone who'll hit on the right formula to remove the spell eventually, but it could take some time. Easily a week."

"Oh, much more than that, I think," Devona said. "He might even still be looking come this time next year."

Morfran's shell had gone completely black now. I wondered if it was a sign of anger, or maybe fear. Whichever, it was clear we were getting to him.

"You don't understand," he said quietly, with an edge of desperation. "The people I work for would be most displeased if I told you anything."

"By 'people' you mean the Dominari, right? I sympathize

with you, Morfran old bug, but all I can tell you is to ask yourself which is worse: talking to us and maybe having the Dominari find out, or going the rest of this year's mating season desperately needing to have sex, but without any lead in your pencil."

Morfran regarded me for a moment, his head cocking back and forth slowly this time. Finally, he let out an edgy buzz of a sigh that already sounded tinged with the beginnings of sexual tension and frustration. "Very well. What do you wish to know?"

We asked the demon some questions, and he answered them clearly, quickly, and concisely. I was fairly certain that he had nothing directly to do with Varma's death—it was clear the Red Tide vampires had been responsible for that—and so I had the werecat waitress bring over the antidote. Morfran practically inhaled the potion, and then scuttled off toward the more carnal section of Madam Benedetta's establishment, no doubt intending to make sure the antidote worked as advertised.

And so Devona and I said goodbye to Lyra, who I wished well in her new profession, and Devona alone (as she insisted) thanked the werecat waitress, and we left the House of Dark Delights to follow up on what we had learned from Morfran. I wasn't looking forward to this—not in the slightest.

We headed for Skully's.

—TWENTY-THREE—

The place was still busy as hell, and there were a few new suspicious-looking stains on the floor since the last time I'd been here. But the atmosphere seemed calm enough now. I doubted it was going to stay that way, though.

Devona and I sat at the bar on two stools suddenly vacated by a pair of lykes who wrinkled their noses in disgust as they left.

"What did you expect, roses?" I muttered as they walked off.

Skully was busy at the other end of the bar filling a human's mug with what looked like honest-to-Christ plain old beer. When he was finished, I caught his eye—or rather eye socket—and he trundled on down to us.

"Hey, Matt! I'm surprised to see you back so soon. Business?" He nodded to Devona, and from the tone in his voice would have smiled if he'd possessed the lips and facial muscles to do so. "Or pleasure? Wait, let me guess. Has to be business, as bad as you look. You shouldn't be in here: you should be over at Papa Chatha's getting fixed up."

"This lady's father lost something, Skully. Something important, and I'm helping her look for it."

"Oh?"

"Her father's name is Galm, and the object is called the Dawnstone. Sound familiar?"

He shook his fleshless head. "No, should it?"

"Yes, because according to my source"—who was at that very moment probably, as he put it, "expending a great deal of fluid"—"you're responsible for its disappearance from the Cathedral. Or at least your bosses the Dominari are."

Then something happened which I'd never seen before. Tiny pinpricks of crimson light began to blaze deep in the cold darkness of Skully's eye sockets. "I think maybe you'd better leave, Matt, and take your new friend with you."

He started to turn away, but I grabbed his pudgy, hairy wrist and stopped him. "I know there's a Dominari-run lab upstairs, Skully. A lab that's been awfully busy lately cranking out veinburn."

Skully yanked his arm away. "Your mind has finally rotted through, Matt, you know that? All that's upstairs is my room and some extra storage space."

Skully and I looked over the bar at each other for a moment. I knew his silver broadaxe wasn't far from his reach.

"If that's true, then you won't have objections to my taking a look, now will you?" And before Skully could respond, I jumped off my stool and ran-limped as fast as I could toward the narrow flight of stairs to the right of the bar.

Head aside, Skully has a fully fleshed body. A little too fully fleshed, and I thought given my current state, we'd be evenly matched when it came to speed. But even with his modest bulk, Skully was able to grab his axe from behind the counter and leap over the bar and come after me before I made it halfway to the stairs.

He shouted my name, and I turned in time to see him raise his axe over his head, the silver glinting even in the bar's dim light. "Don't make me hurt you, Matt. Please."

"If you don't want to hurt me, I have a suggestion: put the axe down."

"I can't do that, Matt."

I became aware of the whole bar watching us act out our

little drama. It was like a replay of earlier in the day, only instead a murdering lyke, I was now facing a friend. A friend who was about to bring a very large, very sharp axe down on me, but a friend nonetheless.

"I can't let this one go," I said. "It's too important."

"And I can't let you reach those stairs."

Stalemate. I had little in the way of surprises left in my pockets, and nothing that would take care of Skully. Hell, I wasn't even exactly sure what he was, and I didn't have the first clue as to what sort of weaknesses he might possess.

"So what do we do now, Matt?"

"I figure you can just stand there, and I'll watch as Devona cracks you over your bony noggin with a barstool."

"C'mon, I'm not gonna fall for—" The stool seat connected with his skull with a sharp CRACK! and Skully dropped his axe, which embedded itself solidly into the floor with a loud thunk like a poor man's Excalibur returning to the stone. A second later, Skully crashed down beside it.

I quickly examined him. He had a tiny jagged fissure in his skull, and the lights in his socket had been extinguished.

Devona set the stool down. "Is he unconscious?"

"Who can tell? But he's not moving right now and that's good enough. Let's go." I continued toward the stairs, this time with Devona at my side.

Skully's patrons didn't know what to do at first. They merely sat and stared. Then one particular Einstein among them shouted, "Hey, free drinks!" and a stampede for the bar commenced. I hoped Skully wouldn't get stepped on too badly, even if he had been prepared to turn me into filet-o-zombie.

We hurried up the stairs as fast as my bum leg would allow us, and exited onto the second floor. The short hall had only three wooden doors, all closed. I turned to

Devona and touched the side of my nose. She nodded and inhaled.

"That one." She pointed to door number two.

"That one it is, then." I took out my gun, which was now loaded with purely ordinary bullets, stepped to the door, and tried the knob. Locked.

"As a macho type, I'd ordinarily kick the door in myself," I said, "but seeing as how you're quite a bit stronger than I am . . ."

She smiled and came forward. She leaned back and executed a swift, powerful kick to the middle of the door, which exploded off its hinges and flew into the room.

She stood back and I rushed past her, fighting the urge to shout, "Police!" Instead I said, "Nobody move!" Hardly as satisfying, but it was the best I could do under the circumstances. At least it still fulfilled my quota of tough-guy talk for the day.

There was no one in the room; I kept my gun out, though, just in case. Inside sat a table filled with chemical apparatus: copper tubing, black rubber hoses, beakers, vials, the whole Jekyll and Hyde bit. Next to that lay a stone altar upon which rested various flowers and herbs, along with the gutted body of a dead lamb and the rune-engraved obsidian knife which had done it in. Science and magic, working together to create a better world, or at least a more profitable one—for the Dominari, that is.

"So Morfran was telling the truth," I said. Even with the motivation we'd provided him with, I still hadn't quite believed what he'd told us. You can never trust drug-pushing scum, regardless of species or home dimension.

And then I took a closer look. While there was chemical residue dribbled here and there on the table, the beakers and vials were empty. The blood that had pooled around the lamb was hard and brown, and flies crawled eagerly over the less than fresh but still appetizing kill, which had begun to decay in earnest. And most telling of all . . .

"No veinburn," I said.

"But I smelled it!" Devona insisted.

"The stink's probably gotten into the walls and floor, and it looks like they didn't bother washing up their equipment before they cleared out."

"The least the jerks could've done was gotten rid of the lamb."

Skully stood in the doorway, axe held at his side. I searched for pinpricks of anger in his sockets and found none.

"They left early this afternoon, and took what veinburn they had left with them," he continued.

"This was what you were protecting so fiercely?" I said. "A deserted drug lab?"

Skully shrugged. "I had my orders. And given who my bosses are, it's a good idea to follow orders, even when they don't make a hell of a lot of sense."

I didn't have to ask Skully who his bosses were; I knew he meant the Dominari. "Who worked here? Arcane?"

He nodded. "One of them was. The other was a chemist who'd emigrated from Earth, both freelancers the bosses brought in."

"Was Talaith in on this operation?" I asked.

"Not to my knowledge. The bosses don't like messing around with Darklords. Far as I know, the warlock who worked here did so only for the money."

Did that mean Gregor—as impossible as it sounded— had been wrong about Talaith's involvement? Or was Skully not telling me the truth?

"What do you know about the theft of the Dawnstone,

Skully? And what do the Dominari plan to do with it?"

"The bosses had nothing to do with stealing the Dawnstone. They were working with someone else, someone whose identity I don't know. I wasn't particularly chummy with the warlock or the chemist, but we talked a few times. From what I gathered, this other party approached the bosses with the formula for veinburn, but needed some capital, and the technical know-how to produce it. For providing both, and giving a relatively small quantity of the finished product to their silent partner, they got to keep the formula."

"So the Dominari are probably setting up other veinburn labs around the city even as we speak. Great. Tell me, Skully, didn't it bother you what they were doing up here?"

"Sure it did. Just because a man has to take orders doesn't mean he's got to like it."

It was impossible to gauge his emotional state from his face (or lack thereof), but he sounded sincere. "And you have no idea who your bosses' mystery partner might be?"

"No, and I don't think the warlock or the chemist knew, either."

"How does Morfran fit into this?"

"He's one of the bosses' regular dealers, a small timer who usually sells mind dust. The bosses wanted him to try veinburn out on the market, see how people took to it."

"Which they undoubtedly did, given how addictive it is." I thought for a moment. "You said Morfran's a small timer. Why would the Dominari choose him for such an important project?"

"I wondered about that myself, but like I said, it's best not to ask questions."

"Perhaps because the Dominari's new partner asked them to," Devona suggested. "Because one of his regular customers was Varma."

"Who, fun-loving guy that he was, was probably first in line to try Morfran's newest product," I said. "Which got him hooked—"

"—And after that, he'd do anything for more," Devona added. "Including risk Father's wrath by stealing the Dawnstone."

"This unknown 'partner' probably made the arrangements with Varma himself or herself. The theft of an object of power from a Darklord is far too sensitive an operation to involve a sleazy little bug like Morfran. And then, once we started nosing around, Mr. or Ms. Unknown decides to have Varma killed, in case we get him to talk."

"And if he wouldn't have told us what happened to the Dawnstone, I would've had no choice but to tell Father everything myself. He most definitely would've gotten Varma to talk."

I didn't want to think about what sort of persuasive techniques Lord Galm might have used on his bloodson.

Devona frowned. "What I don't understand is why wait to kill Varma? Wouldn't it have made more sense to kill him as soon as he delivered the Dawnstone?"

"Murdering Varma then would've drawn too much attention too early. Mr. Unknown wasn't worried about Varma spontaneously confessing. Varma would've been too afraid of Galm—and the punishment he would deliver—to admit his crime. It wasn't until we got too close that Varma became a liability and needed to be dealt with."

Devona's already pale skin grew paler. "Then . . . we're responsible for his death. No, I am, because I was afraid to go to Father, afraid of his anger, his disappointment. If I had spoken to Father instead of hiring you . . . Varma might still be alive." She looked like she might cry.

I took her hand. "The only ones responsible for killing

Varma are the Red Tide vampires, and whoever was pulling their strings. Or in their case, wires. Okay?"

She didn't look completely convinced, but she nodded anyway. I figured it was the best I was going to get just then. I turned to Skully, who had been standing silently by while Devona and I tried to piece this mess together. "Do the Dominari have any connection with the Red Tide?"

"No, they're too unstable."

"So they worked directly for Mr. Unknown. I thought as much." There was something important about that particular tidbit of information, but I couldn't quite put my slowly decomposing finger on it. Not yet.

"So where does that leave us?" Devona asked.

"Not much farther along than we were before," I admitted. "It appears Talaith doesn't have the Dawnstone and neither do the Dominari. It looks like Skully's bosses are the only ones who know who does have it, but I doubt they'd be amenable to sharing that information. Assuming we could even locate them." I sighed. "I think it's safe to say that our investigation has run into a very large dead end."

"Uh, Matt?" Skully said. "There's something else."

"What? You know something you haven't told us?" I said hopefully.

"Not exactly. Remember when I told you it was a good idea to follow the bosses' orders? Well, they gave me some instructions about what I should do if the two of you came around asking questions."

He lifted his axe. I immediately trained my gun on the middle of his chest.

"You don't want to do this," I said. His lack of face aside, Skully appeared to be human. A regular non-silver bullet might stop him, or at least slow him down.

"I have my orders." He took a step forward.

I tightened my gray-skinned finger on the trigger but didn't fire. "If you were supposed to kill us, it would have been much easier to lead us up here in the first place. You'd have privacy for the deed and surprise on your side. But you didn't do that; you tried to send us away, and then you tried to physically stop us from coming up here."

Skully's grip on his axe tightened and loosened, tightened and loosened. "So?"

"So I think you were disobeying orders, not following them, when you asked us to leave. And I think it's because you didn't want to have to kill a friend."

Skully gave forth a hollow laugh. "The Dominari and their servants have no friends."

"Then prove me wrong." I lowered my gun. "Go ahead, make like Lizzie Borden. I won't stop you."

I heard Devona draw in a nervous gasp of air, but otherwise she did nothing.

Skully stood silently for several moments before finally lowering his axe. "You're the closest thing to a friend I have, Matt. You're right; I don't want to kill you." He nodded to Devona. "Or her." His shoulders slumped. "But when the bosses find out I couldn't go through with it . . ."

"Don't worry about that," I said. "We can make it seem like you tried to kill us. We'll bust up the lab so it looks like we fought, and then we can clonk you on the head again, this time with your own axe. We'll take off and you can just lie here unconscious until someone comes looking for you— or your customers downstairs steal all your booze, whichever comes first."

"You'd do that for me?" Skully asked.

I smiled. "Hey, what are friends for?"

Just then a solemn, sonorous tone sounded off in the distance. Several seconds later another sounded, and then another. They kept coming every ten seconds, soft and low, reminding me a bit of the lonely, mournful sound a foghorn makes.

"What's that noise?" I asked.

"Father Dis!" Devona swore. "It's the Deathknell summoning the Darklords to the Nightspire—the Renewal Ceremony will start soon!"

It was my turn to swear. We were too late. I was certain whoever had the Dawnstone planned to use it during the ceremony to kill Lord Galm, or maybe even Dis himself, if such a thing were possible. And there was nothing we could do about it. Unless . . .

I grabbed Devona's hand and pulled her toward the door. "I'm afraid you'll have to hit yourself over the head, Skully. Devona and I have to go." I shoved past him, dragging Devona with me, and led her down the stairs, taking them as fast as my bum leg would allow.

"Where are you going?" Skully called after us.

I shouted over my shoulder. "To crash a party!"

—TWENTY-FOUR—

From the outside, Lady Varvara's stronghold is a glass and steel building ten stories tall, which wouldn't be out of place in the business district of any midsize city on Earth. Inside, Demons' Roost is a paean to pleasure, a twenty-four-hour-a-day bacchanalia that makes Las Vegas and Times Square look like kindergarten playgrounds. It's an adults-only amusement park which contains such a dazzling scope and variety of decadence and perversity that it might have given Caligula himself pause.

Beside the mass of partiers, getting inside wasn't a problem. Varvara didn't believe in locking doors or posting guards. Anyone could come in and play, from the lowliest street beggar to any of her fellow Darklords. We squeezed through a mass of beings drinking, drugging, gambling, screwing, eating, talking, laughing, yelling, fighting—often, it seemed, all at the same time.

Devona looked stunned.

"Varvara has a one-word philosophy," I shouted to be heard over the nearest of the three live bands playing in various corners of the room. "More."

"She certainly appears to live by it," Devona said.

The main reception hall of Demons' Roost looks as if it had been ground zero during the explosion of an atomic kitsch bomb. Gaudy pastel-colored carpeting, black velvet paintings in neon-tube frames, mirrored disco balls spinning above . . . We passed a wall collage formed from hundreds of tiny cheap toys from fast-food kids' meals, and soon after that, my favorite piece, a fifteen-foot-tall pewter statue of Elvis gazing benevolently down on a flock of plastic pink flamingos.

"Oh, my," was all Devona could manage to say.

"Quite a change from the Cathedral, isn't it?"

Even with all the tumult in here, the tolling of the Deathknell could be heard. None of Varvara's guests seemed to notice it, or more likely they just didn't care. After all, the Renewal Ceremony had been taking place every year for over three centuries. It was nothing special to them. They were far more concerned with obtaining their next drink and/or lover. But then, none of them knew about the Dawnstone and the use to which it would soon be put—unless Devona and I could stop it.

We pushed, shoved, elbowed, and in a few cases kneed our way through the crowd until we came to the elevators. There were five, all the same, except the last on the left. It had a red button, while the others had white.

I pressed the red button, and it lit. "This is Varvara's private elevator," I said. "It'll take us straight to the penthouse, which is probably where she's at right now, getting ready for the ceremony."

"I'm surprised just anyone can walk up and use her private elevator," Devona said.

"Just anyone can't, but I can."

"How do you rate? No, let me guess: you did her a favor once."

"Not quite." I didn't want to go on, but Devona was looking at me expectantly. "She finds me . . . amusing."

Devona smiled. "Really? How so?"

The dinging chime of the elevator arriving saved me from having to answer. The door opened, and we got on. There was only one button to press, and I hit it. The door slid shut, and we rode upward to the lilting strains of a Muzak version of Blue Oyster Cult's "Don't Fear the Reaper." Varvara's odd sense of humor seemed appropriate given what had brought us here.

"Do you think she'll listen to us?" Devona asked.

"There's no telling with Varvara. She might hear us out, or she might have us executed for bothering her before the Renewal Ceremony."

Devona looked suddenly alarmed.

"Relax; I was joking about the last part." At least, I hoped I was joking. It all depended on what sort of mood Varvara was in.

The elevator glided to a stop and the door opened to reveal a boudoir of silks, satins, and a thousand overstuffed pillows scattered everywhere. Every possible shade of red and pink was represented, and I later learned from Devona that the air was thick with the scents of a dozen different cloying perfumes mingled with a truckload of potpourri. The whole place was like a Barbara Cartland wet dream.

Half of the large room was taken up by a monstrous canopy bed upon which lay the still, naked body of an obscenely muscled man. At first I thought he was dead, but he stirred slightly, and I realized he was only nearly dead.

I stepped off the elevator, and Devona followed. On the far side of the room, a stunningly beautiful redhead with a body that made most centerfolds look like concentration camp survivors stood before a mirrored wall, checking the fit of her outfit—a skin-tight dress made entirely of jade emeralds.

"That doesn't look very comfortable," I said.

Varvara didn't take her eyes off her reflection. "Comfort is not the point." She turned around and examined her rear.

"Then what is?"

"Maximum amount of soul-gnawing envy from all women in the vicinity and maximum number of painfully unendurable erections from all men." She nodded. "I believe this will do nicely."

Varvara turned away from the mirror. "Hello, Matthew." She quickly looked me up and down. "You are aware, I trust, of your achingly desperate need of a makeover? So, what brings you into my bedroom this fine Descension evening? And with such a cute little friend! Don't tell me you want to get a foursome going? I'm afraid I don't have the time, and Magnus—" she nodded toward the insensate slab of beefcake sprawled on her bed—"does not have the energy, and most likely won't for some days to come."

Now that Varvara faced us, her single non-human feature (unless you count her exaggeratedly feminine body as non-human) was evident: her slightly overlarge reptilian eyes. They reminded me of a cobra's: cold, calculating, and always in the process of trying to decide whether or not to strike. She flashed us a dazzling smile that almost, but not quite, wiped away the eerie sensation of those snake eyes constantly sizing you up.

"Sorry to disappoint you Varvara, but I'm not exactly up for those sort of games, if you know what I mean."

She walked over to us, every step runway-model perfect, even with the incredibly steep high heels she was wearing. She leaned forward, nearly spilling out of her emeralds in the process, and whispered in my ear, "You could always watch."

And then she stepped back and laughed.

"Matt told me you find him amusing," Devona said icily. "Is it because he puts up with you cruelly taunting him like that?"

I shot Devona a warning glance. Maybe it was jealousy,

or concern for my feelings, or both, that had prompted her to speak out, but talking like that to Varvara is not exactly conducive to your health.

The demon queen regarded Devona impassively with her reptilian gaze for some time, but Devona stood her ground and stared into Varvara's eyes with equal intensity. And even though I didn't need to breathe, I held my breath anyway.

And then Varvara smiled. "I like you," she said simply. Underneath her words was an unspoken message: I think I'll let you live.

I released my breath.

"I'd really love to stay and chat, but I must dash. Have to help Dis and the other Darklords keep Necropolis going for another year." She sighed theatrically. "A girl's work is never done."

She started toward the elevator.

"I have a favor to ask of you first, Varvara."

She stopped and turned around. "A favor?" She smiled slowly. "Why of course, Matt. We demons love to do favors—for a price."

I held up my hand and displayed Lord Edrigu's mark. "I'm afraid I don't have much in the way of trade right now."

She frowned upon seeing the mark, and her manner became serious. "What in the Nine Hells have you been up to?"

And so I told her.

When I had finished, Varvara said, "I wasn't even aware Galm had the Dawnstone, and now he's lost it. Intriguing."

"You know about the Dawnstone?" Devona asked.

Varvara waved the question aside. "Honey, when you've

lived as long as I have, there isn't a whole lot you don't know." She turned toward the mirror and looked thoughtfully at her reflection. "I wonder if there's a way I can use this to my advantage."

"This isn't the time for scheming," I said sternly.

Varvara turned away from the mirror and her reverie. "While the Dawnstone is a potent token of power, I'm not sure it really poses much of a threat. Still, I suppose it wouldn't hurt to telepathically check with my fellow Lords, especially since the Renewal Ceremony is soon to begin." She nodded to herself as if making a decision. "You two wait here." She turned and headed for a closed door on the other side of the room.

"Where are you going?" I asked.

She stopped. "To a private chamber where I can concentrate more effectively. We Darklords have built up quite strong psychic defenses against each other over the millennia, and it's going to take some effort on my part to get even a simple message past their guard—if I can."

"What about contacting Father Dis?" I suggested.

She gave me a withering look. "Darling, it's simply not done. You don't contact Dis; he contacts you." And with that she walked to the door, opened it, stepped inside, and closed it behind her.

"Private chamber?" Devona said. "That looked like her—"

"Bathroom, yeah. But you have to admit, 'private chamber' sounds a lot classier."

"So what do we do?"

"You heard her: we wait."

Devona went over to the mirror and examined her transparent reflection. "I wish now that I had gone to Father right away. What if we can't stop whoever it is from using the Dawnstone?"

I joined her in front of the mirror, though I didn't particularly appreciate the chewed-up zombie it showed me. "There's no point in worrying about might-have-beens, Devona. All we can do now is our best. In the end, that has to be enough."

She didn't look convinced, so I decided to try to take her mind off her recriminations while Varvara attempted to contact the other Lords. "This is more than just a mirror. It's Varvara's dimensional portal."

Devona took a half step back, as if afraid the mirror might suck her in. "You and your partner came to Necropolis through here?"

"This is Varvara's personal portal. She has a larger one down in the basement, which is what Dale and I used." I smiled. "I don't think we would've lasted very long if we'd popped out into Varvara's bedroom—especially if she'd been busy entertaining company."

Devona stepped back to the mirror. "I've never seen Father's portal. I wonder how it works."

"The one in the basement is pretty simple. All you have to do—" I reached out and tapped the glass three times with my index finger. The mirror shimmered and our reflections were replaced by an image of a park just before sunset—trees, benches, neatly trimmed green grass, birds singing, people walking, holding hands, riding bikes, in-line skating . . . From the trees and the way people were dressed, it looked like late spring. I wasn't sure, though. I'd kind of lost track of Earth's seasons during my time in Necropolis. And then I realized: sunset. Horrified, I tried to push Devona out the way. But she planted her feet solidly on the floor, and with her strength, I couldn't budge her.

"What are you doing?"

"The sunlight!" I said. "You have to get away from the portal before—"

She laughed. "Matt, I'm half human, remember? Sunlight doesn't destroy my kind, it just temporarily nullifies our vampiric abilities."

I wasn't sure, but it looked like her skin was slowly turning pinker, more fully human. I thought it would be a different story if I tried to shove her away from the mirror now.

"So that's the sun," she said in a hushed voice. "It's redder than I imagined, but still quite beautiful." She touched her cheek. "And so warm."

For a moment I thought she was joking, but then I remembered Galm had brought her to Necropolis soon after she'd been born. She really never had seen the sun.

"It's that red because it's setting." And likely also due to pollution in the atmosphere, but I decided to leave that depressing little fact out.

"What are we looking at?" she asked.

"A park. It's a place where people in the city go to get away, feel close to nature, and relax." I smiled. "Kind of like the Wyldwood, only without lycanthropes."

"Everyone looks as if they're enjoying themselves. I wonder what it would be like to be human, fully human, and live in an ordinary house, work at an ordinary job, and go to the park at sunset."

"As I recall, it was pretty damn good." It had been a while since I had seen Earth except in movies that had been imported to Necropolis. But this was a hundred times better—and more heartbreaking—than any movie could ever be. Because I knew that all I would have to do to go there was to step through the glass. I was tempted. If I were going to die for good in the next day or so, at least I could die in the world where I'd been born and lived most of my life.

But I didn't step forward. There was still a chance that I

could save myself. And besides, I don't like to leave a job unfinished.

"Pretty isn't it? Especially for Cleveland." Varvara had come out of the bathroom—excuse me, her private chamber—and was standing behind us. "Still, we don't have time for sightseeing." She snapped her long red-nailed fingers and the park evaporated and the mirror was just a mirror again. Devona looked disappointed.

"Any luck?" I asked.

"No, the fools wouldn't even acknowledge my attempts. Can't say as I blame them, though. I'd have done the same thing; centuries of distrust are hard to overcome. I'll just have to try to talk to them once I get to the Nightspire, I suppose."

"You mean, once we get to the Nightspire," I said. "Devona and I have been through too much not to see this to the end."

"I don't think so, Matt. While you're fun to have around, Father Dis doesn't appreciate tag-alongs."

"The Darklords always bring a retinue with them," Devona said. "My father does, though I've never had the distinction of being part of it."

"So why couldn't we tag along with your tag-alongs?" I asked.

"Our retinues are primarily made up of relatives, high-level city functionaries, and important Earth contacts," Varvara said. "Still . . . I suppose it wouldn't hurt anything."

"And think how much it'll annoy Talaith to see me there," I pointed out.

The demon queen brightened. "There is that. All right, you may accompany me. But we should go now. There isn't much time left before the ceremony starts."

The three of us walked over to Varvara's private elevator.

I nodded to the still comatose Magnus. "What about him?"

"Let him sleep," Varvara said with a wicked grin. "He'll need all the rest he can get for when I return."

The elevator arrived. We got on and began our descent.

Varvara turned to Devona. "Before, you asked—in quite a snippy tone, I might add—what I found so amusing about Matt."

"I was just—" Devona began.

"What I find so amusing about our friend here is that he is a champion of order in one of the most chaotic places in the Omniverse—an undead Don Quixote, tilting at Necropolis' windmills on what may very well be an ultimately futile quest to make this a better place." She smiled. "Besides, he makes me laugh."

"I'm just a guy who does favors for people, Varvara, you know that." I hate it when she talks about me that way. Probably because I'm afraid she's right.

The elevator stopped, the door opened, and we were off to the biggest windmill Necropolis has to offer—the Nightspire.

—TWENTY-FIVE—

Of all the ways I might have imagined traveling to the Nightspire in pursuit of a thief and murderer, riding in the back of a hot pink limousine (with matching interior) wasn't one of them. Behind us was a line of far less striking vehicles, bearing Varvara's retinue, primarily demons, but a few humans—mostly music industry and Hollywood types—who served her as well.

Varvara sipped a frozen daiquiri whipped up from the tiny wet bar by her personal bartender, a creature which resembled a levitating sea urchin, and waved through the open widow at the cheering, and by this point in the festival thoroughly soused, crowds lining the street.

"It's so nice to receive the adulation of the masses, don't you think?" Varvara said. She downed the rest of her daiquiri and told the urchin to mix her another.

Varvara is probably the most popular Darklord, considering she lets her subjects—and anyone who visits the Sprawl, for that matter—pretty much do as they please. I can't say near-anarchy is my idea of effective social policy, but then Varvara's never asked for my opinion.

The driver, who I would've taken for just another pretty muscle-boy if it hadn't been for the ram's horns jutting out of his head, spoke over the intercom.

"I have to slow down, Milady. Several Sentinels are coming up behind us."

Varvara pushed a button on her armrest. "No problem,

love, but when they're past, speed up a tad. We're running a wee bit late."

I turned around, and through the rear window I saw three Sentinels walking in a row down the middle of the street. They weren't running (I'm not sure if Sentinels can run) but they were walking faster than I'd ever seen any of the golems move before.

"Don't tell me," I said. "They're going to arrest us for assault with an exceptionally tacky paint job."

"Remember what I said about you making me laugh?" Varvara asked. "Forget it."

The Sentinels tromped around us and continued down the street, accompanied by boos and hisses from the inebriated crowd. Father Dis' police force wasn't exactly beloved by the denizens of the Sprawl.

"Where are they going in such a hurry?" I wondered aloud.

"They've been recalled to the Nightspire for the Renewal Ceremony," Devona explained.

"How long have you been in Necropolis now, two years?" Varvara asked.

"Just about."

"And you didn't know the Sentinels are part of the ceremony?"

I shrugged. "This is only my second Descension celebration, and I spent the first helping a pregnant witch escape her abusive warlock husband. At one point, he actually switched my personality with that of the fetus, and I—well, suffice it to say the situation took some straightening out, and I missed a good part of the celebration, including the Renewal Ceremony."

"You have to tell about that one some time, Matt," Varvara said. "So many mortals wish to return to the womb, but you're the only one I know who's managed to do it!" And she laughed the rest the way to the Nightspire.

As we approached the slender black needle that was the Nightspire, I noticed something strange.

"Umbriel seems larger than usual."

"That's because it's descending for the Ceremony," Varvara said impatiently. "Really, Matt, are you going to be this tiresome the whole time?"

"More, if I can manage it."

The crowd was thickest as we neared the bridge that led from the Sprawl to the Nightspire. Varvara continued playing the gracious queen parading before her adoring subjects, when a grizzled old man in a yellowed seersucker suit and carrying a sheaf of paper broke out of the crowd and came running toward the limo, and Varvara's open window.

"Oh, no," I moaned. "Not now, Carl."

Carl thrust one of his homemade papers through the window and into Varvara's face.

"Beware the Watchers, Lady!" he shouted wildly, "Beware—" But that's as far as he got before Varvara hit a button and the window slid up. Carl barely retracted his arm in time. He released his "paper," however, and it fell onto Varvara's lap. With a grimace of distaste, she brushed it onto the floor.

"Usually I find Carl's rants diverting, but I'm not in the mood tonight."

"I'm surprised he was able to approach the car at all," I said. "We need to have a talk about security."

"If he had any ill intent toward us, the wardspells on my car would've flash-fried him as soon as he came within three feet." Varvara smiled. "Secure enough for you?"

"It'll do, I suppose."

The ram's-horn hunk drove us onto the bridge. The winds of the Furies didn't rise, but then we were expected. As soon as we reached the dull, gray, grassless earth of the island on the other side, the sonorous tolling of the Deathknell stopped.

I looked at Varvara, but she said, "That merely means that all five Darklords have now reached the Nightspire. I'm usually the last."

"Why am I not surprised?"

The driver pulled up to the Nightspire and parked behind a double row of coaches and wagons—the other Darklords' vehicles, I presumed. The chauffeur came around and opened Varvara's door, and she slid out, taking his proffered hand and allowing him to help her, though she was doubtless the far stronger of the two. Devona and I had to haul our butts out on our own, of course.

The other cars in Varvara's entourage parked behind us, and their occupants disembarked, more than a few of them giving Devona and me dirty looks, obviously wondering who we were and how we rated riding in the front of the procession with their queen—especially when they didn't.

The green flames of Phlegethon which surrounded the small island seemed to flare higher than usual. Because of the coming ceremony? Maybe. The air seemed charged with barely contained energy. I looked up. Directly over the tip of the Nightspire, Umbriel, looking bloated and heavy, continued slowly descending.

Varvara started toward the rectangular entrance of the Nightspire, and gestured for Devona and me to follow. I heard a few mutterings from Varvara's other guests. It appeared we'd usurped yet another honor. My heart would've bled for them—if I'd had any blood.

As we walked, I noticed a driver sitting on one of the

coaches, a shadowy figure in Victorian dress. Silent Jack. He touched his finger to the brim of his hat as we walked by, and I felt a chill run down my back that had nothing to do with whether I had working nerves or not.

As we entered, I thought that if Gregor had wanted Devona to carry one of his children so that he might finally get a look-see inside a Darklord's stronghold, how much more excited he would be to actually learn about the interior of the Nightspire itself. Inside was the same as the outside: featureless black, as if the Nightspire had been shaped from solidified shadow. We walked down a long narrow corridor lit by torches of green fire. Varvara's outrageously high heels clacked hollowly as she walked, echoing up and down the hall. She looked like someone who was trying to appear as if she wasn't hurrying, when in fact she was. I had a feeling we were running more than a "wee bit late," as she'd earlier told our driver.

The corridor let us out into a vast circular chamber which sloped inward the farther up it rose, and I realized that the Nightspire was hollow. But while the inside walls of the Nightspire were of the same unchanging black as the exterior, white marble columns ringed the chamber, and the floor was made of tiled mosaics, all depicting scenes from classical mythology. I'd once heard Dis was the name for the Roman god of the dead. It seemed I'd heard right.

In the middle of the chamber was a large, raised marble dais in the shape of a pentagram. Sentinels surrounded the dais, face out, as if they were guarding it. At a quick estimate, I figured there were maybe thirty Sentinels altogether. I hadn't realized the city had that many. I thought I recognized one, a Sentinel with a faint scar running down its chest, as the one who had taken Varma's body off our hands. I wondered if it had delivered Varma to the Cathedral, and if so, what Galm's reaction had been. I supposed I'd find out soon.

The Sentinels were far from the chamber's only occupants, though. Vampires, lykes, Arcane, and half-visible spirits stood in small groups, talking and sampling hors d'oeuvres and imbibing drinks brought to them by bald, red-robed men and women. That is, the living ate and drank. The dead merely watched them do so. Between two columns on the far side of the chamber, a tuxedo-clad pianist played soft, unobtrusive background music.

"I can't believe it," I said. "After everything I've heard about it, the vaunted Renewal Ceremony turns out to be nothing more than a cocktail party?"

"These are merely the preliminaries to the ceremony," Varvara said quietly. "The ceremony itself will begin shortly."

"Who are the baldies in red?" I asked.

"The Cabal," Varvara said quietly. "Father Dis' personal attendants. And it would be a good idea to avoid calling them 'baldies.' "

"They look like waiters to me," I said.

"They are whatever Dis says they are," Varvara replied. "Don't bother trying to talk to them; they only respond to their master."

"We must find my father and tell him of the threat," Devona said, and without waiting for either of us to reply, set off for a group of nearby vampires nibbling on what appeared to be small animal hearts. Varvara and I hurried after her.

She asked the vampires—who were dressed in overdone Bela Lugosi drag—where Lord Galm was. The vampires (who I took to be out-of-towners from Earth by the way they dressed) pointed to the base of the pentagram dais, where Galm was standing talking to Amon (in his English hunter guise), Talaith, and a thin man with the gaunt face of a mortician. I assumed he was Edrigu. Devona made a beeline, or in her case a batline, toward them.

Varvara caught up to her, and took Devona's arm to slow her down. "I think it would be best if I led the way, dear." From her tone, and the way her eyes flashed, it was clear Varvara wasn't making a request.

Devona looked like she was going to argue, but then thought better of it and nodded. We continued with Varvara in the lead. As we approached the other Lords, the demon queen opened her arms and said, "Darlings! So nice to see you all!"

"And for us to see so much of you," Talaith said cattily as she eyed Varvara's outfit. "Why didn't you just come naked this year?"

"Is that a criticism, or are you voicing a regret?" Varvara shot back.

Talaith reddened but didn't reply. She looked smaller than the avatar which had attacked us in Glamere, older and more tired too. Physically, she appeared to be in her late sixties, with short gray hair, baggy eyes, and sagging skin. She'd looked better before the destruction of the Overmind and the loss of a portion of her strength. One more reason for her to hate me. In diametric opposition to Varvara's skimpy outfit, Talaith wore a simple black and white dress reminiscent of Puritan garb. I wondered if anyone had ever attempted to burn her at the stake. If so, I was sorry they'd failed.

Talaith turned to Devona and me, and her upper lip curled in disgust. "I knew your standards were low, Varvara, but really."

"Watch your tongue, witch," Galm growled. "The

woman is one of my birth daughters." Maybe Devona, as a half human, didn't rate as high in the vampire hierarchy as the fully Bloodborn, but it seemed she was high enough for Galm to object to anyone insulting her.

"I was referring to the zombie," Talaith covered smoothly. She looked to the thin-faced man. "Really, Edrigu, isn't there something you can do about this . . . thing? After all, as one of the undead, he falls under your purview."

The corners of Edrigu's thin lips raised a fraction in what I assumed was meant to be a smile. He appeared to be in his mid-fifties and was bald save for a fine layer of black hair along the sides of his head. He wore a tattered white shroud covered with grave mold, and through the ragged cloth glimpses of not flesh but bone were visible.

"What would you have me do, precisely, Talaith?" His voice was a hollow monotone, a lonely echo in a deserted mausoleum.

"Oh, I don't know. Wave your hand and make him collapse into dust, something along those lines."

Edrigu gave me a look and I felt the mark on my palm itch. He knew he didn't have to do anything to me; I was due to turn to dust soon enough as it was.

"Stop being so tiresome, Talaith," Amon said. "You're still bitter Mr. Adrion and his late partner disrupted one of your little schemes a while back."

"Not much of a scheme, as I recall," Varvara said. "Even if Matt hadn't happened along, I doubt it would've worked."

Talaith glared at them both, but otherwise did nothing. The bantering Darklords reminded me of wary jungle predators facing each other over a water hole. They hated each other and weren't afraid to show it, but this wasn't the time or place to do anything about it. But I could see in Talaith's eyes that she was keeping track of every insult and adding it to her list of grievances against her fellow Lords.

"Father, we must talk," Devona said urgently.

Up to now, Galm had been brooding and not paying attention to the conversation. When Devona spoke, he looked up, startled, as if he'd forgotten she were here. "Not now, child. We received bad news at the Cathedral while you were out. Varma died the final death earlier today."

"I know, Father," Devona said softly. "Matt and I found his body."

The other Lords fell silent and awaited Galm's reaction. Me, I half expected him to destroy us where we stood. But instead he spoke in a voice thick with restrained anger. "Tell me what you know."

Devona hesitated, and then launched into a concise summary of everything that had happened since she'd discovered the Dawnstone was missing.

After she was done, the ice on Lord Galm's glacially impassive face broke and his features contorted in fury. "Varma was a weak, immature man who existed only for pleasure. If the Dominari hadn't introduced him to veinburn, he would have tried it on his own eventually. But if had you come to me immediately, child, I might have been able to locate Varma and use my magics to burn the addiction out of him, quite possibly preventing his assassination." He shot Varvara a meaningful look, and I imagined the two of them were going to have a few conversations about the drug trade in Varvara's section of the city not long after the ceremony.

"But you let your pride as keeper of my Collection interfere with your duty to your cousin—who was fully Bloodborn, I might add."

Devona hung her head in shame. "Yes, my Lord."

I wanted to shout at Galm, to tell him he was being unnecessarily cruel—not to mention just plain wrong-headed—to talk to Devona like he had. But I knew that despite my watering hole analogy, the Darklords' truce didn't extend to me, and I had to watch what I said.

"My Lord," I said, nearly choking on the words, "what of the matter of the Dawnstone?" I hoped this would distract him from berating Devona and also turn his attention to the most important aspect of her story: that whoever stole the Dawnstone likely planned to attack with it during the Renewal Ceremony.

But I was surprised by his response.

"It is of no consequence."

"No consequence! I thought it was an object of great power!"

"It is," Galm admitted, "but one which takes much mystic knowledge and skill to operate. Such attributes are possessed only by my fellow Lords."

"And we would never use such a device," Edrigu said. "Not during the Renewal Ceremony."

"Edrigu's right," Amon said. "It would be one thing to employ the Dawnstone against each other outside of the Nightspire, but to use it here and risk Dis' wrath? Never."

"Not to mention what the effect of using an object of power would have on the ceremony itself," Talaith said. "We need Dis, and all five of us, to maintain Necropolis. If the ceremony were interrupted before completion, the city would fail to be renewed."

"And Necropolis, and all its denizens, would be no more," Edrigu finished. "There'd be nothing left to rule over."

"Besides," Talaith pointed out, "there's no way anyone

could sneak such a powerful artifact into the Nightspire, not with the powerful wardspells Father Dis has placed on the entrances."

"It's far more likely the Dominari have different—but no less nasty—plans for it," Amon said. "But that need not concern us at the moment."

I looked to Varvara for confirmation. "They've got a good point," she told me. "Several, in fact."

It sounded as if the other Lords had managed to convince Varvara. And truth to tell, what they said did seem reasonable. But that didn't mean I bought it. My undead gut told me that despite all the Darklords had said, whoever had the Dawnstone would use it here, soon. But if the Darklords didn't believe us, I didn't know what we'd be able to do about it.

Evidently, Devona felt the same, too, for she said, "Father, please, you must—"

"Forget the Dawnstone," Galm said, icy reserve in place once more. "It is no longer any of your concern, for you are no longer keeper of my Collection."

Devona stared at her father in stunned disbelief.

"You have failed me and failed Varma. From now on you are cast out from the Bloodborn; you are no longer my daughter. Do not return to the Cathedral—if you do, I shall kill you." And with that, Galm turned and strode away.

Devona's eyes filled with tears which she fought desperately. Her hands clamped into fists so tight, her nails punctured the flesh of her palms and blood dripped from her wounds. She was shaking in both sorrow and anger. She opened her mouth—to call after Galm, I presume—but no words came. No matter what she might have said, I knew it wouldn't have helped. Lord Galm had rendered his judgment, and I doubted even Father Dis could get him to reverse it.

I put what I hoped was a comforting hand on her shoulder. I wanted to say something to console her, but it was my turn to be unable to find the right words. Everything that had defined her existence and her very identity for her entire life—seventy-three years—had been stripped away from her in mere moments.

I suppose I should have also been concerned that I'd lost my chance to gain Lord Galm's aid in staving off my final decay. But you know something? The thought didn't even occur to me.

Edrigu, Amon, and Talaith wandered off, the latter looking quite pleased with the way things had turned out. Varvara remained with us, though I wasn't sure why.

And that's when a gong (though there was none in the room) sounded, and through a doorway on the other side of the room, a handsome man dressed in a dark purple toga entered.

And although I'd never seen him before, I had a pretty good idea who he was.

Father Dis.

—TWENTY-SIX—

Everything stopped—the music, the conversation—and everyone turned toward Dis and slowly went down on bended knees. I don't mind showing someone respect, provided they earn it. But the idea of paying homage to a person I'd never meant as if he were royalty (even if in Necropolis he was) really grated. Still, I thought, quite aware of the pun, when in Rome . . .

I knelt along with the others.

Dis strode into the chamber with the easy confidence of someone who is lord of all he surveys and doesn't feel a need to make a big deal out of it. He paused for a moment, smiled, and then gestured for us to stand. Everyone complied, but they remained silent, watching Father Dis and waiting for their next cue.

Dis wasn't what I had expected. There was nothing monstrous about him at all. He stood over six feet, had short curly black hair, a large but distinguished-looking nose, and a relaxed, charming smile. This was the ultimate Lord of Necropolis? He looked more like an Italian movie star.

He walked through the crowd, smiling and nodding to those he passed, stopping once or twice to shake someone's hand (or paw or claw). And then he continued walking— straight toward us.

When he reached us, he stopped and flashed that smile of his. "Varvara, how lovely to see you, as always." He took her hand and kissed the back of it. His voice was a mellow tenor, but with an odd accent I couldn't quite place.

"My Lord," Varvara said solemnly, all trace of the shallow, fashion-crazed party-girl persona she affected gone.

Dis released her hand and turned to Devona and me. "I see we have two new guests this evening. Charmed, Ms. Kanti." He kissed Devona's hand, and she just watched him, flustered. "Mr. Adrion."

I held up my gray-skinned hand. "If you're going to kiss my hand too, I have to warn you, it's seen better days." I couldn't help it; I'm even more of a smart aleck than usual when I'm nervous.

Dis chuckled. "I've seen far worse in my time, Mr. Adrion, believe me." And then the pupils in his warm brown eyes dilated, becoming windows to a darkness deeper and colder than anything I had ever imagined. And then his pupils returned to normal and he shook my hand. "So glad you two could make it tonight. I hope it shall turn out to be a memorable experience for you both."

And with that he left us and walked toward the pentagram-shaped dais. "The time is nigh!" he called out in a commanding voice, the charming host gone, replaced by the Lord of the City. "Let us begin!"

He mounted the dais steps and climbed to the top, and passed through the ring of Sentinels. He took a position in the center of the pentagram and waited. The five Darklords, including Varvara, then joined him, each standing on the point of the pentagram which corresponded to the location of their stronghold in the city, facing Father Dis.

I half expected dramatic music to swell as Dis and the Darklords raised their arms above their heads, but the chamber was silent, the air charged with anticipation. Everyone stood gathered around the dais, watching, waiting. Dis chanted no harsh, multisyllabic words of a spell, made no complicated mystic gestures. All he did was simply look upward—and the Nightspire began to open.

As if it were an ebon flower curling back its night-dark petals, the tip of the Nightspire blossomed open to reveal Umbriel. The shadowsun hovered huge and heavy in the eternal night of Necropolis' sky, its hue no longer pure black but now shot through with patches of gray. It seemed to sag in the sky, as if weary and barely able to keep itself aloft.

The Darklords lowered their hands until they were pointing at Dis. And then gouts of darkness blasted forth from their palms to engulf Dis in a turbulent, writhing shroud of shadow. Dis inhaled, drawing the darkness into him as if it were air, and then, with the Lords continuing to feed him with their shadow, Dis lowered his arms, threw back his head, and opened his mouth wide.

A torrent of darkness surged upward from deep within the being that called itself Father Dis, spiraling up through the interior of the Nightspire, geysering forth from the opening, and streaking across the starless sky toward Umbriel. The stygian bolt struck the shadowsun, feeding, restoring, renewing it. As we watched, the patches of gray began to shrink, and Umbriel seemed to grow stronger and more vital. It was a wonder to behold. A dark wonder, yes, but a wonder just the same.

And then, out of the corner of my eye, I became aware of movement on the dais. One of the Sentinels—the one I'd recognized earlier, with the scar on its chest—was stirring. It moved its thick-fingered hands to the line of puckered flesh, plunged them into the skin, and pulled open its chest. It reached into the cavity and brought forth a crystal a bit larger than a man's fist.

The Dawnstone.

I understood in a flash how the artifact had been smuggled past the Nightspire's wardspells. Concealed within a Sentinel, one of Dis' own guards, it hadn't tripped any of the mystic protections.

Some of the others in the audience had noticed the Sentinel's actions, and were shouting and pointing. If the Darklords and Dis were aware of what was happening, they gave no sign. The Lords continued pumping Dis full of darkness, and he in turn continued feeding it upward into Umbriel.

The Sentinel cupped the Dawnstone in its hands, and a warm yellow glow began to suffuse the crystal.

"It's activating the stone!" Devona shouted. "But that's impossible! A Sentinel is a golem, a mystic automaton without a mind of its own! It can't work magic!"

The Dawnstone's glow was getting brighter.

"Well, this one can!" I said.

People were shouting to the Lords, trying to get their attention, but it was no use. Whether the Lords couldn't hear or couldn't afford to be distracted at this point in the ceremony, they didn't respond. Neither, for that matter, did the other Sentinels, who remained motionless on the dais. Maybe they too were somehow part of the ceremony, or perhaps they needed Dis to command them to action. Whichever the case, they stood by, useless.

Dis' red-robed attendants, the Cabal, dropped their serving trays and rushed toward the rogue Sentinel, their hands flaring with crimson energy. But the Sentinel merely pointed the Dawnstone at the oncoming attendants. A dazzling lance of white light blazed forth from the crystal and washed over the Cabal. They didn't even have time to scream. One second they were there, the next they were gone. Not even dust remained.

A number of the Darklords' guests—the vampires especially—fell to the floor, crying and moaning in pain, injured from merely witnessing the release of the Dawnstone's awesome power. Everyone else either stood in mute fear or was trying to escape the chamber. No one headed for the Sentinel, which was slowly starting to turn around to face Dis and the Darklords.

It looked like it was up to the dead man. I drew my gun, aimed at the Sentinel's head, and fired.

I wasn't the world's greatest marksman when alive, but death has given me a much steadier hand, and my shots hit their intended target. But I might as well not have bothered; the bullets merely scratched the Sentinel's doughy gray flesh.

I decided to try a different target and fired at the Dawnstone. Because of the way the crystal was glowing, it was harder to tell if I hit it, but I believed I did. But instead of being rewarded with the sound of shattering magic crystal, nothing happened.

"I should've known it wouldn't be that easy," I muttered as I reloaded.

The Sentinel completed its turn and aimed the Dawnstone at Father Dis and, along with the five bolts of darkness still blasting into him from the Darklords, a stream of white light struck him full on the chest. The shadow streaming forth from Dis' mouth cut off as the Lord of Necropolis screamed.

Take all the pain in the universe, not just physical pain, but all the mental and emotional anguish you can imagine. Put them all together, double, triple, quadruple them, and you still wouldn't match the intensity of the agony in Father Dis' cry.

And then the ground began to shake, as if the Nightspire

shared its master's anguish. I wondered if the disturbance was localized to Dis' island, or if the entire city experienced the tremors. I feared the latter.

I finished reloading and turned to Devona. "Time to get your crystal back," I said.

She nodded grimly, and we started toward the dais, but before she could get three steps, she stiffened, grimaced in pain, and fell to her side. In my concern for Devona, I momentarily forgot about the Sentinel, the Dawnstone, the Lords and the quaking of the Nightspire. I knelt by her side.

"What's wrong?"

She touched the side of her head and between pain-gritted teeth forced out, "My head . . . feels like it's . . . on fire . . ."

I feared she was suffering from some delayed reaction to viewing the Dawnstone's brilliance. I wanted to help her, wanted to take away the pain, but I didn't know how.

"Forget about me, go . . . stop . . . Dawnstone . . ."

I didn't want to leave her lying there in agony, but I knew if someone didn't do something soon, it looked like we'd all be destroyed. I nodded, squeezed her hand, then stood and half-ran, half-limped toward the dais. I weaved between weeping and wailing guests, my mind racing to come up with some sort of plan of attack.

I couldn't hurt the Sentinel by shooting it, couldn't shatter the Dawnstone. I certainly couldn't physically battle the golem, nor did I have any mystic knowledge that would allow me to attack it magically. And I didn't have anything in my jacket of tricks that would help. If only the damn thing's hide wasn't so blasted tough! Then I could—and then I realized: its skin might be impenetrable, but what about its insides? There was a gaping hole in its chest now where the Dawnstone had been concealed. If I could just get a shot at it . . .

I circled the dais, looking for an angle. It wasn't easy, considering the other motionless Sentinels in the way, not the mention the Darklords and Father Dis. But I finally found a space between a Sentinel and Talaith that, while not perfect by any means, would have to do. I aimed, doing my best to ignore Dis' cries and the chamber's shaking. Steady, steady . . . I fired.

One, two, three shots right into the open gash in the Sentinel's chest. Success! The creature staggered and the Dawnstone's beam winked out. But the golem didn't go down. Instead, it leveled the Dawnstone at me and I was blinded by the crystal's blazing light. I threw up an arm to protect my eyes, but I felt no heat and no pain.

The light extinguished, and I blinked furiously, trying to force my eyes to work again. Within seconds, I could see once more, although my vision was peppered with floating purple and orange afterimages. I took a quick inventory of my body, and as near as I could tell, the Dawnstone hadn't harmed me. I was grateful the crystal produced no heat; otherwise, I likely would have burst into flame.

The Sentinel seemed to regard me for a moment—it was difficult to tell for certain since it possessed no facial features—and then it turned and began descending the dais. I checked Father Dis. He knelt in the middle of the pentagram, obviously shaken. The Darklords were still emitting beams of darkness at him, though, and the Nightspire continued quaking furiously. Dis got to his feet and looked up at Umbriel once more. The shadowsun was covered with gray patches, many more than before, and jagged fissures criss-crossed its surface. The Renewal Ceremony was failing.

Dis opened his mouth and released a shout of equal parts frustration and determination, and pure darkness fountained from deep within him and rushed upward toward Necropolis' dying sun.

The Sentinel, meanwhile, had reached the chamber floor and was stomping toward me, the Dawnstone held at its side in one massive hand. Magic hadn't harmed me, so it looked like the big bruiser was going to get physical. No problem; this kind of fight I understood.

I aimed for the gash and squeezed off three more shots.

The Sentinel took a step back, swayed, and then dropped the Dawnstone, which fell to the floor with a loud clack! but was undamaged. The rent in the golem's chest widened, and out spilled a black flood of tiny hard-shelled insects.

I stared in surprise, and suddenly a whole lot of things began to make sense.

But I didn't have time to reflect on my newfound realizations before the insects were upon me, covering me completely from head to toe. I slapped at them, tore at them, hit the ground and rolled in an attempt to crush them, but while I got a few that way, there were just too damn many, gnawing, chewing, ripping away at my undead flesh. It didn't hurt, of course; I felt a certain distance from what was occurring, as if it were happening to someone else.

And then I couldn't move my left arm anymore, then my right. I fell to the floor, my legs useless. I couldn't see, for I no longer possessed eyes. And my thoughts became erratic and sluggish, and I realized the insects had penetrated my brain.

I experienced a moment of vertigo then, followed by darkness. And then I could see once more, only now I was looking down upon a carpet of insects that were picking clean a rag-covered skeleton, and I understood what had taken place. The insects had destroyed my body and released my spirit. I was dead, for the second time.

I wasn't upset by this development, didn't feel anything about it one way or the other. It just was.

Although I had no body, at least none that I was aware of, I did appear to have a limited range of vision, as if I were still using eyes to see. I wanted to know what the Sentinel was doing and, without being conscious of doing anything other than having the desire, I was now looking at the golem.

It stood motionless while the insects finished their work, and then like a movie in reverse, they flowed back into the Sentinel. When they were all inside once more, the golem gripped its chest wound and pinched it closed, in order to hold the insects in, I presumed, and then stomped back toward the dais where Father Dis and the Darklords still struggled to renew Umbriel.

I watched, unconcerned, as the Sentinel retrieved the Dawnstone and mounted the steps of the dais. The golem then raised the mystic crystal and once more unleashed a blast of light at Dis. The ruler and founder of Necropolis screamed, and the dark power he channeled upward to Umbriel was cut off again. He fell to his knees as the tremors which shook the Nightspire grew even more violent. I wondered idly how long the structure could withstand such shaking, not that it mattered much. Nothing mattered.

And then I felt a pull, as if something were drawing me toward it. I "looked" in that direction and saw a light a thousand times brighter than any the Dawnstone could ever produce. I began drifting toward that light, slowly at first, and then faster, leaving the struggles of the flesh creatures behind me, already forgotten.

And as I neared the light, I heard a voice, a voice that I hadn't heard in almost two years.

It's not like you to leave a job unfinished, Matt.

With a jolt, I remembered the Sentinel and the Dawnstone, Dis and the Darklords, Umbriel and the Nightspire.

And Devona.

Dale was right; I still had work to do.

I turned away from the light and moved back toward the chamber and the struggle taking place on the dais. I had no idea what I could hope to do as a disembodied spirit—I just knew I had to do something. I wished Lyra were here to give me a few pointers. She'd spent enough time as a spirit and probably could . . . And then it hit me. Lyra and Honani, one soul exchanged for another.

I didn't have a spell designed by Papa Chatha to aid me, but I did have a hell of a lot of determination. I concentrated on drifting toward the Sentinel, who was still unmercifully blasting Father Dis with the Dawnstone.

More specifically, I aimed for the gash in the thing's chest.

I slipped into the Sentinel's body and was suddenly aware of another consciousness within it. A fragmented, alien consciousness that I experienced as a million tiny voices whispering back and forth to each other. And then I sensed the voices become aware of me and begin speaking as one, only they weren't whispering this time: they were shouting—shouting for me to get out.

But I wasn't about to go anywhere. I concentrated my entire will on merging with the Sentinel, on becoming one with it. I could feel the alien presence begin to weaken. I took advantage of the opportunity to seize control of the Sentinel's arms.

The alien presence shrieked within my mind as I brought the crystal to the chest of the body we shared, pried open the gash, and aimed the stone within. I sensed that all I needed to do to activate the Dawnstone was will it.

I did.

Light flooded through our shared being, and I could hear the presence's agonized screams, feel its death throes. And then the presence was gone, and the Dawnstone's light grew dim and went out altogether, leaving me alone in the Sentinel's body.

I began to feel my thoughts slipping away then, to feel my very Self begin to dissolve into an approaching night that was warm, welcoming, and eternal.

I didn't care, though. All that mattered was I'd finished my job.

–TWENTY-SEVEN–

I walked down the steps into Gregor's basement, my flashlight on high this time. I half expected him not to be there, but he was, crouching against the wall in his usual position, masses of his children—more than normal, I thought—all around him, covering the walls, floor, and ceiling. The ones scuttling across the floor remained outside my flashlight beam, but only just.

"Hello, Matthew."

"You don't seem very surprised to see me alive, or at least my version of alive. But then you wouldn't be, would you? We never did find the child of yours which Devona carried in her head. She thought it had somehow been destroyed by her proximity to the light of the Dawnstone. But it really escaped while Devona was half unconscious with pain and came back here to report to you, didn't it?"

"Getting into the Nightspire is one thing," Gregor said. "Getting out another. Your surmise is correct."

"Why'd you implant it in her? As a sort of fail-safe device?"

"As a precaution, in case either of you came too close to interfering with the plan. We would have tried to manipulate you into hosting one of us, but we knew you would never agree to it."

"You were right. Speaking of people being right, I'm still shocked that crazy Carl actually reported a legitimate story."

"Even a lunatic is correct occasionally," Gregor said.

"That's what you are, isn't it? One of the Watchers from

233

Outside. Outside the city."

"Yes, but despite our pose as Gregor, it is incorrect to refer to us as separate individuals. We are One."

"That's what I saw back in the Cathedral, when I looked out the window over the Null Plains and saw what I took to be shifting waves of darkness. It was really millions upon millions of bugs, wasn't it? Millions of bits and pieces of you."

Gregor, or at least the part of the Watchers' group mind that appeared to be Gregor, nodded.

I became aware of insects gathering quietly around us. I had no doubt that if I turned to look, I'd find the entrance to the stairs blocked. But I continued talking.

"You know, I always wondered just what species you were. You didn't seem like any other being in Necropolis. Now I know why."

"This dimension is our home, and has been for more years than your birth planet has existed. When Dis and the Darklords first entered this dimension and created Necropolis, we had no idea what had happened, for as One we had no concept of otherness. No concept of invasion. But we learned. We entered the city, tunneling beneath the flaming barrier of Phlegethon, and we spread throughout Necropolis. It took over fifty of your years before we began to understand what had taken place, understand that others had come to our home, had stolen part of it and claimed it as their own. We became determined to do what anyone from your world would do in similar circumstances: repel the invaders and reclaim our home.

"We merely observed for the next century, learning as much as we could about Necropolis and its denizens, their strengths and weaknesses, desires and fears, wants and needs. And when we felt we had learned enough, we decided it was time to begin. We created the guise of Gregor and began trading information. Not because we needed it; we collected more than enough on our own. But because we wished to make contacts with others that would be able to serve us. This is why, incidentally, we aided you over the years, Matthew, in the hope that we might eventually find a way to use you. Unfortunately for us, you proved adept at resisting manipulation.

"At any rate, as the years passed, we slowly, cautiously began to shape the course of events in Necropolis. Through our agents, we helped foment dissent between the Darklords, founded the Dominari and the Hidden Light, established street gangs, encouraged the growth of crime on all levels. We worked especially hard to make sure the Darklords did not cut off all contact with Earth. We wanted not only to make certain the others had a way to leave our dimension, but that the developing technology from their former homeworld would continue to flow into the city to provide us more tools to fight with. And for the next two centuries, we gathered information, made contacts, manipulated, plotted, and schemed. And finally we saw our opportunity."

"The Dawnstone," I said.

"Gregor" nodded. "We have worked hard the last dozen or so years aiding the development of various thaumaturgially enhanced drugs such as tangleglow and mind dust. But when one of our agents created veinburn, a drug so powerful it would prove addictive even to the strongest of supernatural beings, we realized its awesome potential. As Gregor, we made arrangements with the Dominari to begin producing veinburn in limited quantities—"

"And made sure Morfran, who was the supplier to a bloodson of a Darklord, distributed it."

"Yes. Varma, indolent pleasure-seeker that he was, eagerly sampled Morfran's new product. And from that moment on, he was ours. By threatening to cut off his supply of veinburn, we convinced Varma to cooperate with us. He told us anything we wanted to know, all the secrets of his father that he was privy to. Including the contents of his vaunted Collection. And we learned of the Dawnstone.

"We had acquired much mystical knowledge over the last few centuries, and were instantly aware of the potential a crystal that produced actual sunlight would have here in a city of darkness. The Renewal Ceremony was fast approaching, and we realized it would be the perfect time to strike, for if Dis and the Darklords could not revitalize Umbriel—the power source which actually maintains the existence of Necropolis within this dimension—the city would be destroyed and we would finally have gotten rid of the hated others."

"So you had Varma steal the Dawnstone. After using your magical know-how to make sure his aura matched his father's so that he could get past Galm's wardspells."

The insects were all around me now; I was surrounded by solid walls of them. Only the illumination of my flashlight protected me. Still, I did nothing.

Gregor went on. "Varma delivered the Dawnstone, and we resumed supplying veinburn to him. We saw no need to slay him at that time; there was no chance he would report his crime to Lord Galm, and we did not wish to draw any undue attention to the theft of the Dawnstone. Eventually, of course, it became necessary to have him killed in order to keep him from talking to you. He was a pathetic, weak creature, and would have told you everything with little prompting on your part.

"We had previously managed to implant some pieces of ourself into one of Dis' Sentinels, and we realized we could use it to ferry the Dawnstone into the Nightspire and then, once inside, use it to attack Dis and disrupt the Renewal Ceremony."

"So you stuck the Dawnstone inside the Sentinel, and waited for it to be recalled for the Ceremony. Tell me, why did you leave a scar on the Sentinel, even a faint one?"

"Our mystic knowledge, gleaned as it has been in scattered fragments over the centuries, is less than complete. The spells Dis used to create the Sentinels were unfamiliar to us, and we could only heal the golem's flesh so much. We had no choice but to go forward with the plan and hope no one noticed."

I had, not that it had done me any good.

"I should have known it was you all along, Gregor. One of your children was on the wall listening when I first spoke with Devona. You were the only being in the city besides the two of us who knew we were investigating the theft of the Dawnstone, the only one who could have sent the Red Tide vampires to kill us after we left the Great Library."

"We knew you, Matthew. You wouldn't let go of this until you saw it through to the end, one way or another. You had to be stopped. Ms. Kanti was of lesser importance. She would have been killed only due to her association with you."

"How did you manipulate the Red Tide members?"

"They were pathetically simple-minded creatures. To secure their services, we had only to promise them unlimited access to whatever technology they wished. They were no different than Varma, in that regard. They cared only for seeing their lusts fulfilled. Vampires' need for blood tends to make them highly addictive personalities in other regards."

"Thanks for the psychology lesson." The insects were only inches away from me now, and edging closer all the time. "I suppose you were behind all the attempts on our lives?"

"Most of them. Through various agents, we made sure Thokk knew you were in the Broken Cross, and that Talaith was aware of your passage through her realm. And of course, we made certain the Red Tide vampires were waiting for you after you left here. And we had the Dominari order Skully to kill you. Unfortunately the fool prized your friendship more than he feared his masters."

"And the insect we saw in the alley?"

"An error. It was one which we had implanted in Varma in order to keep track of him. The sheer amount of veinburn the Red Tide vampires injected into Varma was enough to affect the child, and slow its escape long enough for you to see it."

The writhing, softly chittering wall of darkness that surrounded my back and sides was only an inch away now. I knew if I swept my flashlight beam around, they would scurry off. But I kept the light shining at my feet. I wanted to lure as many of them into the basement as possible.

"I understand why you misled us into thinking Talaith might be behind the Dawnstone's theft; you wanted to draw attention away from yourself. But why did you tell us the truth about Morfran being a veinburn supplier?"

"Because the best lies are those mixed with some truth. And if the Red Tide vampires failed to kill you, we hoped that Morfran would lead you to Skully, who would finish you off. A hope that was in vain, as it turned out.

"It is a shame our plan failed, but we are nothing if not patient. We came close this time, and we shall succeed the next, whether it be tomorrow or a hundred years from now."

"I'm glad to see you're maintaining an optimistic outlook."

"We would have succeeded if not for you, Matthew. You have a fine, incisive mind and excellent instincts. Join us; help us free our home from the scourge of others which infests it."

"Help you?" I said incredulously. "After everything that's happened, everything you've done, how can you even ask such a thing?"

"Because I have something to offer you, Matthew. I can make you live again."

"You're lying."

"The child Ms. Kanti hosted remained hidden in the Nightspire long enough to witness the Renewal Ceremony completed and Dis reward you for saving his city by removing your spirit from the Sentinel and restoring your body to you. But he didn't return you to mortal life, did he?"

"He said it was beyond his power, that I had been a zombie too long to make me human again."

"Perhaps it is beyond the capabilities of Dis, but it is not beyond ours. Remember what you said when I asked you how you felt about being a zombie? You said you were a freak, trapped in a body that was little more than a numb piece of meat. Cut off from the world around you, on the outside of life. A pale memory of the man who was once Matthew Adrion.

"We can end your suffering, Matthew. Help us destroy the invaders and we shall make you live again."

I didn't respond.

"Surely you have no love for this city or its inhabitants. Your kind regard them as monsters: unnatural, unholy things. You would be doing creation a favor by helping us destroy them."

"After nearly two years as a walking dead man, it's hard to see others as monsters, Gregor."

"Then consider it justice. This is our home; they are trespassers. They have no right to live in this dimension, no right to befoul it with their obscene otherness. Help us be rid of them, and we shall make you a man once more and use one of the Darklords' portals to return you to Earth. Perhaps you will not be able to resume your life where you left off, but at least you may begin a new one."

"Sorry, Gregor, but I can't do that. Maybe Dis and the Darklords shouldn't have built Necropolis here, but they did, and you didn't protest."

"We did not understand! We knew nothing of otherness then! We did not know there were others to protest to!"

"Even so, the city and its people have been here for coming up on four centuries now. Isn't it time you learned to co-exist with them?"

"Impossible! Otherness can not be tolerated!"

"Then there's nothing I can do for you, Gregor. I won't help you. In fact, I'll do everything I can to stop you."

"You'll do nothing. It's a pity you won't join us, but that is your decision. You were foolish to come here alone, Matthew. We destroyed your body once, and we shall do so again—and this time there is no one to restore you. And don't think your flashlight will protect you. While we are creatures of this dark dimension and light does hurt us, there are far too many of us for your feeble beam to kill."

"I don't intend to use my flashlight. And you're wrong, Gregor. I didn't come alone." I clicked off the light and was plunged into darkness.

No insects swarmed over me as in the Nightspire. Instead, there was a rushing, moaning sound that made me think of a cold winter wind blowing across a blood-soaked battlefield. And then I heard the screaming of thousands upon thousands of tiny voices, the same as when I had shone the Dawnstone into the Sentinel's chest cavity, only multiplied to the nth degree.

And then there was silence. I waited a few moments more, then turned the flashlight back on. Its beam revealed Father Dis, standing alone in the now empty basement.

"Are they all gone?" I asked. I was grateful my flashlight had been turned off. I had no idea how Dis had destroyed the insects, and from the horrible sounds they had made while dying, I was certain I wanted to remain ignorant.

"All that were present at this location. I fear many more remain within the city, however, and even if none do, there are uncountable millions more outside Phlegethon's boundaries. I seriously doubt we've heard the last of the Watchers." He sighed. "I was of course aware of them when I led my people to this dimension, but I thought them some sort of native animal life. I never realized they were intelligent. If I had . . . well, it's too late now, isn't it?"

"Can't you do something? Like wave your hand in a godly gesture of omnipotence and smite them?"

Dis smiled. "As I told you when I restored you, there are limits to even my powers. The vast majority of my strength is used to maintain Umbriel and Phlegethon. The Darklords help, of course, but far less than even they imagine. Still, there's no use in letting them know that; everyone likes to feel they're important, don't they?"

"So you were telling the truth when you said you couldn't make me alive again?"

Dis nodded. "Though I was able to see to it that you are in no danger of inevitably decomposing again, provided of course you keep up regular applications of preservative spells. Barring accidents, you might very well exist forever."

Forever. The word had no meaning to me now. I wondered if it ever would. I figured I'd find out.

I showed Dis the underside of my hand. "My little finger grew back, but I still have Edrigu's mark."

"Edrigu had a previous claim on you which I can do nothing about. Be careful what deals you make in Necropolis, Matthew. They are always binding."

And with that he began to fade, like the Cheshire Cat in

a toga, until he was gone, not even leaving behind so much as a smile.

I picked my way through the rubble above what had been Gregor's lair, and walked down the steps to the broken sidewalk. Dis had brought me here after restoring me so we could take care of Gregor before he abandoned his hidey hole, but for whatever reasons, the Lord of Necropolis hadn't seen fit to provide me with a lift home. Not that I was ungrateful: Dis had already done plenty for me. Still, it was rude to leave a guy stranded—especially when said guy had just saved the whole goddamned city.

I started walking. But I hadn't gotten more than a block away from Gregor's when I heard what sounded like a water buffalo moaning in extreme pain coming up behind me, followed by a blat like a strangling trumpeter swan.

I turned and saw a hideous conglomeration of metal barreling down the street toward me. The thing screeched to a stop, and Lazlo hung out the window.

"Sorry it took me so long, Matt, but I had a little trouble getting the old cab running. I ended up having to cobble together a new one from what I could scrounge up in the junkyard. Still, I think I did a pretty good job, don't you?"

I walked over to the bent and twisted thing that coughed and shuddered alongside the curb.

"This . . . is a car?"

Lazlo guffawed. "You really kill me sometimes, Matt, you know that?" He shook his head. " 'This is . . . a car?' That's rich! C'mon, hop in!"

I climbed into the passenger seat—once I figured out how to get the door open, and Lazlo said, "Where to, pal?"

"Demon's Roost," I answered. I had to talk to Devona, and see if I could get her to change her mind.

—TWENTY-EIGHT—

I found Devona standing alone in front of Varvara's bedroom mirror, looking at the image of a park at nighttime. Blue-white fluorescent lights were lit, and small clouds of insects flitted around them. Even with the competition of the city lights, the stars were visible in the sky.

"Those are real stars, aren't they?" she asked without taking her eyes off the scene before her. "They look different from the illusion in the Wyldwood. Crisper, brighter."

"Yes, they do."

"You know, I've never really experienced night before. I thought I had, living in Necropolis, but what we have here isn't true night, is it? More like a perpetual gray. Night seems more peaceful, soothing. And, even though everything is quiet, somehow it possesses a life, an energy, all its own."

"Maybe that's your vampire half talking. After all, the night—true night—is a vampire's natural environment. Still, I know what you mean. The night is special."

"I wish there was sound to go with the image," she said wistfully. "Birds singing . . ." She turned to me. "Do birds sing at night?"

I smiled. "Sometimes."

She turned back to the mirror. "Good. Birds singing, leaves rustling in the wind . . ."

Horns honking, brakes squealing, people shouting . . . but I decided not to mention these. Why spoil the moment?

Devona took my hand and we stood silently and drank in the night.

After a time, she said, "At first it devastated me when Father removed me from my post and cast me out of the Bloodborn. But now . . ."

"What?"

"Now I see it as an opportunity. I've spent all my life in Necropolis, most of it cloistered away in the Cathedral, tending a dusty collection of someone else's memories. I think it's time for me to create some memories of my own, don't you?"

"I think that would be a very good thing." I hoped my words sounded more positive than I felt.

She let go of my hand and brushed her fingers against the mirror's glass. "Time to explore the other half of my heritage, to get to know my mother's world, the world I was born into."

She turned to face me once more, but she didn't take my hand again. "I have you to thank for this, Matt. If it wasn't for you—"

"If it wasn't for me, you might not have been excommunicated," I finished.

She shook her head. "That likely would have happened no matter what. Father never cared for me, I see that now. A creature like him is incapable of caring. I failed in my duty, and I had to be punished. It was as simple as that to him. Never mind that I served him well for thirty years. That's only the blink of an eye to a being such as he." She turned back to the mirror. "Thirty years . . ."

I had come here hoping to change her mind, to persuade her to stay. And maybe I could've done that. But I no longer wanted to.

"I could come with you." I didn't sound very convincing.

She smiled and touched my cheek. "That's sweet of you, Matt, but you know it wouldn't work out. You'd still need preservative spells."

"I could come back and get them."

"Magic functions reliably in Necropolis because Father Dis wills it so. On Earth, magic is haphazard. There's no telling how long a preservative spell would last. You might decompose after only a few hours."

"Or I might not. I might be fine."

"I don't want to take that chance. I don't want to lose you."

If anyone had told me I'd be having a conversation like this a week ago, I'd have said they were crazy. But even though Devona and I had known each other for a short time, the link we'd established in the Wyldwood made it seem like we'd been together for years. And seeing her go was breaking my unbeating zombie heart.

I almost said it then, almost said, *Then don't go. Stay with me.* But I gritted my teeth and held the words back.

"So tell me," she asked, "what is Cleveland like?"

What could I say? That it was known as the Mistake on the Lake? That people still talk about the time the heavily polluted Cuyahoga River caught fire?

"It's a nice place," I said. "I think you'll like it."

She smiled. "I'll come back and visit, Matt. And someday, when I've experienced my fill of Earth—and perhaps Father is prepared to forgive me—I'll return for good."

Maybe. Or maybe she'd fall in love with Earth and never want to leave. "I'll be here," I said simply.

And then she leaned forward and kissed me. I couldn't feel her lips against mine, couldn't feel their softness, but that didn't matter. No mere physical contact could ever compare to the link we experienced in the Wyldwood.

"You take care of yourself, Matthew Adrion." Crimson tears welled in the corners of her eyes.

"You too."

And then she stepped through the mirror and was gone. I wanted to watch her walk through the park a bit, wanted to see her initial reactions to physically being on Earth for the first time since she'd been a baby. But as soon as she was through, the portal became a mirror again, and I was left staring at my now only slightly gray-tinted face. My reflection was dry-eyed, but that's only because a zombie's tear ducts don't function.

"I thought it best if the portal closed as soon as she passed through."

I turned to see the demon queen sitting on the edge of her bed. She was dressed in a skimpy red silk gown with a Chinese dragon embroidered in gold encircling the waist, its tail—which served as the robe's belt—clutched in its mouth.

"I should have known you couldn't pass up spying on us," I said bitterly. "I hope you enjoyed the show."

"I have only arrived this moment, Matthew. I placed a small spell on the mirror to let me know when Devona had gone through. I know nothing that occurred between the two of you."

I looked into Varvara's snake eyes and tried to decide if I could trust her. Maybe she was telling the truth, but if she was, she might very well have enchanted the mirror to record our farewell scene for later playback. But even if she had, I found it hard to care just then.

"Thanks for letting us use your private gateway, Varvara."

She grinned, and the embroidered dragon around her waist winked. "It's the least I could do for the savior of Necropolis."

"You can cut out that kind of talk right now. There was a job that needed done, I did it, and that's the end of it, okay?"

"Of course, Matthew," she said innocently. "Whatever you say."

I sighed. I knew I'd be lucky if she didn't address me as Savior from now on.

Her manner grew serious. "Are you all right, Matt?"

"Of course I am, Varvara. I'm a zombie; I don't have any feelings, remember?"

"Right. I forgot."

I knew Varvara didn't believe it, and for the first time in a long time, neither did I.

Lazlo was waiting for me in his cab outside the main entrance to Demon's Roost. The street was mostly empty now; only a few drunks sleeping it off in the gutters were left. The festival was over.

As soon as I climbed in the back, Lazlo said, "Where to, pal?"

Where to indeed? Not Skully's; I knew it would be better for him if I didn't show my face around there for a while, not until he had patched things up with his Dominari bosses. The Broken Cross? Not my scene. Papa Chatha's? I was sure Papa would be glad to learn I had avoided the final death, but I really didn't feel much like talking right then.

"Why don't we just drive around for a while?"

"Sounds good." Lazlo pulled away from the curb and, for a change, drove almost sanely away from Varvara's stronghold.

I settled back in my seat, looked out the window at the scenery of the city—my city—going by, and thought of a starlit glen.

—ABOUT THE AUTHOR—

TIM WAGGONER has published more than fifty stories of fantasy and horror. His most current stories can be found in the anthologies *Civil War Fantastic*, *Single White Vampire Seeks Same*, and *Bruce Coville's UFOs*. His first novel, *The Harmony Society*, has been published by DarkTales Publications, and he is currently working on projects for both White Wolf and Wizards of the Coast. He teaches creative writing at Sinclair Community College in Dayton, Ohio.